GONE BEFORE GOODBYE—LOVE AND MYSTERY IN THE 6-OH-3, BOOK 1

The police are stumped. Was she a runaway careening toward disaster or the victim of a predator preying on teenage girls?

When rebellious seventeen-year-old Lisa Grant vanishes from her bedroom in New Hampshire, her guardian, Teagan Raynes, becomes ensnared in the frantic hunt to find her alive. Search dogs lose the girl's scent at Pretty Park, where another teenager disappeared three months ago. Teagan and the police fear a stalker is using the park to track and abduct young girls. Soon a mysterious death threat arrives for Teagan, and she reluctantly puts her faith in the lead detective, the notorious Noah Cassidy.

Praise for Nora LeDuc

TRUST ME: "The suspense built steadily and unpredictably. Trust Me is a must read." ~ *Long and Short Reviews*

~*~

DEAD WOMEN TELL NO LIES: "This author writes an outstanding romantic suspense. One of the best I have read in a long time. I would absolutely recommend highly—5 Flowers—I loved this book! It's on my keeper shelf!"~ *It's Raining Books*

~*~

"*STAGING MURDER* absolutely kept me glued to my ereader. I was caught up in the suspense, quite curious about the murder, the threats and what they all meant for Ava." ~ *Jennifer Porter, Romance Novel News*

~*~

"Impressively crafted, *PICK UP LINES FOR MURDER* is an enjoyable suspense thriller." ~ *Josee Morgan, Apex Reviews*

~*~

MURDER CAME CALLING: "A Night Owl Romance Book Review TOP PICK!"

~* ~

MURDER BY HEART: "Tension begins on the first page and doesn't end until an unexpected culprit is revealed in the last few pages. This cleverly crafted story is filled with sexual tension that neither the hero nor the heroine wants to recognize and an abundance of action as they try to outwit a vicious killer." ~ *Donna M. Brown for Romantic Times Book Reviews*

~*~

LOVE'S WICKED JEWEL: "Several of the scenes contain wry humor that binds all into a tidy bundle of compelling and suspenseful romance." ~ *Faith V. Smith, Romantic Times Book Reviews*

GONE BEFORE GOODBYE

NORA LEDUC

GONE BEFORE GOODBYE

Copyright © 2014 Nora LeDuc

Cover Art by Beetiful Book Covers

Formatted by IRONHORSE Formatting

Contact Information: NoraLeDuc@yahoo.com

Publishing History 2014
ISBN-13: 978-0-9892090-8-3
Published in the United States of America

DEDICATION

To Susan and Linda who tirelessly answered all my how, when, where, and what questions. Thank you for sharing your awesome knowledge with me.

CHAPTER 1

Lisa Grant was trapped in the dead zone, aka Pretty Park. That's what the nerds called this place in Hawick Falls, New Hampshire.

No one remembered why or who named the park. "Stick that fact in your history books," Lisa mumbled to herself she kicked the burnt-out sparkler leftover from last night's Fourth of July firework celebration and scanned the open space under the lights.

Where was Travis? She never should have snuck out to meet him so late at night, but it wasn't fair she'd been grounded for 'talking back'. She was seventeen, not a little kid, and should be allowed her opinions.

The shriek of a cat from the woods nearby startled her. She clenched her jaw. *Come on, Travis.*

She should have hitched a ride with him, but she'd wanted to keep him guessing if she'd come. He'd made a big deal about tonight, like something special would happen. She checked her phone one final time, no messages. No way was she texting him.

Already, she'd wasted more than half an hour hiking the almost two miles from home and standing around to be blown off. If she called the house and admitted she was stranded, Teagan, her legal guardian— no, her guard— would find out she'd taken her phone and slipped out. Lisa would be jailed in her room for the rest of the summer.

Who could she call? Travis had been her one loyal friend, and

1

he'd deserted her. A jab of pain struck her, and she swallowed the lump of misery.

It didn't matter; she'd always been on her own. Still, she was sure Travis was different.

She thought he'd loved Lisa Grant, the unlovable child abandoned by her parents in foster care when she was two.

She pivoted around, taking in the jogging path, the lit tennis court on the rise to her left, and the vacant playground in her right. Beyond lay the run-down ball field. She was totally alone in the empty park. If anything bad happened to her, who would know? Goose bumps broke out on her arms.

She'd give Travis five more minutes before she bolted. A breeze carried the sound of a croaking frog and the warning of rainfall. Lisa paced past the lamppost and brushed against a piece of paper tacked on the pole. Pausing, she glanced at the laminated sheet. Moisture had seeped inside the plastic cover during the rainy spring and hot, humid June and July, but she recognized the fading image of the missing fourteen-year-old girl with a gap between her two front teeth. Kara Linn's picture had popped up everywhere during April when she vanished at dusk walking her dog in a park.

This park. Everyone knew horrible things happened to girls who disappeared. Gooseflesh crawled over Lisa's arms. She should never have come. Anyone could hide in the woods across the street and watch her.

Screw it. She was going home.

Movement by the court lights caught her attention. Travis? She let out a breath of relief. Everything would be okay. He must have parked in the lot behind the hill. She'd forgive him for keeping her hanging around after he begged to get back together. Maybe he'd bought her something special for tonight. It could be a necklace. She'd wear it the first day of school. They'd walk side-by-side through the halls and sit next to each other at lunch. After classes, they'd ride around in the cool car Travis was going to buy. Lisa ran her damp hands over her cutoff shorts and smiled. She didn't care that he wasn't on the honor roll but more likely on the detention list. She loved him.

The figure paused beneath a light, twenty feet from her. The beam spotlighted a short man, wearing a T-shirt and sweatpants that hung on his body. White hair touched his shoulders. The guy was too old to be Travis and kinda creepy.

Don't go into the park after sunset. The caution screeched in her mind. Parents claimed criminals and crazies roamed the place at night. Why hadn't she listened? What if the guy was a freaked-out murderer who wandered the park searching for victims? What if he'd kidnapped Kara Linn?

Lisa's throat grew dry. She shrank from the light. She shouldn't have worn a white shirt, too obvious in the dark. Nah, forget Travis and shirts. That guy was coming closer. She turned and headed away along the path. The wind picked up and whipped strands of hair across her face while thunder rumbled a caution overhead. She tossed a glance over her shoulder; the man was moving in her direction. Sweat broke out on her forehead and ran down her face. This was Travis's fault.

Why didn't you come, Travis? I love you. No, he left me in the park, by myself at night. I hate you. We're done forever. Why'd you ditch me in this scary place?

Once she got out of here she'd throw away the stupid heart bracelet he'd given her. She wished she could rip it off her wrist now. Tears filled her eyes and blurred her vision.

She swiped at them and broke into a trot. Cool drops of rain splattered on her head. *Great, a storm was rolling in.* Claps of thunder and flashes of lightning struck on both sides. She clenched her hands at the sound of running behind her. He was following. He—

She stumbled as her foot touched a broken branch on the ground. Something hit the heel of her shoe. For a second, she wobbled, and then righted herself. She glanced over her shoulder. Her wallet had fallen out of her pocket. No. No. Her life was inside.

The man rounded the bend.

Forget it. She'd come back in daylight and find it. She increased her speed. Had Kara fled on this path too? Would Lisa's picture be on the next flyer nailed on a pole? She gulped, and her heart threatened to leap from her chest.

The city sidewalk appeared through the rain like a finish line. A few more feet and she'd be out of the park. The chilly drops soaked through her shirt and caused more goose bumps. Trees lining the trail swayed together. The rustle of their leaves whispered, "Faster. Faster."

She reached the vacant walk near the road and peeked behind her. No signs of the creepy guy. Phew. She paused to catch her breath. The homes on the other side of the street were dark. Lightning sizzled across the sky, and in the flash, he appeared.

She gasped. He was less than ten feet from her and blocked the way. He grinned a toothless smile and licked his lips. She whirled around and fled.

Beams from a set of headlights emerged in the blackness. "Please, please stop." She darted into the lane and waved her arms.

The vehicle slowed and halted. The driver's window rolled down with a mechanical whine.

"I'm trying to get home," she blurted, struggling to keep the hysteria out of her voice. "Will you take me?"

The sound of locks popping up answered her prayer before the caution burst into her thoughts: *Never take rides from strangers.*

But this was no stranger, and tonight, if anyone asked who gave her a ride, she'd say, "My savior."

Lisa hurled herself into the front seat. The door locks clicked shut.

CHAPTER 2

Lisa Grant had been missing forty-eight hours, and Teagan Raynes, Lisa's guardian, couldn't cry any more. Teagan had promised Aunt Sophia, before she passed away, to take care of the troubled teen, her aunt's foster child.

How could Lisa have disappeared without a clue? Was she a runaway? She talked about living in a big city like Boston, but in the distant future. Worse, had someone snuck inside while they slept, crept upstairs, and entered Lisa's room? Had Lisa awoken and become paralyzed with fear, as something dark stole across the floor to her bed and covered her mouth to drown her screams?

Nausea climbed up Teagan's throat. No. Refocus. Block the image. She'd vowed today would be different, had to be different. No more being a victim frozen on the stupor highway. She'd gotten up this morning, hunted up a skein of purple yarn, and tied a purple bow around the maple tree in the front yard. Purple was Lisa's favorite color.

What should she do next? Aunt Sophia always knew what to do. If she were alive, she'd be leading every search group and making every decision.

Teagan sighed and listened to the eerie silence in the kitchen. Two days before, teams of law enforcement invaded the house. They searched from the cellar to the attic. She'd hung out at the table with the FBI techie, who'd been consulting on another missing girl, Kara Linn, and now was helping them. He tapped her phone and waited for Lisa or an abductor to call about a ransom. Teagan had little cash, but the investigators explained that people went to any lengths to obtain money in exchange for a kidnap victim. Meanwhile, a stream of techies scoured for prints, fibers, or hair.

Last night, everyone had left, but the wiretap remained, a reminder nothing was solved. Even the press pulled back and seemed satisfied to check in with the police. Lisa. Gone.

Teagan's anxiety blew up in her chest. It stole her breath. Controlled her body. Her heart raced, threatening to burst. *No. Concentrate on a peaceful place.*

She closed her eyes and pictured the ocean with the waves rolling onto the beach. The image lingered in her mind for a second, and then Lisa was lying on the sand. Blood trickled from beneath her still form, across the opal grains, and turned the granules scarlet.

Teagan opened her eyes with a gasp. Life was a horror fest.

Breathe. Inhale through your nose and exhale through your mouth the way you were taught.

The attack finally eased. She scanned the room to ground herself in normalcy. On the fridge, a magnet held the color-coded map of Hawick Falls. Each shaded neighborhood marked the places the volunteers posted their flyers. People she didn't know, or hadn't seen in ages, saw the posters and sent her emails and cards offering support. She'd never be able to thank them all.

She inhaled the scent of cinnamon from the geranium above the sink. The zesty fragrance comforted her as she sank into the ladder-back chair. After several minutes, she swallowed the fear blocking her throat. Teagan stared at the clutter, which hid the red-and-white-checkered tablecloth. Notes for the vigil, leftover snacks, and messages covered the tabletop. The mess resembled her mother's organizational system. Aunt Sophia wouldn't rest until she straightened the chaos. But what good was neatness unless it brought Lisa home?

At the end of the table, the teenager's chair sat empty. Tears spilled from Teagan's eyes. Several lost minutes later, she stretched across the jumble for the tissues, her constant companion. "I don't know how this happened, Aunt Sophia. You've been gone six months, but it feels like an eternity."

Teagan's thoughts drifted to the day she first arrived in Hawick Falls, nineteen years ago to live with her aunt. She was seven. Aunt Sophia had welcomed her with a hug and an explanation about Teagan's big job: learn to use the calendar. Life with her aunt revolved around the times and dates of her meetings. Her aunt had been a great coordinator and the one everyone elected to chair an event. Informal and formal gatherings were often held at the house. Teagan's favorite night was Friday when the women's group met to knit and chat. They gave her candy and kisses

And then there was Lisa. Life with Lisa consisted of highs and lows with little middle ground. Only Teagan's lingering, vivid memories of life on the street before she moved to Hawick Falls provided her with the patience and a way to reach the sixteen-year-old. Lisa ate up Teagan's childhood stories of meals at the Sharing Kitchen and sleeping in tents by the river with her mother. The unforgettable memories were anchored by the emotions of fear, loss, and love for her mother.

And now Lisa was missing. Was the teenager wandering the streets reliving Teagan's homeless days? Had she romanticized her own past instead of pointing out the dangers while trying to bond with Lisa? She should have been lecturing Lisa on the gnawing hunger, and the continuous fear of nowhere to sleep to escape the cold, rain, or snow. Never mind the scary people who smiled, but when you looked away, eyed your few belongings.

From the corner, the chiming of the clock announced the noon hour. No need to clear a space for lunch. She didn't want food. Teagan ran her fingers through her hair, snagging a black strand on her opal ring. She should have combed it this morning, but what did a tangle matter? No, she wasn't on autopilot like the previous days. She worked through the knot with her fingertips.

The quiet of the kitchen yanked on her nerves, and her silver bracelets jangled louder than normal when she moved. She controlled her anxiety and walked into the living room to settle on the tan sofa. She clicked the remote. The screen above the fireplace leaped to life. "An Amber Alert has been issued for a local seventeen-year-old, Lisa Grant. Officers are going door-to-door, interviewing the neighbors."

Too much reality. Teagan switched to the twenty-four hour shopping channel that had kept her company over the sleepless nights. The daytime hostess was chatting up a product, but Teagan's attention faded and her mind flitted from idea to idea.

She'd dreamed of teaching children and enjoying a close circle of friends. She'd own a home, pay her bills, and date reputable men. What she wanted most was to put behind her the remembrance of the crazy woman, her mother, roaming the streets of Hawick Falls.

The dream had come true, but fallen apart with Aunt Sophia's demise. Five years after moving away, she was again living in Hawick Falls, where a TV movie was the evening highlight. Her new friend on the screen urged viewers to order before the musical tea kettles sold out. Teagan hit the off button.

The questions and ideas continued to jumble in her thoughts. Was Lisa alive? Scared?

Near? Maybe, Teagan's negative comments about Lisa's boyfriend, Travis, drove her off. Teagan sighed. The other missing girl, Kara Linn, vanished three months ago, and the police had no clue of her whereabouts. Would the girl's existence become a distant memory used by parents to warn their kids of the dangers that lurked in Hawick Falls?

Teagan rubbed her burning eyes. She had to stop the unhelpful musings. Yes, she'd post a social media page and remind people to search for Lisa. But first, the mail should have arrived. There was the slim chance Lisa mailed her a letter confessing she'd run off. The notion was doubtful, but not impossible.

In the hallway, she unlocked the door. On the street, a postal truck crawled up the block of New England style houses with sprawling porches, rectangular ranches, and modern Cape Cod homes. She grabbed the envelopes from the mailbox attached to the beige clapboards, stepped inside, and closed the entryway.

She sorted through the ads and bills to the last piece, a large white envelope. The sender used a printed label addressed to her. What was this? She ripped open the flap and pulled out...a holy card?

The picture of Mary Magdalene decorated the front. Someone must have sent a prayer for Lisa? Teagan flipped to the other side and frowned at the words.

Tu sequens morieris

Someone wrote to her in...Latin? Strange. The prick of sweat stabbed the back of her neck. She sat on the sofa and scooped up her phone from the coffee table. As she searched online for a translation, she dug into her memory of high school Spanish to help crack the code. Tu was you and morieris had something to do with death and sequens translated to—

Her breath whooshed out of her. She dropped her cell on the cushion, but the phrase stared up from the screen.

You die next.

CHAPTER 3

A little after noon, Detective Noah Cassidy drove toward the brick Hawick Falls Police Station next to Itsy Bitsy Pre-school. Across the street at Bud's Variety Store, cars overflowed the parking lot onto the road. Anyone could guess the day without a glance at the date. Bud held the annual July eighth firework sale in the barn behind his business.

Noah entered the rear of the hundred-year-old station house. The city's twenty-five thousand taxpayers had refused to renovate the building at the past three municipal meetings. Heat and body odors from the holding pen greeted him as he passed through to the large squad room. Vacant desks alerted him that the chief had assigned most of his full and part time department of forty-five men to search for the missing teenager. The few remaining uniforms paused to greet Noah. He saw the wariness and the big question in their eyes. How had he handled the second anniversary of his family's deaths?

They were scrutinizing him for warning signs of stress or a meltdown. He'd be the first to admit he'd been unable to function when the date rolled around last year. This anniversary, he'd kept it together. *Too bad, guys. You'll have to find your entertainment somewhere else. I'm back from vacation and I'm going to solve my case. You'll see.*

He acknowledged them and continued onward. The sound of tapping on keyboards and the buzz of voices on phones returned.

Paul, the newest patrolman with the baby face and large glasses, spun away from his desk as Noah approached. The officer was young and inexperienced, but eager.

"Hey, Cassidy. Good to see you." The man paused and blinked several times as if he felt the awkwardness of the situation.

"Thanks." The tight sensation in Noah's chest grew. "What's up here? Any news on your bored teenagers feeding the expired meters?" he asked, turning the subject to work and Paul.

"They're leaving printed cards on windshields. The message informs drivers they've been saved from the tyranny of Prince John's traffic tickets by the Merry Men who added time to their parking meters. When the chief learned how few fines we'd collected and how many dollars the kids' actions drained from the traffic school fund, he doubled his ulcer meds." The patrolman glanced around as though he expected to discover someone listening over his shoulder. "Don't use the word merry unless you want to pull the night beat."

"We'd be in real trouble if it were Christmas. Thanks for the warning." Noah strode across the scuffed wooden floor to the quieter space of Chief Banks' office. The compass in the pocket of his blue-black BDU pants pressed against his thigh. He reached up and straightened his collar. The sooner he was back at work, the sooner his days would return to normal.

He was ready for inspection and his meeting with the chief. Noah's blond hair was trimmed short, and his clothes were clean and ironed. He needed a case to get his mind off his past family troubles. His job provided him a place to belong, unlike when he was a kid.

Back then, he'd tried to hide his shame over his father's drinking. Noah still shuddered over the memory. After his mother left them, dear old Dad insisted on proving he was the good parent. He attended school conferences slurring his words or not showing up at all. At night, he needed help to get himself into his bed, and the next day, he staggered around town trying to find someone who'd sell him more beer. There was a whole list of his father's offenses.

Noah had sworn growing up he'd prove he was nothing like his old man. People would respect Noah Cassidy, and he'd help those who'd been wronged by others the way he'd been. Once he'd made that decision, his path to law enforcement was unavoidable.

Yeah, he'd almost blown it once and regretted the incident. People seemed to have an easier time remembering the bad about you. Noah raised a hand to the door and saw his gray cuff was frayed.

His wife, June, had insisted on shopping for his clothes even when he protested he'd buy his own. "You always buy the first shirt that fits. A detective should dress to impress." Her face beamed as she held up the bag with the mall store, Men's More for Less, printed across the bag.

"Who am I impressing? The criminals?" he'd asked and given her a kiss.

His wife's face faded, and a pain settled in his chest. Since her death two years ago, he couldn't predict when bits of their past would surface to spark the hurt and regrets. If only he'd been with her the day she'd gone out on the boat. Instead he'd skipped out to do paperwork.

He forced his misgivings into silence and knocked on the office door.

"Come in."

Noah walked into the eight-by-ten-foot office and crossed to the desk where the sunlight shone from the single window above the chief. A bookcase of law books stood in a corner and diplomas and certificates decorated the beige walls.

His boss wore a crisply starched, white shirt as though he expected a surprise inspection from his former military years. He kept his head bent over a form beside the computer, probably giving the document his legal eye. When confronted by the press or defense lawyers, he spouted off laws wheeler-dealer prosecutor-style. Chief Banks was a tough, by-the-book leader.

The hum of the window's air conditioner filled the silence. A floorboard under Noah's feet squeaked when he stirred. He'd forgotten to avoid the plank loosened by nervous officers shifting from foot to foot.

The chief raised his head, and the green eyes in his long face narrowed with a frown while he ran his gaze over Noah. "You missed our morning briefing."

"High winds delayed takeoff, sir. I returned as soon as my flight got into the Manchester airport. My drive north took an extra thirty minutes because of the summer traffic on the interstate."

The chief stabbed a finger at him. "Next time, book an earlier departure. Are you ready to work today?"

"Yes, sir." Noah didn't bother protesting that he couldn't have predicted the weather or road conditions. Not that it mattered. The last question was prompted by the chief's concern over Noah's mental health.

His boss sat forward in his chair and snapped, "Right answer. You're needed here. We've another missing girl. The FBI acts as consultants on both cases now."

The chief's voice held steady, but Noah caught the man's wince on the word 'another'.

"I understand, sir."

"We're putting most of our resources into the search. After the dead ends in the Kara Linn disappearance, I don't need to remind you the city is clamoring for an arrest and for the girls' safe return. The media roasts us every day." He grabbed the paper from under a file and slapped it on the desk in front of Noah. "One of the editors, Vic Taylor, is Kara Linn's uncle, and he uses his blog and daily column to keep track of the days she's been gone. The guy's odd, but he has a knack for pressing the right buttons to set off public reaction."

Under the headline '**And Now There Are Two**', Noah read aloud the first paragraph. "Why do we no longer hear Kara Linn's name mentioned or details of a search for her? The police prefer to focus on parking meters. Are they more precious than the missing children of our community?"

Since the chief handled criticism like a sore he constantly picked until it grew worse, Noah chose his words with care. "I don't think the editor understands the scope of our investigation. The fact we continue working on Kara Linn's case isn't as obvious as when we went door to door. Any connection between the two teenagers?"

"We've found none so far."

"One missing girl is unusual for Hawick Falls. Two seems too much of a coincidence for them to be runaways." If they could discover similarities, they might find a single predator.

"Taylor describes us as heartless and inept." The chief tossed the front section into the wastebasket. "All the readers' letters to the editor condemn the police department. I expect pitchforks and torches instead of cameras and lights at the next news conference."

"I read up on the last girl's disappearance during my flight. Has the crime line gotten any action?"

"We've followed three hundred tips. We checked out every one from the weird neighbor who cuts his grass in the middle of the night with a flashlight to the guy who threatened to blow up his mother-in-law's car. An elderly couple swore they saw Lisa at the bus station, but the girl they ID'd turned out to be a teenager traveling to her grandmother's." The chief pulled a sheet out of a file and handed it to Noah. "Here are her basic facts"

Noah studied the sheet while the boss talked.

"Lisa Grant disappeared sometime on the night of the fifth or morning of the sixth when she was reported missing. Black and pink hair, light brown eyes, weight one hundred and ten pounds and five foot six. Her guardian for the past six months, Teagan Raynes, reported the girl was last wearing denim shorts and a white T-shirt when last seen."

Noah tried a different tact. "Do we have an intruder theory?" Was she a new Elizabeth Smart abducted from her bed?

"No evidence supports forced entry or a struggle. Lisa slept alone on the third floor. No ladder, trees, or trellis near the house or prints on the ground." The chief passed him a picture of Lisa's bedroom and her folder.

Noah noted the windows and door locations. The room size suggested an intruder could get in and out quickly, but going down three flights of stairs with an unwilling teenager was risky even if someone memorized the layout.

"We're done canvassing the neighborhood. State Police questioned the eight registered sex offenders in the area. Your partner's notes are in your file and dropbox, Cassidy."

"What do we know about the guardian?"

"Miss Raynes is a local, who moved to Massachusetts, but returned this winter to care for her aunt. She died two weeks later from leukemia. Since her return, Raynes got a job at the elementary school. At this time, she's not a person of interest. No one else lives in the home."

"Any chance the girl's a runaway?"

"Everyone swears Lisa never mentioned taking off, though she had dreams of working in Boston or New York City. She had little cash and no credit cards. Miss Raynes had confiscated Lisa's cell phone, but it was no longer in her bureau where Miss Raynes put it. The cell, Lisa's wallet, and house key didn't surface in the search. We developed the theory Lisa lifted her phone before she vanished. Miss Raynes reported Lisa carried her key in her wallet wherever she went. The judge issued a warrant for the phone records yesterday, and I've a man working on the call history."

Noah scanned the first page of his partner, Denny Hines', notes. "No useful statements from other foster children in her previous homes."

"Not a damn thing. Lisa's boyfriend, Travis Bodell, says he knows nothing. He shows up each morning for an update. He flips between a civil, mature discussion to an out-of-control rant that we need to work harder and find Lisa sooner. We can't predict which Travis will show up."

"Strange behavior. Counseling?"

"His guidance counselor described him as a teen with poor self-image, who has weak social skills but isn't violent."

"He sounds like every high school kid to me."

"Travis admitted he argued with Lisa on her lunch break the last day she was seen. He maintains he hasn't glimpsed or heard from her since the fight, but until he's ruled out, he's a person of interest."

"Lisa Grant disappeared without a clue."

"The girl vanished faster than a bullet from a Bushmaster rifle. You and Hines focus on Grant. I've got another team searching for the Linn girl. Continue pressuring Travis. He lives with his uncle, Seth Bodell. He's threatened to lawyer-up the kid if we question Travis again and turns deaf when we explain his nephew wants to talk to us. Uncle's earned a rep as unreasonable. Seth went to All Saints on a sports scholarship and was a star for a couple of years until he suffered two broken legs. He used to ump for a few teams in Hawick, until he got into too many arguments.

"So the uncle's a fun guy. His nephew may have inherited his temper. What's the story on friends who'd hide Lisa if she ran?" The chance of finding her safe was better if she'd taken off on her own.

"She's been in nine foster homes since she was two, and she

ages out of the system on her birthday next month. Lisa left a trail of disruptive behavior in her past placements."

"You mean no one put a candle in the window for her."

"Sophia and Teagan Raynes were the girl's last stop."

"A girl with poor impulse control and judgment would be easy prey for the wrong person, and not a happy ending."

"I requested a clearer picture of Grant." The chief seized another section of the *Hawick Falls Citizen* from under a stack of folders and dropped it on top of the desk.

The article on the plane had omitted Lisa's image. Noah stared at the fuzzy photo of a slim teen. A pixie-sized woman with long hair reaching past her shoulders stood beside Lisa. Raynes looked young for a guardian. Raynes. The name and face were familiar. Curious, he brought the picture closer.

"When I asked if you're ready to work, Cassidy...well, your family will always be missed."

The chief's admission left Noah speechless. His boss always lectured the men, "When it's personal, keep it at home."

Had the chief expressed sympathy when June and Kimmy died? His wife had supported his every decision. Many labeled her traditional, but June was proud to be Mrs. Noah Cassidy from the moment they married. His daughter had been the sunshine in his life with her smiles and giggles.

Noah searched his memory and recalled days buried in a haze after their deaths. The chief's calls and visits had seemed focused on when Noah would return to work. Was his boss acting like a normal human being now?

"Hines is at All Saints High School interviewing Lisa's teachers." The chief chucked the rest of the paper into his circular file by his desk. "I need you to go to Miss Raynes' house before you join him. Her address is listed in the report. Ten minutes ago, she called in that she'd received a death threat. She sounded flustered and upset. I sent the patrol over on a welfare check, and they've reported she's safe and secure. You will need to document today's evidence."

Noah checked Miss Raynes' residence. Eighty-six High Street was located in the village section of Hawick Falls and three blocks from the small, popular neighborhood grocery. People joked, if you're lonely drop into Muffy Mart and you'll meet someone you know.

"I planned to head to High Street," the chief said, "but we had a collision on Purgatory Road involving an oil truck. I'm going to the accident to inform the EPA that none of the fuel leaked into the ground. These rules tie up our manpower." The chief tapped his fingers and frowned. "Fish and Game will drag the Bearclaw River, and the staties and volunteers will comb the footpaths in the southeast parts of the city today. We've managed for a Guard helicopter to fly over the rougher terrain."

One hundred twenty-two miles of trails stretched through the Appalachian White

Mountains. Unexpected weather often stranded experienced hikers. The teen's chances of survival were reduced if she'd chosen to walk her way through the nearby mountains unprepared. He turned to leave.

"Oh, Noah, one more thing. Father Matt Hastings, a family friend, will be with Miss

Raynes, too."

Noah swung around to the chief. "Mercy, a priest is coming?"

The chief narrowed his eyes at him, but Noah didn't bother to apologize for the hostility in his voice. He'd never kept it a secret from his boss how his father, once an altar boy, had been messed up by his parish priest's unwanted attentions. Noah was an adult before he had understood the impact of the abuse on his father.

"People turn to their church when they're in crisis, Cassidy. Lisa works part-time in the church's office, and I expect you to keep your personal feelings to yourself."

He knew that name, Father Hastings. "Isn't he the priest who was rejected for a job as a bishop because of an affair?" Seemed like the guy had his own crisis to keep him busy.

When the chief scowled at him, Noah added, "I overheard a few community members mention the fact." Everyone he met. The fling had been the talk of Hawick Falls during the long, boring winter. Townspeople rotated the names of different women for the scarlet-letter role. A rumor flew that the police had arrested a bagboy at Muffy's for running a betting ring on the woman's identity.

"We don't investigate sins," the chief growled. "Otherwise, we'd have to double the force. So, bring those girls home, restore faith in our department and prove your worth."

"Glad you don't expect much."

"Save the jokes. Get going."

Noah's adrenaline revved up. He savored challenges. He stuck the folder under his arm and crossed the wooden floor to the exit. What was the quickest way? Hawick Falls was nestled between the White Mountains with their breathtaking peaks and the sparkling, clear waters of the Lakes Region. Noah loved the place, but not the crowds of tourists the landscape and outlets at the north end of the city attracted. The visitors flocked to stores at the noon hour.

He'd take the Falls Back Road. Being a townie, he always drove the shortcuts or less traveled routes. The road ran parallel to the winding river and ended near the cascade in the village. Sister Mountains to the northwest overlooked the valley.

"Cassidy, I have one more thing."

The edge in the chief's tone warned him his boss had saved the slap on the wrist for last.

"Buy a new shirt. We're not the Rag Squad."

You look handsome in your gray shirt, June whispered from the past. The hitch of pride in her voice swirled in his memory until pain bit into him. He rubbed a hand over his face. "Yes, sir."

Noah shoved the scene out of his thoughts. He headed out of the office, keeping his thoughts focused on the case. Now what items would a teenage girl grab when she left her house? She'd grab her phone. If only the rest of the case came together as easily.

He exited into the sunlight. The warning echoed in his mind. *Restore faith and prove your worth.* Noah's family had been destroyed in the boating accident, but he was determined not to let life break him and end up like his father.

CHAPTER 4

Teagan raced across the tiled entryway when the bell chimed. All she wanted was to show the police the threat she received this afternoon. Maybe it was an important clue that would lead to Lisa, and to the arrest of the person who'd sent the holy card.

Caution slowed Teagan at the last moment, and she cracked open the door. "Chief Banks, I—"

She'd met the Chief of Police and this wasn't him. At five feet tall, she was often the smallest individual in the room, but this male must stand about six four and could make an average sized adult feel short. He'd rolled up the sleeves of his gray-button-down shirt, which seemed to emphasize the mass of his arms. In his hand, he held a manila folder.

He raised a brow and removed the sunglasses over his light blue eyes. "Miss Raynes? Chief had an emergency."

She tilted her head and looked closer.

"I'm—"

"—Noah Cassidy." The name hurtled past her worries and fears. She opened the door wider. "You worked as a counselor at Camp Mighty Joe." She'd had a wicked crush on him. Whenever she heard an oldie love song from that summer, she thought of him.

A forgotten memory popped into her consciousness. They were camped on the mountaintop. A canopy of twinkling stars stretching forever above them, but she barely noticed or breathed. Noah

Cassidy sat less than a foot from her.

Now he moved impatiently, and she stuffed the scene back into her teenage memories. Although he seemed calm, his gaze roamed over her neighborhood as though he was taking in everything around him or ready to take down a suspect. He tapped his index finger against his thigh.

Yes. Noah Cassidy was a man of action. She would have chosen him from a lineup to search for Lisa. At Mighty Joe, his sense of humor and ability to push his campers to do their best while having fun made him a favorite counselor.

"Mighty Joe was a popular camp." He stared at her like he was searching through faces and names in his minds.

Of course, he wouldn't recognize her. She'd attended Mighty Joe fifteen years ago. She was eleven. Aunt Sophia thought weeks spent in the outdoors would be character building. Teagan did her best to win the camper of the month award and not disappoint her.

"You might know me by my camp nickname, Munchkin." She wrinkled her nose over the moniker.

"Thanks for the reminder, but I'll stick with Miss Raynes, and I remember you." He flashed his badge. "But I'm not a counselor anymore. I'm a detective on the Hawick Falls Police Force."

She must be very memorable by the way he changed the subject, but her conscience reminded her he was here to find Lisa and that was important.

"Please, call me Teagan or I'll feel like I'm in the classroom."

"All right, Teagan. I'm following up on the threat you received."

"Two officers came earlier about it. Is the chief sending everyone and anyone? I mean, we need consistency. Lisa is missing, and I get a warning in the mail. We're not trying to get a cat out of the tree."

"Everyone who works the investigation shares information. Don't worry. We're a team, pulling to bring Lisa home and keep you safe."

Lisa home. She averted her face while struggling with a lump in her throat. After a second, she swallowed and regained control. "If you could wait a few minutes for Father Matt, I'd appreciate it. He's like a member of my family." She swept a gaze up and down the block lined with maple trees and orange daylilies. Nowhere did she spot Matt's ten-year-old Suburban rattling on the road. "I guess he's running late. He had to meet with an engaged couple before they went to work."

Detective Cassidy crowded closer, and set off Teagan's alertness to him.

"Mind if I come inside instead of talking on your front porch?" He inclined his head toward the hall.

"Sure." She was rambling about Matt, but if he didn't arrive soon, she'd have to face the death threat discussion without his support. She shuffled back a step as Noah entered the hallway.

"Is the bow on the tree for Lisa?"

"Yes. I wanted to share a reminder that she's still missing."

A meow brought Teagan's attention to her pet. The black cat sat at the detective's feet.

"Is your pet okay?"

"That's Jogger. She was a stray and lost part of her ears to frostbite. That's why she appears a little strange. She used to wander out of an abandoned building and join me when I jogged."

"Got it. Does she cry all the time?" He stepped back and frowned as though the meowing bothered him.

"Say hello and she'll stop."

"Hello...cat." He frowned and patted the air above her head. The animal rubbed against his legs and ceased crying.

Jogger dogged Teagan's heels as she led the detective into the living room. He stopped in the middle of the floor and scanned the interior. She shot a fleeting glimpse at the coffee table with her stash of aspirin, tissues, and eye drops, sitting on the tabletop and then focused back on the detective.

He was taking in Aunt Sophia's mismatched furniture like a prospective homebuyer. Her aunt never threw away a furnishing if it was usable and she'd have dusted and vacuumed before she let him inside. Teagan sucked in a deep breath. At least Aunt Sophia wasn't around for Teagan's temporary lapse in cleaning. "Is something wrong?"

He shrugged. "Old habit. The place looks fine to me." He gestured to the bookcase on the wall above the sofa. "You've got a lot of books."

"What?" Teagan pivoted around. The shelves contained an eclectic collection of dictionaries, classics, how to books, and biographies. "I've read most of them. When I was growing up, my aunt insisted we have our library hour before I watched TV."

"My father owned tons of books."

"Don't tell me." She held up her palm. "He was a teacher or librarian."

"Mechanic."

So much for guessing a stereotype or that she possessed psychic abilities. She shoved the footstool in front of the red rocker, and Jogger settled on it for a nap.

"How are you doing?" he asked.

"I dropped out of teaching summer classes." That was off track. She wet her lips and started again. "I'm surviving. People I've never met have posted hundreds of flyers throughout the city, and we're planning a vigil." She tapped the ends of her fingertips together. "My mind imagines terrible things happening to Lisa. I don't know how to turn it off."

"Each person has a different strategy. Many talk with a therapist."

"Everyone has been open to talking to me."

"Not quite what I meant."

"Good, because it's been awful and I don't recommend it. So far, I've learned zero about where Lisa went, but I've heard plenty of horror stories about girls who never came home." The jangle of her bracelets reminded her to stop her nervous habit of waving her hands around. She dropped her arms to her sides. The detective looked cool and unaffected by the heat or her wandering speech. At least he was looking at her, not the room decor.

"I can't sleep or eat without worrying about her." Teagan's body shook with the overflow of emotion for Lisa, mixed with memories of her first infatuation. "I'm babbling. Sorry." She pressed her damp palms against her tan Capri pants to keep them still.

"You should take care of yourself, Teagan. Becoming sick won't bring Lisa home."

The genuine concern in his voice surprised her, and she reconsidered Noah Cassidy. Maybe he was still the boy who radiated strength and confidence. A certainty hit her. This man would find Lisa.

"Did you remember something?"

She averted her gaze while she censored her thoughts. "I've been asking myself where Lisa would go. I've racked my brain for days." A cramp knotted in her neck, and she relaxed her shoulders. "I've ruled out her parents. They don't live near Hawick Falls, and they're in and out of jail. She wants nothing to do with them."

"Any chance your parents or relatives would take her in?"

"My father..." She shrugged. "He left my mom and me when I was a baby. My mother vanished years ago and has been presumed dead. Aunt Sophia was my last living relative as far as I'm aware." She frowned. "We weren't the model for the Brady Bunch."

"Not many of us are."

"Lisa was so excited about her adoption on her birthday next month that I can't believe she'd run off."

"Lisa didn't feel she was too old to be adopted?"

He had a lot to learn regarding foster kids. "She wanted a family, relatives, and a place to belong. It's common for children who weren't released for adoption to embrace the law allowing adults to become part of a home. My aunt adopted me when I was seven."

His eyes widened with surprise. "In my job, I only find out about the grown-ups using the legal process to cut someone from the will." He crossed the carpet to the mantle and paused.

Why was he studying Aunt Sophia's picture? "Do you have a question, Detective?"

"What? Oh, is that your aunt?" He stepped aside and pointed at her photo with her upswept, auburn hair.

"Yes. Next to her is my Uncle Nick, her husband. He died after their third wedding anniversary. Is the photo important? You seem distracted."

"I'm just getting background information. And this is you with your aunt?" He gestured to her college graduation picture in a smaller frame. Teagan wanted to wince when she looked at her younger self with her hair frizzed out two feet.

"We were at the Keene State College commencement." After that day, she'd never expected to live in Hawick Falls again because she was off to conquer the world. The surprise was on her.

The detective cleared his throat, drawing her attention to him. "If you don't mind, we can discuss your threat."

A pain stabbed above her eyebrow. The afternoon heat had

intensified the headache that had started with the holy card. She swiped at her damp forehead and crossed the flowered rug to the bay windows. "I'd like a little fresh air before we talk." Or she'd pass out. She yanked on the sill's lock without success. Sweat trickled down her neck, and her head throbbed. "We don't have AC, and I can't find the fans."

"Allow me." He set the manila folder on the upholstered chair and scooted behind it.

His long fingers grasped the catch, and he flipped the pane upward with the ease of flicking a switch.

Dust flew off the ridge and landed on her white shirt while a breeze rushed inside. She sighed with relief and brushed off the grime. "I'm glad Aunt Sophia's not here. She'd hate for a visitor to see dirt in her house." She glanced up to find Noah watching her with unmistakable dark heat in his eyes. She swallowed and awareness filled her every pore, even the air she breathed.

He broke eye contact and stepped away from her. "I'll never tell anyone. Pinky swear." For a second, a grin softened the hard lines that had formed in his tan face since his younger days, and the desire disappeared from his eyes.

Had she imagined the expression in his gaze? One thing was certain. He was a good-looking man who oozed coolness. "You're handy to have around." She forced lightness into her tone to hide her true thoughts.

"You'll find a few who disagree," he said in a sober voice.

What had he meant by his comment?

"We should sit and talk." He motioned toward the sofa.

"Okay."

He chose the chair at the head of the room while she perched on the couch across from the fireplace. He dug a pen out of his shirt pocket and opened the file on his lap. "We can go over a few basics before Father Matt arrives. Tell me about the threat you received today."

Teagan's thoughts turned to the holy card she'd place behind the frame on the mantle. She wanted to wait, but who knew when Matt would appear? She linked her fingers and cupped them around her knees to hold herself together. "As I've explained to the two officers who arrived earlier, at lunchtime I—"

No sooner had the words left her lips than the doorbell rang.

CHAPTER 5

The doorbell rang two short rings followed by one long. Jogger sprang from her stool and padded to the hall.

"Aren't you going to answer?" Noah asked her.

"Father Matt's here. Aunt Sophia gave him a spare key when she was ill before I returned. He brought her magazines, medicine, and food. I told him to keep the key. He helps out if I can't be around for a repairman or checks on Jogger. When he knows I'm home, he rings to let me know he's coming inside."

The sound of footsteps in the hall announced the priest was in the house.

He appeared in the living room dressed in black pants and shirt. He wore his collar, which meant he'd been working. Jogger paused near the priest to let out a meow and returned to her stool after a pat.

Teagan gave Matt a quick hug. As she stepped away, she caught Detective Cassidy leaning forward, his gaze fixed on them, and his lips twisted downward. What was wrong with him?

"Any news, Teagan?" Matt tilted his silver-haired head and peered into her face. His wide blue eyes communicated hope, and the familiar scent of evergreen mints couldn't mask the cigarette smoke lingering around him.

"No word from Lisa, but Detective Cassidy is here." She gestured toward him.

Matt crossed the room to the detective with an outstretched

hand. "Sorry, I'm late." He scanned the detective's features, but his expression remained stoic.

"Stacey, the church secretary, stopped me with a few questions before I left." After they exchanged handshakes, Matt settled on the sofa next to Teagan. He removed a white envelope from his pocket and set it on the sofa's arm. Had he found something about Lisa?

"You're joining the search too, detective?" Matt asked.

"Detective Hines and I are partners. I was away until today."

"Since the introductions are done," she said with a tight smile. "I'll explain the reason we're together." She glanced at Matt who gave her a nod of reassurance. "As you know, Detective, I received a death threat in today's mail." Her stomach did a flip-flop. She wet her dry lips and blurted, "The card was addressed to me and said, 'You die next'."

Noah blinked and she guessed what he was thinking. Was Lisa already dead?

Teagan blinked away the tears stinging her eyes and drew in a calming breath. "The sender printed out the words and omitted a signature, of course. Matt encouraged me to report the threat immediately."

"You discussed it with Father Matt?" A dent formed between the detective's brows.

Was that strange? Matt was her closest ally now that her best friend Lucy was gone. "Uh, yes, he called me right after I read the note."

"You just happened to call?" Noah fixed his narrow gaze on Matt.

"I'm helping with the vigil and wanted to discuss a few details. I've known Teagan since she was little," the priest added. "We trust each other."

Cassidy's lips formed into a flat line of disapproval. "From now on, relay information only to law enforcement. Detective Hines and I will take care of the threat, not Father Matt."

She didn't like Noah Cassidy's stern reprimand or how he seemed to be hinting she shouldn't count on Matt. A long-ago memory of a younger Matt handing her a peppermint at the Sharing Kitchen flashed through Teagan's mind.

Her temper boiled. "Matt is the most reliable person I know."

Matt rested a hand on her arm. "The detective's right."

She bit her lip to stop the protest and folded her hands together. She could be diplomatic, especially since Lisa's return depended on this man. "In the future, I'll trust you both."

All right, she was semi-diplomatic.

Noah frowned at her. "Father, I'd appreciate you letting me handle the matter from this point. It's for your safety, too."

"I'll do whatever you suggest. My goal is the same as Teagan's. Bring Lisa home to us."

"Glad to hear, Father. Teagan, who do you think sent the threat?"

"Lisa's boyfriend, Travis, might have mailed it. I disapproved of Lisa and Travis going out," she confessed, putting her irritation behind her. "Their relationship was unhealthy. Lisa wanted to change her life, and she did raise her grades, but socially, she didn't fit in at All Saints. Travis was a loner and Lisa's lack of popularity was unimportant to him. In fact, it added to her attraction. They had each other. I urged her to look beyond him to school clubs, other boys and girlfriends. Travis took my idea as a personal insult." Remorse pinched her. She should have kept quiet and let their teen crush run its course.

"Travis feels unwanted," Father Matt interjected. "The Bodell family belongs to my parish, and I'm familiar with his background. His mother lives in Rhode Island, but confesses she can't deal with the boy. His father, who lived in Hawick Falls, drowned a couple years ago. Travis moved in with his single uncle, who wasn't happy to inherit a teenager. You can understand why the boy is bitter and acts out."

"Makes sense," Noah agreed while he flicked a glance at Matt's hand on hers. "Do you believe Lisa ran off with Travis the night she disappeared?"

She sighed. "Lisa insisted they were finished the last day I saw her, but she and Travis broke up at least once a week. The longest they stayed apart was nine days in May."

Was she wrong and an angry Travis was holding Lisa somewhere? Teagan imagined Lisa bound and locked in a closet. She blocked the image and concentrated on the detective.

"The boy never harmed a soul," Father Matt said. "He raises his voice when he's upset, and ten minutes later, he's contrite."

Detective Cassidy's expression remained unreadable. "Teagan, have you had any trouble with anyone in your past or present? An ex, a neighbor, friend?"

"Me?" She shook her head. Did she come across as a magnet for psychos? How much did he know about her life? He was staring at her with eyes that were inscrutable. She dismissed the thoughts to answer him. "My neighbors were friendly, and I've no hard feelings with the last man I dated. The only person I've had any difference with is Jake Clark. We argued when his girlfriend, my friend, Lucy, left him. He thought I was interfering in their lives, but we agreed to disagree and called a truce."

"Interfered how?"

"I objected when he treated Lucy like a maid, except a maid would have gotten paid. She moved away to start over when she realized their relationship wasn't the type that lasted."

"He forgave you for getting involved in his life?"

She hesitated. "He's not angry with me. Would I trust every word out of his mouth? No. Except for Travis, I don't know anyone mad at me, let alone someone who wants me dead." She shook her head and ran faces and names through her mind. No, she wasn't wrong.

Cassidy glanced at the open file. "Lisa disappeared Monday night or Tuesday morning from her third-floor bedroom. No one else is on that level with her?"

"She slept upstairs for privacy."

"And the last time you saw Lisa, Father Matt, was on Friday?"

Was he pointing a finger of suspicion at Matt again? What was wrong with the detective? Matt was a priest and their friend. He'd never hurt Lisa. Teagan turned toward Matt who showed no signs of offense.

"Right," Matt confirmed. "In the summer, Lisa worked in the church office five days a week. I spoke to her after her last lunch with Travis at the mall. She was upset he didn't pay for her meal, but she calmed down in a few minutes when I asked her to name his better qualities."

"What were those?" Cassidy asked.

"Lisa felt he was supportive, faithful, and planned to get a job to support them in their future." The priest fished in the white envelope and pulled out a photo. "Teagan told me you needed a recent picture of Lisa. I brought one from her Confirmation in May. She always ducked when she saw a camera. I didn't give her a choice that day." Matt held out the photo of Lisa's attractive, dimpled face framed by dark hair with pink streaks. One brow was drawn up as if to say, is this for real?

"Lisa started a new life at All Saints High," Matt told him. "Unlike in her past, she did her school work and attended classes."

The detective set Lisa's picture on top of his file and studied it. "You look like you're related. Black hair, dimples, brown eyes—"

"We're not blood relatives." Teagan touched her shoulder length, dark curls.

The detective tapped the edge of the picture against his palm. His shoulders sank forward. Then he rubbed a hand over his face and rose. "I'll send out her new picture, but I want to urge you, Miss Raynes, to report anything suspicious. Don't hesitate."

"But—"

"Listen to the detective." Matt patted her shoulder in reassurance. "I can take over the vigil."

"No way, I need to do it for Lisa." She'd go crazy doing nothing, and she wanted to make a personal plea to the media. "I have to attend. A family member always says a few words." Aunt Sophia would be up front and center if she were alive.

"I'm sorry, I have to leave." Matt edged forward on the cushion. "But we can set up a neighborhood watch around your house, Teagan and talk more about the vigil later."

"We should keep the volunteers looking for Lisa, not looking at me. Please, let's not waste the donated manpower. Put the volunteers to work searching." The meeting wasn't turning out as Teagan hoped. Their attention had shifted to her. "The police will be at the vigil, right?"

"We plan to be present. You can designate someone to read your statement to the media if you want."

Matt stood and hovered over her. "We'll keep looking for Lisa. I've a friend who'll post the newest flyers across the state, and I spoke to the bishop. We can set up a platform near the church steps Friday night for the speakers. The men's group has a phone tree we'll use to alert everyone in the parish with the details. I'll notify the press."

"And I'll be there." Lisa might be listening somewhere.

Noah twisted his lips in disapproval. "I'm sure Father Matt thinks you're safe at his church, but I can't guarantee that. My job is to find Lisa and keep everyone from getting hurt."

"This is my decision, not his." She resisted the urge to stamp her foot. What was wrong with Detective Cassidy? He gave off a hostile vibe when he spoke about Matt.

"Fine," Noah said. "I'll take you to the vigil."

"Teagan," Matt interrupted her before she could respond to Noah's last statement. "Before I leave, I have good news for a change. An anonymous donor from the parish is donating a five thousand dollar reward for tips that lead to Lisa."

Teagan jumped to her feet and hugged Matt. "Thank you for coming especially after I asked you to go home the other night and not spend more hours worrying about me."

"There's no way I wouldn't worry."

"I want a list of people and schedules for the evening of the vigil," Noah said in his no-nonsense tone as he rose. "We can't take any risks with lives."

The detective was making her nervous. She released Matt, fought the impulse to dash across the room, and close the curtains.

Matt extended a hand to Noah. "I'll email you a copy of the agenda for the night of the vigil. My parishioners will help with anything you need. Just call me."

"I will. The chief will want to address the public at your event, too." The detective shook Matt's hand, and then dug out two cards from his pocket. "Here's my contact numbers and email. Use them if you remember anything else." The detective handed his personal information to Matt and Teagan.

"I'll walk you out," she said to Matt. A moment alone with him would calm her jagged nerves.

"Don't bother. We'll talk." He gave her a reassuring smile.

She snuck a peek at Noah, who watched them openly. His gaze followed Matt out of the room.

His scowl and tight mouth warned her he wasn't thinking positive thoughts. "Let's get to the main business, your threat. Where is it?"

"I stuck it behind my aunt's picture for safe keeping." She went to the mantle and pulled out the holy card in a baggie. "I kept the envelope too. The Post mark is local."

She handed it over and saw him blink twice. "I know you bag evidence," she explained.

"Thank you, *CSI*." He examined the envelope. "We'll work on tracing it." He held up the four-by-seven inch card.

"The picture on the front is Mary Magdalene." Teagan crossed her arms over her chest and stared at the drawing. Long, dark hair framed Mary Magdalene's face. She wore a blue gown and gazed into a mirror by candlelight. Her folded hands rested on a skull in her lap. Teagan fought the shiver creeping up her back.

"Fill me in on Mary Magdalene, so we're on the same wavelength. I don't have a religious background."

"She was a sinful woman who Jesus forgave when she repented."

"Magdalene sounds like a lot of people I know. Only they try to repent in front of the judge." Noah turned the computer printed message to the backside. "How common is a Holy Card?"

"When I was younger, pretty common to buy from a church store. Now you can order them online."

It's in...Latin?" He squinted at the message as if it would change before his eyes.

"Don't you keep a file of criminals who make these threats?"

"Sure, I'll read up on suspects who correspond in a dead language on a holy card." He scrubbed a hand over the light stubble on his chin and lowered the bag.

Now she'd said the idea aloud, it did sound absurd. "I understand. I'd hope you track all illegal actions."

"We don't usually have dead language ones in Hawick Falls, but I'll check the database. The FBI might have a few."

"I've a tip for you. Lisa and Travis were in Latin class together."

"Thanks. I'll follow up on that tip, and I'll fill you in soon." With his free hand, he dug out keys from his pocket and started across the room.

"What are you going to do?" His visit hadn't helped her learn anything. Instead, he was leaving her more unsettled. She wanted him to stay, talk to her about how Lisa would be home soon, and to look at her again with that simmering expression.

She wiped a hand over her eyes. She was going off the deep end. The man was doing his job, not looking for a date.

He turned toward her. "I'm going to interview their teachers." His phone went off in his jacket pocket, and he glanced at the number. "Excuse me. I need to take this call." He ducked into the hall.

Teagan started to gnaw on her nails. He might be discussing Lisa. She jumped up and lingered a few feet from the hall's threshold. The detective's back was to her.

"I'm near Muffy's. I'll be right there. Clear the store after taking the names and addresses of everyone inside. We'll question the employees first. Let's hope we get lucky." He clicked off his cell and his gaze landed on her.

"News of Lisa?" Did the guilt over eavesdropping show on her face?

He hesitated then answered, "We haven't found her." He reached for the doorknob.

Teagan darted into the hallway. "Please, give me a hint. Is it about her?"

"I don't pass on reports until I'm certain they're legit."

Something was going on, and she couldn't sit around the house a minute longer. "I'll go with you and find out what's happening." She needed her keys to lockup.

"You stay here, and I'll brief you when I'm done." He laid his palm on her shoulder. "Is there someone who'll stay with you?"

She was aware of the fact he was touching her. Her pulse leaped. What was she doing? She wasn't eleven. She stepped away. "I just need Lisa back safe and sound. Please, I can't stand not knowing what's happening."

His jaw tightened. "I'll fill you in ASAP."

From the front window, she watched him drive off. Talk wasn't what she wanted. Action and results were what she craved. She'd get them. How hard was it to go to the store? She could do this. She paced for four minutes before she grabbed her keys and purse from the entryway table. In her pocket was her St. Jude's medal. The saint of the hopeless always comforted and reminded her that miracles happened. Maybe today was one of those days.

She jumped into her car and headed for Muffy Mart.

CHAPTER 6

Teagan Raynes occupied Noah's thoughts while he drove down the hill to the village center. She'd arrived at camp registration years ago looking more like a cover model for a kids' fashion magazine. He'd hoped she'd have fun because her size and coordinated sportswear indicated she wasn't the type to win the outdoor challenges. Man, had he been wrong.

She had more heart than all the Mighty Joe's counselors and campers combined. Every morning she arrived early at circle, always neatly groomed and ready. Teagan came out on top in each activity from hiking to small crafts to swim contests. She'd intrigued him before with her spirit and cute face. Now she'd grown into a damn, attractive woman, and one who could cause a major distraction. He'd worked hard to start his life over after losing his family. He sure didn't need a female sidetracking his concentration, especially with the chief's current mood.

He held Teagan's image in his mind for another second. The shadows in her eyes worried him. What horrors was she imagining about Lisa, and how many of them would come true?

He wanted to remove the darkness and the pain from her eyes, and he'd do his best to accomplish it. Hitting the pedal, he sped to Muffy's.

****

The town hall, library, two gift shops, St. Jude's church, and a scattering of indie stores composed the business hub of Hawick Falls and the place Teagan headed. At the intersection of High and Main Streets, she slowed for the stop sign. In the distance, the twin mountains looked down on the village center. Their rocky tops were decorated with the modern technology of cell towers that had replaced the ancient fire tower.

Traffic was sparse until Teagan merged onto Main. She expected to spot Noah's black sedan. Instead, Lisa's unsmiling face posted on the telephone poles stared back at her. The volunteers had done an excellent job of spreading the news, too excellent. Nausea swirled in Teagan's stomach, and she adjusted the AC vent to allow the cool air to fan her.

A block before Muffy Mart, vehicles slowed and jammed together on the two-lane road. A cop on duty waved people onward. He shook his head when a driver signaled to turn into the store. In the parking lot, she spotted three cruisers with Hawick Falls Police written across their sides, and at least eight blue uniforms swarmed around the outside of the concrete building.

She passed the real estate office and Bennie's Hardware, where people clustered together and craned their necks toward the action. Bennie, a short middle-aged man, was pointing to the market. His baldhead made him stick out in the group. St. Jude's Church stood across from the hardware store. Their lot was filled with press vehicles and cars owned by the locals who lounged on the nearby granite slabs that bordered the falls. She drove onward.

Near Pretty Park, she found an empty spot to pull over. She jumped out and hit the lock on her keychain. The sweet fragrance of the red rose bushes bordering the commons hung in the air.

Teagan slung her purse over her shoulder and jogged toward Muffy's. Had the police discovered a big clue? Why else would Detective Cassidy run off to the store? Her throat constricted when one possibility surfaced in her thoughts. What if they'd found Lisa and it was the worst news?

"Teagan Raynes, stop."

Travis' uncle, Seth Bodell, drove next to the curb in a rusted truck that smoked oil from the tailpipe. She swerved in surprise. Where had he come from? Was he following her? He leaned out his open window with a sneer on his face. Blaring music poured out of the cab, and he shouted over the country twang instead of turning it down.

Seth had the dark good looks that drew women, but his disposition was a date repellant. He bared his yellow teeth like a trapped animal, and his brown eyes blazed with anger in a shadow-whiskered face. He flicked ash from a cigarette onto the road before he signaled for her to wait.

She'd rather dodge cars on the interstate. She picked up her pace and wound through pedestrians. Seth hollered at her again, but his radio and the roar of a passing motorcycle with a loud muffler drowned out his words. His curled bottom lip and the fury in his voice assured her that leaving him with his exhaust fumes was a better plan. Ahead, the traffic light flashed green. He'd drive on when she stopped for the walk signal.

Teagan halted at the intersection. Seth slammed the brakes and gunned his engine while he fastened a sick smile on her. Was he imagining running her down as she crossed the street with witnesses present? Her heart thudded in her chest.

"Cut the dumb act, Raynes," he yelled to her. "You set the police on Travis."

Don't make eye contact with him. She scanned the area for a quick shortcut.

A sports car pulled up behind him and tooted for him to move.

Seth didn't budge. "I know it was you. You hate my nephew."

No signs of the police. They were at Muffy's. If she did an about-face, would Seth bang a U-ey and follow her? A ripple of fear shot up her arms. No, she could walk the street if she wanted. He was a big bully. Anger flowed through her and replaced the fears. She bit down on the urge to tell him where to go.

Mature people do not hold screaming matches in the streets.

"I remember, Aunt Sophia," Teagan muttered.

The driver behind Seth blasted his horn.

"I won't forget." Seth took off with a screech of tires.

She shuddered with relief. When the walk light changed, Seth had zoomed halfway up the next block. She detoured between two buildings and across an alley to arrive at Muffy's back lot. The place was thick with law enforcement snapping pictures. Officers with bent heads seemed to be examining the paved ground behind the store. Two employees in their moss-colored smocks gestured while talking to a cop.

Lisa's voice replayed in Teagan's head. "Trevor lost his bag boy job at Muffy Mart just because he arrived ten minutes late to work a few times. He doesn't care though. He's happy he won't have to wear that dumb girl's apron."

Across the yard, a police officer yelled to another to follow him. A policeman wearing latex gloves stood inside one of the twin dumpsters and shoveled the contents into the rear of a pickup. Something bigger than booting a car was happening at the grocery store.

What was in the dumpster? Lisa's clothing, blood, an arm? Her stomach protested and Teagan looked away to the officers who drove stakes into the ground, unwound yellow tape, and attached the bright ribbon to mark the boundary. A knot of blue uniforms clustered together in the center of the lot.

She ducked under a crime scene strip. One major hurdle tackled.

"Ma'am." A young officer with dark glasses approached her. "You're not allowed beyond the yellow line."

"I need to speak with Detective Cassidy."

"Only law enforcement permitted inside the taped area. You have to leave, ma'am."

"Teagan." Detective Cassidy strode toward her through the maze of workers.

"I informed her she needed to go back," the officer told him.

"I'll take care of Miss Raynes, Paul." Cassidy's mouth was a slash in his face.

The policeman nodded and left.

"Teagan, what are you doing here? You're contaminating a possible crime scene."

"Crime scene?" A heavy feeling sank in her chest while dizziness whirled in her head.

He swept his arm around her shoulders and propelled her to the sidewalk on the other side of the police line.

As soon as he paused, she took a deep breath and asked, "What did you find? Is it…Lisa?"

He released her, but stayed less than a foot away. "A stock boy found her phone behind the dumpsters. We're not circulating the information to the public, yet. I'm telling you as a courtesy to family."

Her cell? "How did Lisa's phone end up by the store's trash? Did they find anything else?" She couldn't stop from glancing toward the dumpster where they were harvesting the garbage.

"The men are still working and searching," Cassidy said. "I believe her phone was tossed by someone in a hurry or careless. They didn't check if it landed in the container."

She wet her lips while a sliver of hope grew in her chest. "So you didn't find any other signs of Lisa?"

"We're looking for evidence at this point. Where's your car? I'll walk you back."

"I'm parked near Pretty Park." *They found her phone, not Lisa. Stay positive. She's still alive.* Teagan shoved stray strands away from her face with a shaking hand. "Noah, Travis worked at Muffy's for a couple of weeks last winter."

"Teagan. Teagan."

She raised her head to the sight of the familiar woman rushing to her. Oh, no, they didn't need her at the scene. "Stacey?"

"An old friend?" Noah fixed his gaze on the blonde dressed in a short-sleeved pink dress and high heeled sandals, trotting toward them.

"Stacey Smith. She's the church secretary, twenty-three and wouldn't enjoy you calling her old no matter how you meant it." Teagan sighed, dreading the gossip Stacey would spread. "She's efficient but loves to share what she learns with others and adds her own unique twist."

"I'll handle her." He moved in front of Teagan like a linebacker.

Stacey tried to peek around Noah's huge body. "Teagan, are you okay?"

"Are you lost?" Detective Cassidy asked, refusing to budge.

The blonde widened her blue eyes, and then her features softened. "What's going on? Why are the police at Muffy Mart? Is something wrong with Teagan?" Stacey stretched her neck to attempt a glance at Teagan.

She stepped in front of the detective, and Stacey looked her up and down. "I'm fine," Teagan lied. Nausea mixed with her attraction to Noah was making her unsure how she felt, except on display. "This is Detective Cassidy, who is investigating what happened to Lisa."

Stacey's eyes seemed to enlarge to twice their size. "What happened to her? Did you find out? It's taken you forever. If you don't mind me saying."

"I mind," he said.

"Huh?" Stacey's forehead knit into a wrinkle of confusion.

Cassidy crowded forward, forcing Stacey to back up a step. "This isn't gossip central. We're conducting a police investigation at the Mart. That's all the information I can release."

Stacey frowned then stuck out a well-manicured hand. "Excuse me, I've been rude. I'm Stacey Smith, a friend of Teagan's and you're …an officer?" The blonde bounced her gaze off Teagan and back to Noah, giving him a smile that faded when he ignored her extended palm.

"I'm a homicide detective. Good to know your name if I should ever need to confirm your identity."

"What? I don't understand. You mean, if I was dead?" Stacey flinched and covered her open mouth with a hand.

"Stacey," Teagan said with a tinge of exasperation, "we should leave, and let the officers do their work."

"Right," Cassidy confirmed. "Miss Smith, you should go."

"Sorry to intrude." Stacey tossed her blonde head. "I was at Falls Pizza, and everyone was wondering about the police roaming around Muffy's. I decided to walk over for a better view." She gestured to the store.

"Miss Smith, law enforcement is here for a reason. This is an investigation, not an Internet café."

"No problem, detective, and I'm always available for you." Stacey gave him a small smile and licked her lower lip. "Teagan, I'll drive you home."

"I have my car."

"Then call me." Stacey wagged a finger at her. "Let me know you're okay when you get there."

"Stacey, I'll be fine driving four blocks."

"If you remember any helpful information, pass it along to the tip line," Cassidy said to Stacey.

She rested a hand over her shapely hip. "I look forward to helping in any way." The secretary's sandals clip-clopped down the sidewalk.

"Oh, Miss Smith," he called to her.

Stacey whirled around.

"Vale."

"Excuse me?" Wrinkles creased her forehead. "Valet? Are you talking about parking?"

"It's another way to say goodbye. Never mind, keep truckin' in the same direction."

Teagan leaned toward him while keeping her gaze on Stacey's disappearing figure. "Did you think she'd answer in Latin if she sent my threat?"

"Sometimes an unexpected move works." He faced her. "You forgot a word when you described Stacey."

"Blonde?"

"Flirt. She's the church secretary?"

"Matt hired her because she had trouble finding employment and needs guidance in her life. Her route seems...bumpy. She's had a number of jobs but hasn't held one for long. I don't have much patience dealing with her, but she was always nice to Lisa. I try to remember that fact when I speak to her but often forget, like today."

"She's interesting. By the way, are you a linguist?" He raised one brow and waited for her answer.

She relaxed her shoulders. "I looked up my Latin threat on the Web. I'm not multilingual though I took Spanish and my aunt kept an old missal with the Mass in Latin in our bookcase."

"Light reading."

"What about you, Mr. Vale?"

"I've been brushing up for a conversation. You never know when I'll meet a Roman." He laid a hand on her arm when she started forward. "Once you're home, stay locked in your house."

"In other words, continue what I've been doing since Lisa disappeared." No, she was done being a hermit. "I've been thinking that Travis taking Latin makes him a prime suspect."

"I bet several people can look up or learn a simple foreign phrase, including Father Matt."

What? Her temper rose, but she swallowed her protest when she noted a gathering of Muffy's employees standing near the dumpster watching Noah and herself. She turned her back to them. "What's up between you and my priest?"

"He's a person of interest. Lisa worked at his church. He was close to your family. Both gave him opportunity."

"That's just stupid." She struggled to manage her anger. "Matt doesn't hurt people. He helps them."

"I'll keep your opinion in mind." His voice was quiet, controlled and unconvinced.

"Matt was like a father to Lisa. He wouldn't kill an ant." She blew out a breath and gained control of her emotions.

"Teagan, I suspect everyone. I get paid to think that way. When I have time, I'd be interested in how you two became such good buddies. Now you should go home."

"Well, I have a suspicious nature, too. I inherited it from my mother, and I can be useful. I'll confirm the phone you found belonged to Lisa." There. He'd need her to stay. She tilted her chin up.

"Your presence isn't required at the moment."

Someone shouted his name from across the lot, and Teagan recognized the local TV channel's anchor.

"I'll be back after I take care of the media. Wait here." He turned on his heel, strode to the other side of the tape, and disappeared.

She tapped her foot and became aware the crowd had grown, and the majority was staring at her like she was a reality star in an action shot. Bet they were hoping she'd break down crying and add to the entertainment.

Teagan closed her eyes as pain stabbed at her forehead. She needed to rest for a bit. Wandering to the yellow tape, she waved and attracted an officer's attention. "Please inform Detective Cassidy that Teagan Raynes left."

She headed for her car. On the way, she stayed alert for Seth Bodell's return, but he must have found other people to taunt. Thank goodness.

Stacey Smith was lingering near Teagan's hybrid as she approached. She slowed and breathed deeply while she adjusted her attitude. Today, she'd had little patience to deal with the secretary, who might mean well, but never, censored her thoughts.

The young woman trotted to her. "Did they get a clue or a lead?"

"The   police   aren't   releasing   information.   They're investigating." Teagan dug into her pocket for her keys. She winced as another ripple of pain pounded above her brow.

"Are you okay? You look awful, like you received bad news. I don't get why else they closed Muffy Mart and chased away the customers unless something big went down at the store. Who would they suspect? Everyone shops at Muffy's."

"I have no idea. My head hurts, and I'm going home." Teagan walked to the driver's side.

Stacey shadowed her.

"That detective I just met, he has a reputation for being short-tempered and flipping out."

"As long as he finds Lisa." Would this pounding in her head ever end?

"Everyone said it was caused when his family was killed in a boating accident a couple of years ago."

"What?" Two years ago, Aunt Sophia was diagnosed with cancer, and their emails and phone calls changed from talk of home to doctor appointments and treatments. No wonder she never heard about the deadly accident.

"He went gunning for the guy who ran into them."

Stacey's statement brought Teagan's thoughts back to the present. "Gunning?" She heard the shock in her own voice. She still remembered the fistfights at the homeless sites and hiding behind her mother when a newcomer had invaded a regular's campsite.

"Oh, I don't know if the detective was going to shoot him for real, but who cares when he's so hot looking? Besides, it was almost two years ago. Of course, only a therapist would understand what sets him off now, and he does carry a gun."

Was it possible Noah had grown into a violent person? No, he wouldn't have kept his job. Hawick Falls didn't employ vigilantes. Why was she listening to Stacey? Teagan unlocked her door, but Stacey's gossip left her with an uneasy feeling. If only the girl would leave. "Please, go eat your pizza. I'm going home."

"I want to help. You're under a lot of stress. I'll call Father Matt. You're alone in that empty house. I'm sure he'd hang with you for a while."

Teagan tightened her hand on the door handle. "Stacey, don't bother Father Matt. I need quiet."

"He seems to like when you bother him." Her blonde brows came together as though she were puzzling over the fact.

Was she hinting at something? "He's a person whose work is to aid people who can't help themselves." Teagan tossed her purse on the passenger seat. "I'm not one of them since I'm capable of driving."

"Really, Father Matt won't mind going to your house if you're ill. He'd like to be with you when you receive the terrible news. His job is to counsel and support the weak."

"I don't need company, and Lisa is coming home." Teagan slid into the driver's side and slammed the door, which proved to be a mistake. Her temple throbbed more.

Stacey jerked back, a scowl on her face. "You almost took off my head."

At the moment, Teagan wished she could take off her own. She motioned Stacey out of the way and merged onto the street.

While she drove, questions rotated through her thoughts. Why would Lisa throw away her cell? If she'd lost it and someone found it, why not return or keep the phone? Teagan didn't like the answer. Something terrible had happened to Lisa.

The lump in her throat grew. Tears blurred her vision when she turned into her driveway.

A cruiser pulled in behind her. The young officer who'd stopped her when she crossed the yellow line climbed out and approached.

Teagan wiped her eyes. "Are you here about Lisa?"

"No, ma'am. Detective Cassidy sent me to see that you arrived safely when I informed him you'd left. I'm to check your residence before I leave."

She nodded and the policeman walked her to the front door and insisted she wait for his all clear before she entered. The seconds ticked into minutes, but at last, he announced no one was inside and bid her good day.

Alone in the hall, she leaned against the door, exhausted. "Lisa, wherever you are, stay alive and come home."

Jogger's meow answered her.

Teagan swept her up. "Jogger, we've people to call today. Someone must have seen Lisa."

Detective Cassidy sent one of his men to check on her safety. A small thrill rippled through her. She shook her head. He was an officer of the law. Stacey's warning that he had a bad tempter floated in her mind.

What had he done to earn a notorious reputation and was Stacey's version of the story even true?

Chapter 7

How long had she been shut up in the dark? Hours, Lisa guessed. Her throat was raw. She doubted a whisper would come out after screaming and blubbering forever for help. Water. Just a drop. She imagined the cool wetness sliding past her cracked lips.

Concentrate. Get yourself out of here.

With effort, her numb big toe bent. Somewhere, she'd lost her flip flops and her blouse and shorts—all her clothes. Even her bracelet was gone.

The tingling in her body signaled she could move. Lisa wriggled around in the damp coldness until her feet hit a wall.

Was she in a locked coffin? Please, no. Tears spilled down her face and into her mouth. "Please, God, get me out of here."

Maybe if she pressed her shoulders against the top, the lid would crack open. There had to be a way to escape.

A slamming noise broke through her thoughts. What was that? A door in the earth? She slowed her breathing and listened while a slice of hope cut through her.

Mutters traveled through wherever she was confined. Someone was speaking, but Lisa didn't understand a word. Was it a man or woman?

The voice fell silent. She should yell. But what if it was the monster who'd put her in this hellhole? What—

Sobs mixed with mumbles interrupted the questions spiraling in her head. It sounded like a child crying for her mother.

"No, no. Don't. I want my mommy. Mommy." The child's pleas turned into screams.

An icy chill raced through Lisa.

The shrieks continued. Lisa gritted her teeth while terror rode up her spine. God, help me. Help the girl. Get her and me out of here before I start whining for my mommy. I'll do everything I should. I promise. I'll never leave my room. Please, God. I won't argue with Teagan again. I'll do whatever she or my teachers ask me. Lisa shivered and prayed until a deadly silence fell.

Suddenly, the wall near her feet swung open. It was a door. She blinked in pain as a beam of light hit her eyes. Squinting, she croaked, "Don't hurt me."

CHAPTER 8

Two hours later, Noah jumped into his car and drove away from Muffy's. He called his partner at All Saint's High School, where he was finishing interviews with Lisa's teachers. With luck, the Latin teacher would already be on his partner's interview list and offer them a lead.

"Hey, it's my long lost sidekick." Denny Hines' voice came in loud and clear over the phone. "I missed your ugly face," Hines said.

"Yeah, it makes yours look good." Noah could always count on Hines's support even when Noah was wrong. The man was like a brother, on or off the force.

"How ya doing, Noah?"

"Afraid I need to go back to therapy?"

"Doesn't hurt to talk to someone." Hines' tone changed from light to serious.

"Done that. More than once. The first time, I was in grammar school. I had to visit the guidance counselor when I got into too many fights at school. She told me to use my words not my fists. I smartened up. Now I use handcuffs."

"Well, you picked the right job."

"Damn straight. Are you up to speed on the search at Muffy's?"

"The whole East Coast knows about Muffy's. The teachers are stopping by to ask me what's happening."

"You seem to have survived."

46

"Chief told me to sit tight. Said he'd call again if you found anything besides the phone. I take it I'm continuing my interviews since I haven't heard from him."

"The chief's finishing up at the Mart, and nothing but Lisa's cell showed up behind the dumpster. At the moment, I've a few questions for Lisa's Latin teacher. Did you talk to him, yet?"

"Must be your lucky day, Detective Cassidy. I'm about to meet the man in ten minutes, though I don't expect to learn any new details. All Lisa's teachers described verbal run-ins with her in their classes. Come on down to the principal's office and join the fun."

Hines' sunny disposition shone through. When he'd worked patrol, the neighborhood nicknamed him Officer Friendly. His easygoing nature, boyish red-hair and freckles made him an approachable favorite.

"I thought I was done being called to the office. I'll be there in five." Noah drove through the blocks of single and two story residences separated by trees for privacy. The neighborhood closest to the school contained newer homes. A few of the houses sported metal roofs in different colors, ready for the harsh northern New Hampshire winter. Miniature American flags decked out the green lawns and blooming flowerbeds. The Fourth of July parade used All Saints for the gathering and starting points, and the residents had decorated for the holiday.

A flock of turkeys emerged from the woods on the corner. Noah stopped to allow them to trot by. While waiting, his thoughts cycled back to Teagan. She seemed to have a stubborn streak, but he suspected her doggedness had gotten her through tough spots in the past. The blush that pinked her cheeks when she was mad or flustered, he'd found eye-catching. Never mind the curves she couldn't hide in her simple summer clothes. A spike of heat caught him in the gut as the roar of a biker's muffler broke into his thoughts.

On the road, the turkeys had made it to the other side and loitered near the woods. He hit the pedal and the sprawling All Saints High School came into view. In the lot, he cut the engine.

A Seth's Landscaping sign with contact info was tacked to a telephone pole by his parking spot. In another month, he'd change his ad to Seth's Cordwood. The address told Noah this Seth was

Travis's uncle. He seemed to vary his profession to match the season.

The chirp of birds filled the air as Noah walked up the front sidewalk to the entrance. Inside, the odor of floor wax and the middle-aged receptionist wearing bright pink glasses welcomed him. After he flashed his ID, she directed him to the first office around the corner.

Noah entered through a glass door, and Denny Hines jumped up from behind a wooden desk and greeted him with, "About time, Cassidy."

"I'm just in time if you've taken over the principal's chair." Noah took in the bookcases, computer, phone, couch, and file cabinet. A large analog clock on the opposite wall faced the desktop. Noah pointed at the glass divider separating them from the hallway. "Not too private."

"I guess they want to show the administration is accessible."

"It's more like the fishbowl approach to education." Noah sat on the blue couch against the transparent partition and stretched his long legs in front of him.

Hines reclined in the office chair and put his hands together behind his head. "I'm getting a vibe sitting in this seat. It's kind of a power trip."

"Don't travel too far on your journey. Teagan Raynes received a death threat through the mail today. It was written in Latin on a holy card."

Hines let out a whistle and dropped his arms. "Ah, that explains your meeting with the Latin teacher. His name is Jake Clark. And a warning on a holy card is strange."

"Did you learn that last idea at the police academy or church?"

"Academy Lesson 101. You must have been absent that day. I interviewed Jake Clark's ex, Lucy Watson, by phone if you're interested in her. Miss Watson is a friend of Teagan Raynes, knew Lisa, and was often in their home."

"Hit me with the rest."

Hines flipped through his notes, putting his finger under a line in his notebook. "At first, Lucy Watson thought Jake was a generous caring man. When she figured out the caring was only for himself, she broke up with him. But she doesn't see him as a kidnapper." Hines scanned down the page and read aloud. "Jake never displayed violent behavior and showed more interest in his books and plays than in young girls." Hines glanced up. "Lisa rarely interacted with Jake when they visited."

"I've heard the same, 'he didn't do it', from the wives and girlfriends of guys who were cheating with underage females," Noah said. "No leads from Miss Watson, at least at this time."

"I learned one more interesting thing about him," Hines said. "Jake got his job at All Saints based on the recommendation of Father Matthew Hastings or Father Matt as everyone calls him."

"Are Jake and Father Matt good friends?"

"Like Toad and Frog. How's Miss Raynes doing?" Hines plunked his pad on the desk. "She acted shell-shocked when I spoke with her."

"Today, she was functioning. She reminded me we both went to Camp Mighty Joe." Teagan's face with her eyes darkened by pain surfaced in Noah's thoughts.

"Camp?"

Hines' question refocused Noah. "It's a topic for another time. What's a holy card for anyway?"

"The cards usually have prayers on them, not death threats. They're popular at funerals. It sounds as if someone involved in a church would send it."

"Kind of throws the light on Miss Raynes' close friend, Father Matt. What's the deal with the priest?" Noah recalled how Father Matt had given him the once over when they shook hands. Was Noah seeing more than was there?

"Father Matt's a lifer in the clergy. Similar to other priests, he's been assigned to different parishes, and by all accounts, all his parishioners have loved him. According to one report, he sang in parish musicals put on as fundraisers and they hit record ticket sales."

"Instead of the singing nun, we have the singing padre. What else?"

He's been great at organizing parish members who volunteer to search for Lisa," Hines said as he ran through his notes. "I confirmed his alibi for the night Lisa disappeared. He was at the home of a dying parishioner from noon to the next afternoon."

"The exact hour of her disappearance isn't nailed down. What about his relationships…with women?"

"He was clean until reports emerged of an affair at St. Jude's. They coincided with his name being submitted for bishop. He denied a relationship."

"But he didn't get the position." Noah tapped his fingers on the desktop.

"True. I interviewed his secretary, Stacey Smith, who also worked with Lisa Grant in the church office. She doesn't have much of an alibi for the night or morning when Lisa Grant went missing." Hines consulted his scribbles again.

"Miss Smith went to her job, drove home, and spent a few hours on her computer before going to bed. The next day, she arrived at nine a.m. as usual." Hines lowered his notebook. "The secretary is part of the 'I-love-Father-Matt' club and had the same observations about Lisa Grant as others. Lisa is smart, mouthy, and engaged in lots of fights with her boyfriend, Travis. Before she vanished, Lisa had lunch with him. She returned angry because Travis was too cheap to buy her a burger and announced they were done. She was unable to work until Father Matt calmed her down."

"I met Stacey at Muffy's. She doesn't seem like the church employee type."

"Last year, she was laid off from a dental office, where she was a receptionist. The dentist retired. She's been in the parish office for eight months."

"Don't tell me, she's the woman in the Father Matt rumors?"

"Who knows if the mystery woman exists? Religion can be a political beast and members' motives are as convoluted as in the secular world."

A knock interrupted their conversation.

The door opened and a tall, lanky man entered without waiting for an invite. He wore a navy blue blazer and khaki pants. He rubbed a hand over his clean-shaven chin as though checking for a hint of a whisker. Over his shoulder, he'd slung the strap of a leather briefcase.

"I'm Jake Clark." He shoved up the wire-rimmed glasses sliding down his long, narrow nose. He was good looking in an academic kind of way, which explained Lucy Watson's attraction to him. Noah pictured the teacher wearing a tweed jacket with patches on the elbows and smoking a pipe before a blazing fire.

Jake glanced from one of them to the other. "Should I be

worried that two detectives want to interview me?"

"We're following procedure. Detective Cassidy is my partner, and I'm Detective Hines. You're the Latin teacher?"

"I am." He sent a searching glance over Hines and then seemed to be studying Noah until Hines asked him if he was ready to talk.

"I'm here to do my civic duty," Jake assured. "You've been taking a lot of heat from the public about those missing girls." His large smile revealed even, white teeth.

Jake thought they were sharing a joke. Noah's skin prickled with dislike. "You should worry about yourself, not us. We have a few questions about Lisa Grant."

"I've nothing to hide. I've been employed by All Saints for five years, and I teach summer school four days a week, Monday through Thursday, until mid-August. Lisa was in my classes during the year and this summer. She needed the practice for Latin II." The teacher flicked a glimpse at his watch. "Will this take long? I'm hoping to catch the afternoon show of *Midsummer's Night Dream* at the Indie Theater. It's in Italian. Thought I'd give my translation skills a workout and skip the subtitles. You know how it is."

"No, we don't," Noah said. Was this guy for real? "We don't have hours to waste sitting around in a dark building."

Jake's smile disappeared at Noah's rough tone, and his gaze wavered with uncertainty.

"We'll be done before you can say goodbye in French." Hines motioned Jake to a seat.

Noah's partner was definitely playing the good guy, which worked well since the teacher had already gotten on Noah's nerves. The guy's Indie Theater talk and acting like his time was more important than a missing girl put him in the scumbag category.

Jake relaxed in a student chair facing Hines. "Will I have to sit under a hot light while you threaten me with your nightstick?"

Noah pinpointed his gaze on Jake. "We don't carry nightsticks."

"Of course, not." The teacher stretched out his legs.

Noah rose and leaned into his face. "We prefer tasers. They're more painful."

"You're joking, right?" The man swallowed and threw a wide-eyed glance at Hines. "Detective humor." Hines folded his hands on the desk. "Tell us about Lisa Grant."

Jake tidied his blazer while composing himself. "Before we begin a formal interview, I brought something to share." He dug a book out of the brief case. "Travis Bodell attends my summer class once in a while." Jake shook his head. "He always sits in the same place. Today, I looked in the desk and found his Latin text along with this note stuffed inside the pages." Jake opened the cover and pulled out a ripped page from a notebook.

Noah took it and read the words written in red ink. "I love you. But I cry. Slash slash you cut my heart with your lies. Our fights slice it into little pieces. Soon you will hurt until you cry. But we'll be free to bleed our love until we die."

Whoa, what a find. Noah handed the paper to Hines. "Travis wrote this?"

Jake shrugged. "It's his handwriting and his book. Not very good either. I can't imagine who else would write it."

"We'll need to verify his script," Noah confirmed. If it was by the kid, the composition showed a little about his state of mind. "We'll take his book, too. Does Travis always express himself like this?"

Jake let out an exasperated breath as he handed over the tome. "I've never held a conversation with him. He barely utters a sound. I know Lisa better."

Hines bagged the letter and book. "Tell us about Lisa."

The professor adjusted his glasses. "She'd taken Spanish at her previous schools and received dismal grades." Out of the corner of his eyes, Jake tracked Noah pacing around the room and angled his body toward the door. He appeared ready to run at any moment.

"So she signed up for your class," Noah prompted.

"We viewed Lisa's education differently at All Saints from the public school system. I encouraged her to enroll in Latin to improve her grades and college admission prospects."

"Was she competent?" Noah agreed with Lucy Watson's assessment. The man was all about himself. Noah walked the floor, unable to sit while the Latin teacher spoke in his pretentious manner.

Jake twisted toward him. "She's intelligent and pulled a B, but she stayed after school for tutoring sessions with me and worked for the grade. Her foster mother, Sophia Raynes, insisted she put in the extra study time, and you don't go against Sophia. She had a big effect on the girl. Lisa idolized her. Everyone knew and respected Sophia. Lisa thought that was cool. I'm sure she's the main reason Lisa straightened out."

"Mr. Clark," Hines said drawing the man's attention to him. "Did Lisa ever mention problems or a place she wanted to visit?"

"No. Once in a while, she asked my opinion on curfews or the school's dress codes. She seemed curious and was often anxious about being popular, which isn't unusual at her age. She was out of her depth socially at All Saints despite Sophia's help. Lisa was more likely to frown at someone than smile. Given her history, I understood."

"You always got along with her?" Noah asked, pausing in the front of Jake.

"We sometimes disagreed. When I mentioned her pink hair didn't fit the image of an All Saints student she called me prehistoric."

"Must have made you mad." Noah glared down at Jake.

"Of course not. Lisa and I could discuss a topic in a civilized manner."

According to Hines, Jake was the only one of Lisa's teachers who didn't have a run-in with her. Yeah, like he believed that.

"Detective Cassidy," Jake said. "Did you attend parochial schools?"

"Me?" Was Jake about to tell Noah he was less educated because he didn't go to a private school? He wouldn't put it past the pompous ass. "Hawick Falls Public. I'm a product of our taxpayers' generosity."

"Then you don't know." Jake's voice held a tired note. "I've taught for ten years. Students at All Saints aren't perfect. I've been sworn at, had a chair tossed at me, and graffiti sprayed on my car. Lisa's response was on the mild side."

"Mild, huh? Where were you on the evening of July fifth?"

"I'm impressed." Jake sat with his hands linked in his lap. "You operate the same as detectives in the movies. If you need my alibi, I spent the evening at home reading while I listened to Verdi's Requiem."

"Cheerful music."

"You're familiar with it?"

Jake probably thought a detective in Hawick Falls was too ignorant to enjoy Verdi. "Not my type of music. My old man liked it. Let's get back to Travis Bodell. He wasn't a student with potential?"

The teacher's lips tightened, and his smugness disappeared. "Travis was failing and resisted help. He was supposed to attend summer classes, but blew off at least one or two days each week. I don't know how Travis made it as far as he did in school. Father Matt tried to intervene last fall, but the kid wouldn't listen to him either. Teachers often gave him a break because of his home situation, but I doubt he has enough credits to graduate next June."

"How about his home life?" Noah asked.

"The boy lives with an uncle, Seth Bodell, who's not involved in his life unless he wants to complain. Seth doesn't put much value on education. He once told me at a parent conference that he graduated high school and never went further. The man has never impressed me as much of a scholar, but his customers claim he delivers what he promises and works hard."

"Seth wasn't much of a role model for a high schooler."

"He thought the school would take care of Travis for him once Seth got the boy a financial scholarship. Too bad Travis didn't inherit his uncle's athletic abilities."

"Tell us about what he thought of Lisa," Hines said.

"Seth didn't approve of Travis going out with Lisa, and Teagan didn't support Lisa dating Travis. I'm surprised the kids stayed together all year, but I heard they had lots of fights."

Noah's radar picked up. "How did you learn this fact?"

"Teenagers love to gossip even to teachers. A couple of my students witnessed the couple arguing at the food court and reported it to me. I gather it was the day she was last seen."

"We'll need your students' names."

"They quit the summer session and won't be around until Labor Day. Their parents took them out of state for the rest of the vacation. I've no idea where."

"We'll find them," Noah said. "We're detectives. Write down their information."

Hines ripped off a piece of paper from his notebook and passed it to Jake.

"What is your relationship with Teagan Raynes?" Noah leaned a hip on the corner of the principal's desk and folded his arms. The man didn't seem like someone who'd be her friend.

Jake sat forward in his chair and used the desk to scribble the names of his pupils and their parents while he talked. "Teagan and I had a few disagreements when she inserted her views into my personal life."

"What does that mean?" Hines asked.

"Teagan sided with my ex when she and I had a difference of opinions, but I'm over it."

"Over it?" Hines persisted.

"My former girlfriend, Lucy Watson, and I had a discussion and worked out our issues before she left Hawick Falls. I've moved beyond our relationship. It's embarrassing to admit, but I use the Internet for dating, and I've learned a lot of younger women are interested in mature men like myself."

He liked younger women. Why was he volunteering this information?

Jake handed over the paper. "The secretary can give you their home addresses and phone numbers. As for my dates, nothing serious so far, but I'm willing to give the new experience a few more chances."

"Lucy and Teagan were good friends?" Noah hovered over the man, forcing him to tilt his head back to speak to him.

"They attended meetings together, and afterward, they'd shoot over to the coffee shop where they discussed how much or how little attention I paid Lucy."

The two women only talked about Jake. Was the guy an egotist or was he omitting key parts?

The teacher continued with his discourse. "Teagan preached my relationship ideas were passé because I expected Lucy to cook and clean for me, but we simply believed in a division of duties. On my part, I shopped for our food and paid half the costs."

"Hold on, what meetings?" Noah glanced at Hines, who shrugged.

"I'm surprised you don't know." Jake's eyes gleamed with a gotcha.

Hines sat forward at the desk. "Get to the point, Mr. Clark."

Jake let out a breath. "Excuse my bluntness, but it's the best way to describe their pasts, and I do emphasize pasts. Teagan and Lucy were drunks. They belong to AA."

Drunks? Was he calling them names to get back at them? "We better find proof you're telling us the truth," Noah said in his deadly voice. "We'll be checking your alibi for the night of Lisa's disappearance and following up with AA. One thing about me, Jake, I don't like people who lie."

CHAPTER 9

A short nap cured Teagan's headache. After an hour, she created and posted the Bring Lisa Home page and used a picture of the maple tree with the purple bow for her cover photo. When she finished, she settled upstairs in her bedroom and began her list of places to search for Lisa. The coolness of the night was refreshing. She sank onto the pillows propped against the headboard. She'd removed her bracelets that jingle-jangled with each movement. Maybe when her days were calmer, she'd wear them again.

Thoughts of her conversation with Stacey kept pulling her from her task. How bad was Noah Cassidy's temper? Had he really gone gunning like a cowboy in a western?

She shook her head. If Aunt Sophia were alive, she'd lecture her on listening to gossip. Noah probably had another woman in his life by now, and even if he didn't, she wasn't into rough, testosterone-filled men.

Across the room, her bulletin board came into her direct line of vision. Keepsakes and memories cluttered the cork. Her friends had moved to places with more opportunities and variety than Hawick Falls. The bright lights of the big cities had lured them away, but the memories of her former days were tacked on the board. Dance recital programs and the menu at the waitress job she worked during college were just a few reminders of her past.

The picture of her first boyfriend still hung on the display. His wide mouth smiled from his tanned, round face. Aunt Sophia had lectured her to throw away the photo, but she'd resisted. She'd been unable to let go of that initial excitement. At the time, she'd thought he was the world's cutest boy. They dated for three months of her junior year at All Saints.

Her past dating life followed a similar pattern. She'd fall for someone and then feel he wasn't right for her. Her counselor told her that relationships were affected by her past insecurities, but knowing her history hadn't solved or changed her problems. She bet Taylor Swift wouldn't catch up to her in the breakup arena.

The last guy Teagan dated had lasted a record twelve months. When they broke up, he'd warned she'd never have a permanent relationship because she didn't think she deserved love.

"Amateur shrink," she muttered. What did he know? If only Lucy was around for a late night talk. If only she hadn't moved. Her friend had been forced to take an evening job in a chain hotel when she didn't find other work in Manchester. Lucy slept during the day. Sometimes, she texted Teagan when work slowed, but nothing this evening.

It was after midnight when she wiped perspiration off her forehead and shifted her attention to the noise coming from the ceiling. What was causing that scraping sound? She scanned beyond the pumpkin-colored walls to the spot overhead—Lisa's bedroom.

A quiver of fear passed through Teagan until a new idea popped up. A squirrel must have gotten into the house. One or two had discovered a way to enter in the past. The rodents had caused a mess.

She'd better get the animal out before it destroyed Lisa's room. Teagan laid her list on the nightstand and scooted to the side of the mattress. A bat flitted by on a breeze that floated through the open window. Above, the scratching grew in intensity.

You die next.

Teagan jumped off the bed, slammed and locked the window. She wanted to rip the words out of her brain. Her cell phone lay on the ivory spread, tempting her to call Noah Cassidy. He'd briefed her by phone after law enforcement finished at Muffy Mart. The police found no other traces of Lisa. He promised to stop by in the morning. His assurance had given her a moment of pleasure, until he reproached her on leaving the mart without waiting for him to return so he could assign a patrolman to follow her home.

Okay, she wasn't up for more of his reprimands. She'd handle a small furry animal. *What if it's not a rodent?*

She slid her cell phone into her Capri pocket and grabbed her .38 Special from the locked gun case on the cherry bureau. Aunt Sophia had been a marksman who'd insisted Teagan learn to shoot once she reached the age of eighteen. Despite wincing over each shot, she became an expert.

Her mother could have used a weapon. Memories of sleeping in the woods at the homeless camp with their belongings tucked between herself and her mom for safekeeping flashed through Teagan's mind.

"We don't trust anyone," her mother had lectured Teagan.

And she didn't. At least not without years of proof, they were the good guys. She loaded one bullet and put on the safety. With a deep breath, she squeezed the grip and tiptoed out of her room.

The hall nightlights her aunt kept plugged in because of her night blindness lit the way to the stairs. Darkness hugged the walls. Stifling heat hovered on the staircase. Sweat stung her eyes as she crept upward.

She halted on the top step. Another light bulb burned on the empty third floor passage. Moonlight shone from the window at the end of the hall. She pressed her ear against Lisa's door and listened.

The grating sound grew louder.

Nerves shrieked for her to retreat. She released an unsteady, "Hel-lo?"

The noise stopped, giving her courage. "Look out, rodent, I'm coming in." She clenched the gun in a damp palm while twisting the knob with the other.

The door swung open. She squinted into the dim light. Lisa hated the dark and had picked up on Aunt Sophia's penchant for the small plug-ins. She'd installed two. Teagan paused in their soft glow, and the moonlight shining through the three floor-to-ceiling windows. While she scanned the bedroom, she blinked away the sweat rolling down her forehead.

The scent from the newly painted purple walls clung to the humid air. Lisa's bed stripped of blankets and sheets for lab testing, lay naked in the center of the room. The spot on the desk where her laptop rested was vacant.

A spasm of grief cramped her stomach. *Please come home Lisa. Let everything be normal again.* Teagan recalled Lisa's room the evening before her disappearance. Rock music had blared from her iPod. Lisa sat crossed-legged in her cutoff shorts and white T-shirt on the lavender spread. A large poster board, glue, and magazine pictures of teen stars surrounded her. Teagan felt like she'd entered another land.

The teenager held up the scissors and pointed them at her. "An intruder has entered my turret."

Teagan wiped a hand over her face to dislodge the image of the pink-and-raven haired girl, who believed Travis was her prince who'd love her forever.

The scratching began again near the flooring.

"Hello?" Teagan forced firmness into her voice and raised her weapon.

A meow answered.

"Jogger?" Teagan relaxed her shoulders and lowered her weapon. "Where are you?"

The cat loved to prowl the house at night. Dark time meant playtime to the animal.

Another meow came from the corner behind Lisa's desk, which was spotlighted by the moonlight from the bank of windows under the house's eaves. Teagan peeked over the desktop. The animal's large yellow eyes stared up from beneath the heat register.

"Jogger, how did you get inside the furnace duct?" The cat must have entered through an uncovered vent and gone exploring. The officers had looked in every cranny and opened or detached everything movable in their search for Lisa's phone or wallet in case she'd hidden them to retrieve later. If only they'd found her cell in the house. For sure, Lisa would never toss the phone she'd worked and saved to buy. She treated it like a best friend.

Teagan set the gun on the iron-framed bed and crouched down on her hands and knees to remove the grill covering.

"You're okay, Jogger," she whispered and snatched the scrawny cat up in her arms, "but you scared me to death."

Her pet let out a loud meow.

"No more wandering through the dark." She'd scout out the missing grating tomorrow. Tonight, kitty stayed in her room.

As she straightened, a movement on the lawn caught her attention. She froze. A figure emerged from the trees separating the rear of the property from the road. The shadowy shape crouched beside the angel statue. His back blocked her complete view, but he seemed to be searching for something. Then he rose and stalked toward her home.

Teagan ducked closer to the wall.

Fighting the urge to bolt, she forced herself to lean forward and peered out the pane. She was horrified, yet mesmerized; she couldn't tear away her gaze. The dark form prowled the perimeter of her house.

Was this a burglar hunting for a way to enter? What if it was the person who sent her the threat or took Lisa? The hairs on the back of her arms rose and the air left her lungs.

She gasped deep breaths while the form moved closer, bent, and seemed to be studying a cellar window.

The windows were locked, weren't they? What if she'd forgotten one? She tightened her grip on Jogger. Her pet hissed, squirmed free, and raced from the room.

In the yard, the trespasser slithered into the woods. Relief and something else drew her closer to the window. The swagger of his body triggered recognition.

Chapter 10

The chill woke Noah. He gritted his teeth and raised an eyelid. The large bedroom with his dresser, bed, and TV appeared normal. A pile of clean laundry sat in the basket by his bureau. The temperature in the room had dropped to jacket weather thanks to the ancient air conditioner blasting in the window. Reaching down, he yanked up the sheet while he held onto the fragment of the dream about his mother.

He didn't remember much about her, except the night she'd walked. He'd woken to the sound of their car driving away, and remained awake in the gloom waiting for her to come back. That's when the house changed.

No more fights over his father's drinking. He just drank. No more pillows over Noah's head to block out their arguments while he tried to sleep. After she was gone, he stayed awake thinking of reasons why she left him.

His father told him she'd come back in a day or two. She'd never returned.

The year he got his driver's license, someone called from a small town in Vermont. The caller was on the Cemetery Committee and working on tracking relatives of a destitute woman, who'd died the previous winter. She'd been buried in a grave for an indigent. A clerk emailed Noah's father a picture of the deceased, and his father confirmed it was his wife. His old man had scraped together the money from somewhere and mailed a check for the burial fee and a small gravestone. After he dropped the envelope in the post office slot, he recited a few lines from a Robert Frost poem and that was the last time he spoke of her.

Noah and his father had one thing in common. They'd both lost women.

Now there were times when Noah couldn't remember little things about his wife. How she sounded when she was angry or tired. Memories of Kimmy were frozen in time and reminded him his little girl never had the chance to grow up, get married, or have her own child.

His musings turned to Teagan Raynes. He'd thought of her over the years when his mind drifted to camp. His counselor job and his place on the staff had given him a place to belong and faith in himself. As for Teagan, she'd been too young for him then. However, he couldn't deny the punch of attraction to his gut when their eyes connected recently.

He tossed on his side. No use thinking about her. She was out of reach. The press would love to hear he was sleeping with the victim's family. Vic Taylor's headline would scream preferential treatment. He dismissed the idea and debated opening a window to allow the warm air in to fight off the cool. At his cell's ringtone, he shot upward and grabbed it from the nightstand.

"Noah Cassidy?"

"Here." His breathing slowed while his mind snapped into work mode.

"This is Teagan Raynes."

Teagan! He sat up straighter in his bed. The white numbers on his radio clock read one a.m. Rubbing a hand across his eyes, he asked, "What's happening?"

"A trespasser was walking around my yard a few minutes ago. I think he wanted to break in."

"Are you in danger?"

"No. He left. I can hang up and wait until morning."

"I'll be right there. Don't let anyone inside. Call 9-1-1 if he returns." Noah jumped into his clothes. As was his habit, he touched the picture of his chubby two-year-old daughter on the bureau before he left.

The streets were deserted as he drove from his ranch style house near the south end shopping plaza. He headed down the main road. No jam up at the rotary at this hour. The residences were dark.

As he approached Teagan's home, he recognized the priest's Suburban in her drive. Late night, an attractive woman and an infamous priest together—was he about to learn more about the relationship between Teagan and Father Matt? A surge of irritation ate at him. He was beginning to dislike this silver-haired man who pretended to be holier than thou with his calm voice and friendly touches. Why was she turning to him? The police were what she needed.

At her front door, Teagan greeted Noah with another apology for calling late. At least the priest didn't meet him. Noah took an ounce of satisfaction in that and the fact Teagan was unharmed.

"I'm here because I should be," he reassured. "Can I come in?"

She nodded and stepped aside. "I hope I didn't wake anyone else at your place."

"I live alone."

"Oh, I thought, I mean. Never mind." She blushed, whirled around on her heel, and led him across the living room.

Her awkwardness reminded him of his few attempts to speak to her years ago at camp. It had been obvious she had a crush on him, but he'd thought of her as just a kid.

Inside the kitchen, red curtains brightened the white walls and cabinets. Father Matt sat at the end of the table like the head of the family. Annoyance clawed at Noah's guts, and he mentally stomped on his feelings. What was it to him if Teagan was the woman in the priest's life? She was an adult, and he'd witnessed worse relationships between men and women and felt nothing but sadness for most of them.

"Father Matt, you're here, again." Noah crossed the room to the priest who was drinking a cup of tea.

"Teagan phoned me, and I drove over to be sure she was safe."

She raised a finger when Noah opened his mouth to complain. "I called you first, detective."

Noah couldn't resist at least one more shot at Father Matt. "It's convenient that St. Jude's is only a couple of miles from here." He pulled out his notepad and pen from his jacket, conscious that Teagan was frowning at him.

"Where were you when the trespasser came into your yard,

Miss Raynes?"

"I was upstairs in Lisa's room. The cat was stuck in her bedroom. When I went to get her, I looked out the window and a person emerged from the woods behind the house."

"Describe this person."

She shifted her eyes away for a second and back. "He wore dark clothes and a hoodie."

Noah turned to the priest. Father Matt was dressed in his usual dark clothes minus his collar. "Where were you, Father Matt?"

He blinked several times as though confused. "I was asleep at the rectory."

"What can you tell me about holy cards?"

"If you need one, I can provide one. They've fallen out of popularity. I mostly give them out at when I call on the ill, visit the little children at school, or someone has passed away. Anyone can order them online. They have beautiful artwork and many people collect them. Excuse me. But do these questions pertain to the trespasser?"

"Not that I know. Just collecting a few facts."

"Father Matt wasn't creeping around my yard or mailing me threats." Teagan tapped her palm against her thigh, and her frown deepened.

"When Teagan called and reported she had a prowler," Father Matt said, bringing the attention to him, "I encouraged her to contact the police."

"But I had already called you, Detective Cassidy. Save the lecture. I didn't want to be alone while I waited for you. How about I name the person who was sneaking around my yard?"

"You can ID him?" Was she kidding? "Sure would have saved a lot of time if you'd told me when we first talked. We could have issued a BOLO on him already." At their puzzled looks, he added, "Be On the Lookout."

"I'm not one hundred percent positive. I couldn't make out his features, but from the way he moved I'd guess it was Travis. I've no idea why he'd want to enter my place or slink around in the dark."

"Lisa's former boyfriend was sneaking around your property at midnight?"

"I'm pretty sure."

Defense lawyers loved doubt. "Was the outside light on?"

"The light doesn't reach past the steps, but the moon is full."

"You recognized him by the moonlight?" Prosecutors would rip out their hair and go bald over her statements.

"Yes. Travis' walk is distinct. He swaggers or sways side to side when he moves like he doesn't have a care in the world."

Great. Noah only needed a lineup where a guy swayed in the moonlight. He stuffed his notebook and pen into his pocket. "Did Travis ever threaten Lisa?"

"No."

"I've never seen him be violent or verbally abuse a soul," Matt confirmed.

"No emails, texts, or phone calls where he warned he'd get even or hurt you or Lisa?"

Teagan looked at him like he'd grown two heads. "No."

"I agree with Teagan," Matt said.

He was hitting a big zero. "My team will search tomorrow in the daylight. I'll be here, too."

"You won't look tonight?" The pupils in her brown eyes grew to twice their size, and she bit her lower lip. "I'd feel better if you made sure he was gone."

"All right. Where's the light for the backyard?"

"The switch is on the wall." She turned on her heel and walked to the rear door.

Father Matt rose from the table.

Noah cut in front of the priest. "Father, you wait here. The fewer people who disturb the area, the easier it will be for my team to find evidence when they investigate."

"I'll wait." The priest spoke in his unruffled voice, but he remained standing instead of sinking into his chair while Noah followed Teagan.

A yellow bulb lit the way in the mudroom. She flipped the switch by the green slicker hung on a peg by the door. The yard lit up for a few feet and then disappeared into the dark.

Noah crossed the porch and went down the wooden stairs to the lawn. The short grass would produce little proof of a footstep.

"I'll show you where I first saw him." Teagan stepped out onto the stairs.

"I need you to stay put." He pointed to the top step and pulled his penlight out of his pocket.

She stopped and gestured toward the copse of trees in the shadows. "The trespasser appeared near the cherub statue and crouched down by it. I couldn't see what he was doing."

Noah headed in the direction she indicated. He could use an angel himself. Overhead a cloud smothered the moon, and nighttime insects buzzed in the summer air. Oaks and maples grew beyond the reach of the light on the far side of the flower gardens.

"Go more to your left," Teagan called to him.

He moved five paces, scouting the ground with his beam.

"That's the place." She folded her arms over her chest and gripped her elbows. "He entered from the foliage and slunk past the figurine by the rosebush." The lawn softened the sound of Noah's footsteps. He pointed his flashlight over the plants and searched. Scattered rose petals lay on top of the undergrowth, but nothing told him if it was from a person brushing against the bush. His best chance for a print would be in the dirt. He inspected the ground. Masses of vines and leaves grew together covering the soil. So much for finding a clue. "When did you last weed?"

"I'd guess the fall of 2012."

"Give me mercy," he muttered.

"Find something, detective?"

"A toad. I doubt he wanted to break in." He scanned the sculpture with his light, but nothing obvious showed. Tomorrow his men would pore over the yard and garden. "Did your trespasser have a flashlight?"

"No, but remember the moon was bright." She craned her head upward. "The clouds have rolled in."

Next she'd be describing a werewolf. "Then where did he go?"

"He walked around the house and seemed to be studying the cellar windows. I couldn't see him when he went to the north side.

Noah edged toward the residence and shone his penlight around the building and the ground under the windows. No signs of disturbance. He aimed the beam into the buffer of woods. He should have brought his police force flashlight. Next time. Beyond was another street and neighborhood. Pocketing his flashlight, he returned to the porch.

The distant howl of a dog grew in pitch as he reached Teagan.

She rubbed her arms, and strain pulled her mouth downward.

"Father Matt and I checked the windows and doors while I waited for you to arrive. Everything is locked tight."

They had time to search the house? Father Matt had run right over. "How about the basement?"

"We didn't go there, yet."

"Let's go inside, and you can show me the cellar."

"Is Travis gone?" she asked, not budging. Her gaze darted around the yard and landed on him.

"I doubt he'll come back," he said to ease her fears. If he possessed the ability to read criminals' minds, he'd earn a fortune and boost his arrest record. "I've a question for you. Are you in AA?"

Her eyes widened, and then, she tightened her lips. "I am. I joined during my party days in college. Is that a problem or have something to do with tonight?"

"Means we have more people to interview." He was looking into every connection for a lead. "I'll need their names."

"Anonymity is a rule in our organization." She drew up ramrod straight.

"I get it. My old man belonged to the group."

"Did he find sobriety?"

Noah shrugged. "He died in a boating accident two days after joining."

She pressed a hand against one of her reddening cheeks. "I'm sorry."

"Forget it." His dad's troubled history could fill a library.

She relaxed her stance. "I joined because of my mother and for me."

The hoarseness in her voice alerted him to the current of pain underneath her admission. He also sensed she was trying to apologize by sharing info about herself.

"Mostly my mother drank, but if someone offered her a freebie drug, then she'd accept the high. It's how we ended up on the streets when I was five."

"I understand." He never would have guessed from her appearance at Camp Mighty Joe. She gave him the impression of a kid from a solid middle class home who always had it all together.

She glanced back at the house as though she wanted to go inside and avoid his questions. "My aunt tried to trace my mother for a couple of years after she disappeared, but then decided my mom would turn up if she needed money."

Teagan inched toward the doorway, and he guessed her confession time was over.

"I'll show you the stairs to the cellar."

He walked beside her into the mudroom. "By the way, I searched the data bank for death threats in Latin. In the last twenty years, pig Latin was as close as I came. I guess a dead language isn't popular for threats in New Hampshire."

"Thanks for looking." She entered the kitchen and he followed.

Father Matt jumped up from his chair and fixed a hopeful gaze on them.

"Detective Cassidy didn't find anything." She picked up her pet, who ran meowing across the kitchen. "I wish you talked, Jogger," she said, bending her face over the cat. The tension in her shoulders eased as she held the animal.

"I'll head below now," Noah said. "Do you have bedrooms or other living space downstairs?"

"We use it for storage." She snapped a light switch on the wall and opened the door beside the mudroom. "Yell if you need help."

"What and ruin my tough guy reputation?" He raised his brows in mock shock before going down the wooden steps to a concrete floor. Within minutes, he did a round of the musty cellar, which appeared to be full of old furniture and trunks piled around the furnace. A rickety futon and wicker chair rested near the locked bulkhead. Canned goods were lined-up in alphabetical order on shelves. Nothing of great value. Four rectangular windows were shut and locked. If the trespasser wanted to get in, he could have broken a pane and slipped into the home. Why hadn't he entered?

The question gnawed at him while he climbed upward and joined Father Matt and Teagan in the kitchen. They sat at the table, their backs to him and heads together. The priest was whispering to her. Were they praying or involved in a personal conversation? Whatever they were doing, they looked too cozy.

"No signs of tampering downstairs," he announced and moved toward them.

Teagan sprang away from the priest and forced a smile. "That's a relief. Thank you."

"I recommend installing brighter outside lighting ASAP."

She rose while locking her fingers together at her waist. "I'll make it look like a landing strip."

"Don't signal any planes," he said drawing closer to her. "Any possibility Lisa was your trespasser??"

"I'm sure it wasn't Lisa. She moves with a natural grace."

"We'll agree you saw Travis for now. Did he see you?"

"He never looked up to the third floor. Why'd you ask?"

"I wondered if he fled when he spotted you. How tall was he?"

"He was Travis' height, about five eight and lanky." She raised both brows. "What else can I tell you?"

He could have broken or pried open a cellar window and crawled through if he tried. "Did Travis leave anything in the house that he'd want?"

"Nothing comes to mind."

"Okay. Try to get some rest before morning." The pastor sat relaxed in his chair with one arm resting on the table. Was he staying the night? "Are you leaving, Father?"

"If Teagan feels safe."

"I'm fine, Matt. You should go home. Tomorrow's your day to serve breakfast at the soup kitchen."

She knew his schedule. Noah added the fact to his mental list about the priest and

Teagan.

Father Matt stood. "If you change your mind and want company, you have my number." He crowded closer to her as though he expected her to kiss him goodbye.

Noah felt the now familiar twist of annoyance. He stepped forward to break up their little parting scene. "Teagan, remember, call the police if you need help. The night patrol will be near."

"I'm reassured she's in capable hands," Father Matt said. "God be with you, Teagan. Detective, good evening. I'll lock up."

"I'm worried about Father Matt," Teagan said when the sound of the front door closing told them the priest had left the house. "The bishop is discussing the possibility of closing the parish because of financial problems. St. Jude's would combine with a church in another city and Matt might be transferred."

"Concentrate on yourself, Teagan. On Lisa." Talking about the poor priest was not something Noah planned to encourage, but his curiosity and the detective side of him pressed for more. "What is your relationship to the priest? Don't tell me, friends."

"We are," she protested and fisted her hands. Then she expelled a deep breath. "Years ago, Matt was the pastor of a parish in Manchester that ran a soup kitchen. My mother and I went to eat there almost every day. When my Aunt Sophia arrived looking for my mom and me, Matt hooked us up."

"And that's how you came to live in Hawick Falls?"

"Eventually. My mother refused to move in with her sister, but she let me go. Matt often visited us. Ten years later, he became the pastor of St. Jude's. If it weren't for him, I'd have ended up in foster homes like Lisa." She searched his face. "I could have been Lisa."

She owed the priest. He understood gratitude and the bonds formed by the emotion. "Got it." Not that he approved. "But who's the woman?"

"I don't understand." She narrowed her eyes.

"The one Father Matt had the affair with?"

"Matt wouldn't break his vows."

"Was he interested in younger females?"

"You mean Lisa?"

"Lisa or anyone you know?"

"Matt never had an affair. He cared about Lisa's welfare, nothing else. He wasn't involved in her disappearance. He's family."

His instinct told him she was telling the truth. "I had to ask, Teagan." He wasn't sure why he'd asked or why he was relieved she wasn't the scarlet woman. As the chief had reminded him, they didn't investigate sins.

"I understand." Her hostile tone softened. "But the gossip's not true." Her shoulders slumped forward, and she took a step toward him. "Now I need the truth. You believe Lisa will be found?"

"We will bring her home. Let me worry about finding her."

"I promised Aunt Sophia I'd take care of her."

Another psychological chain bound her.

Teagan dropped her gaze. "I keep thinking she's out there in trouble, not far away, and crying for me to save her. If only we can figure out where." She raised her gaze. Misery swam in her eyes. "Why can't I locate her, if I hear her calling me?"

"The mind often plays tricks on us when we're in a crisis."

"Maybe. It's horrible to feel trapped and unable to escape." Sadness lowered her last few words to a whisper.

"We'll bring her home."

She tilted her head upward. "I appreciate your help, especially at this hour."

The sincerity in her voice pulled him closer and a current of raw hunger suddenly ran through him. He wanted her and didn't care if it was a good idea or not. He reached out and touched her face. Her lips parted in surprise.

Lips he needed to kiss. The hard hum of lust flowed through his veins. He craved her, and she was right in front of him. He smoothed back a stray strand of hair. With his thumb, he traced the curve of her cheekbone, and every cell in his body ached.

A voice in the back of his mind warned him, move away.

Only a few more minutes and he'd leave. He edged closer with the urge to run his palms up her bare arms and then skim the open vee of her shirt.

From the kitchen came the ring of her phone.

She swallowed and motioned with a wild gesture to the other room. "It must be Matt checking that I'm locked in and safe."

Before she could move, the ring ended. She dipped her head, breaking eye contact. "I'll call him back."

Noah inhaled a harsh, ragged breath and stepped back. He was on the job and supposed to be helping her, not helping himself to her. "I should get going." He walked to the window to give himself time and space from Teagan. "My men will arrive by seven a.m."

"Thanks again, Noah."

Her gratitude eased his conscience until the chief's voice pushed into his thoughts. *No distractions.*

"I'll walk with you to the hall and lock up."

He tried to ignore his pounding pulse and the fragrance of her fruity shampoo while they walked together. She held the door for him, and then shut it behind him. The click told him she'd flipped the deadbolt and would soon call Father Matt.

The last idea snapped him back into work mode. He didn't have time to sit around and pray for a miracle like the priest. Noah climbed into his car and hit the number on his cell phone. "Hey, what are you doing sleeping? Get up. We've got a night stalker."

CHAPTER 11

Lisa's hands and feet were bound to the pole above her head. A wire collar was secured around her throat and attached to a leash bolted to the table. The wire dug into her skin when she moved.

A yellow light bulb dangling from the ceiling left shadows in the corners of her musty, windowless prison and hid the monster hovering nearby. She'd given up fighting when Monster Man first choked her into unconsciousness.

When she regained her senses, the monster was doing gross things to her that hurt. *Please, God, stop him.* Tears spilled down her cheeks. A hand came toward her and she flinched.

He squeezed her shoulder.

His touch made her cry harder. She wanted to go to sleep, wake up at home, and hear Teagan calling her to get up for school. Please, God, wake me anywhere but here.

Her tormenter's face never moved or showed emotion, but those cold eyes peered at her with an icy gleam of excitement when she begged or sobbed. She hated them the most.

Fingers came around her neck and squeezed. Not again. She gasped for breath. "Won't fight."

The grip eased. The monster's hands groped her breast.

She shot a glance at the small door on the reverse side of the bookcase full of tools. Tools that weren't used for work. Her coffin, the hollowed-out space in the earth, was behind the shelves.

When finished, the monster would shut her away in her tomb,

in the blackness. She'd go crazy, if she didn't die first. "Don't put me back in—" She blurted out the words and felt the monster's energy rising. Fear rose from her chest and blocked the rest of her begging.

The fingers threaded through her hair yanked. She gasped in pain.

Tears rolled down into her mouth. "I want to go home. I'll never tell what happened. I'll say I was lost. Please. I won't tell."

The monster stared at her.

"I promise. Just let me go home. I'll tell everyone I was hurt. Couldn't walk. Lost my phone."

He released her and grabbed the electric prod resting against the bookcase.

Cold fear raced up her spine as he approached. Her gaze froze on the prod. Pain. More pain was coming. "I won't whine. I'll—"

A gleam widened those eyes, enjoying her begging, anticipating the torture. The Monster got off when she pleaded.

Scum. She drew back her head and spit into the uglier eye on the right.

A volley of cusses and swears filled her ears before the metal touched her breast.

"N—" Pain and spasms ripped her body.

CHAPTER 12

After Noah picked up Hines, they headed for Travis Bodell's place north of the village to surprise and question their person of interest. Noah filled in his partner on Travis' possible visit to the Raynes' house, and Teagan and Father Matt's denial that Travis threatened Lisa.

"No reported violence in his family either," Hines said. "The letter in his Latin book might have been about Lisa, his father, or his mother."

"Yeah, a shrink would agree with you. He could claim he was writing song lyrics and offer us his autograph."

"I'd like him to offer us the truth."

"Not likely, Hines." Noah concentrated on driving. At this late hour, the sidewalks were empty and soon disappeared. The lake came into view as they crested the hill.

Noah remembered the days when he was young and he and his old man waited for a full moon so they could fish at night. His father joked the moon lit up the water just for them. The scent of the damp ground merging into the water hung near the shore. On hot evenings, heat lightning would streak across the sky.

They'd sit in his dad's boat for hours, their lines bobbing, listening to the nighttime sounds of the frogs and insects, and the swoosh of the water lapping against the rocks. Oh, and then, there was the pop of the old man's beer tops opening.

A car puttered by at the thirty miles-per-hour speed limit, and

Noah banished his childhood past. His father was gone, and the good residents of Hawick Falls were asleep in the early morning hours.

"When we find the Grant kid, want to take a day off to fish?" Hines said from the passenger seat.

"You're on." His friend loved the water as much as Noah did.

Hines had grown up further south in a land locked town, but he took right to the lake.

A moose emerged from the woods a few yards in front of them. Noah hit the brake. At over eight feet tall and over a thousand pounds, a collision with the bull meant serious damage to his vehicle and possibly worse for the animal. In their headlights, he threw a glance at them and then ambled across the road.

"Don't want to run into him." Noah watched as the moose disappeared into the woods.

"Hope he makes it through the hunting season," Hines said. "I heard Mrs. Johnson hit a moose on Goat Hill. She was mad because the EMTs were asking her if she wanted the meat instead of asking if she was hurt."

"Was she injured?"

"Nope. Car was totaled along with the animal." They headed down the hill.

"What's your gut reaction to Teagan Raynes?" Hines asked him.

"Reaction?" He pictured Teagan's surprised face when he'd first touched her hair, and his hunger for her grew. She was nothing like June, who waited for him to lead the way. Teagan would agree to stay put, then change her mind, and rush into the situation.

"Yeah, you know," Hines said, interrupting Noah's off track musings, "those gut instincts that help us wrap an investigation."

Right, the case. He was glad the dark hid his expression while he omitted his true gut response to Teagan. "Miss Raynes is intelligent and seems genuine." An image of Teagan attempting to pry her window up popped into his mind, the sun glinting off her dangling pendant by the open vee of her shirt, exposing a hint of what was underneath.

"What did you think of her at camp?"

Noah searched for a noncommittal answer to Hines' question.

"I barely remember her, except she wore clothes that looked like they were ordered from a catalog, not the usual cut-offs and T-shirts like the rest of the campers. I'm pretty sure we didn't talk unless I was speaking to her group. I was a counselor, too old and too cool for her."

"Too bad the cool part's changed." Hines grinned.

"In your warped opinion, but as far as the priest goes, he and Miss Raynes seem overly friendly," Noah said, redirecting the conversation to the key persons and away from his feelings about Teagan. "She claimed they're friends. I'm still figuring out what she means."

"Father Matt could star in that old movie my wife watches whenever it's on TV. What was the name?" Hines snapped his fingers. "*The Thorn Birds*. The priest fell in love with a girl who was way too young."

"At least Raynes is not a teenager, but Father Matt is always around her. He was in her kitchen when I arrived tonight."

"Where would he be late at night except accessible to one of his congregation who is in trouble? You sound angry over the priest's availability, Cassidy."

"I'm suspicious. You got to admit the Father doesn't have the best reputation with women." Teagan and Father Matt shared a bond that the priest used to cut others out when he was around. Was Teagan the woman in the rumors? Had he been wrong about her honesty?

"Most people were happy the priest wasn't a pedophile." Hines's voice interrupted Noah's musings.

"That's sick." Noah tightened his grip on the steering wheel. "And isn't watching that movie sacrilegious, Hines? You are a Catholic, not a heathen like me."

"I didn't write the story. If I did, I'd be rich, and you'd miss having me for your partner. You should count your lucky stars I can't write."

If his partner ever had a sour moment, he recovered in seconds. "I've got a lot of catching up to do after taking vacation."

"Vacations are overrated. Most people spend it fighting with whoever they're with."

"Thanks for the tip. I'll be sure to avoid inviting someone along." Noah hung a left on to the road with older single-family houses. The aged structures needed fresh paint and repairs. He slowed to take in the house numbers on the mailboxes in his headlights. They were close to Bodell's.

"Another problem with vacations, you need money," Hines added.

"Right, cancel the cruises."

"If you did go on a big trip, I'd expect to be invited for picture night when you got back. Why don't you come over for supper and bore us with your time-off stories. How about next week?"

"People don't hold picture nights anymore, Hines. I spent my vacation holed up in a mountain cabin out west. No photos. Anyway, you should have gotten right to the point." Noah shook his head over his friend's lame attempt to bring up the invitation. "I try to break the habit of eating while solving a major case. Tell Chelsea thanks, but I'm fine. You guys should stop worrying about me."

The image of the dark-haired Chelsea standing on his doorstep with a casserole after June's funeral floated into his mind. Chelsea had been the first to show up and offer sympathy when the news broke of the accident.

Through the past two years, she'd also introduced him to her single friends. He'd appreciated her efforts and gone on a few dates, but none of them eased the pain or guilt that lurked beneath the surface.

. "My wife worries about everyone who's alone," Hines said, pulling Noah back into their conversation, "but I told her you had us."

"Don't expect me to start hugging you."

"Save your appreciation for my wife, but I give her the hugs."

"Give her one for me." Noah shifted in his seat as the problems of the case returned and ate at him. "Teagan and Father Matt believe Travis sent the holy card."

"The kid's climbed to first spot on my person of interest list." Hines dug up his interview notes on his phone. "Travis Bodell's uncle, Seth Bodell, is forty-six and self-employed. He picks up construction jobs when he can. He's worked on a number of buildings in town from the addition to Muffy's to the Activity Center at St. Jude's."

"I've seen his partial résumé hanging on a tree by All Saints

High School."

"Me too. He's good at marketing. He was arrested twice for drunk and disorderly. Last time was three years ago. Since then, he's kept a low profile. He reported various relationships with women, but no permanent ones." Hines lowered his phone. "Maybe his nephew will continue the family arrest tradition."

"Then we'd have another happy ending." Noah parked in front of the brown, two-story house with sagging steps. The neighborhood was known as lodging for those unable to afford the upper and middle-class village home prices. Every few years, a flat lander who planned to make big bucks through criminal activities moved into the area and was surprised when a uniform knocked on his door with an arrest warrant for illegal drugs. They assumed the Hawick Police Force couldn't tell the difference between a tomato and a marijuana plant.

"I bet Seth will be happy when we wake him." Hines jumped out of the vehicle.

"Yeah, if he suffers narcolepsy."

They strode up the chipped brick walkway, rang the bell, and waited. In the dark, the moon shone over them, and their shadows stretched toward the two trees in the front yard.

Noah banged on the entry. "Mr. Bodell, it's Detectives Cassidy and Hines."

Hines turned to Noah. "I'll go to the rear and—" The sound of footsteps, and the sliding of a chain cut him off. An outside light snapped on overhead. The door cracked open an inch, and the barrel of a rifle appeared in the aperture.

"What is it?" a threatening voice yelled.

Noah's hand went to the butt of his firearm under his jacket, and he fought the itch to shoot out the spotlight on them.

"Seth Bodell, I'm Detective Hines. We met before at the station, and this is Detective Cassidy. We need to speak to Travis. Can you put your weapon down, Mr. Bodell and get him? We've come to talk."

A bulky man with the shadow of a beard opened the door wider and shot them suspicious looks. He wore a gray T-shirt and plaid drawstring pants.

From his physical appearance, he'd be perfect to play an angry Paul Bunyan in a movie. Some women might fall for his woodsman profile.

"Kinda late to talk. Why are you here?"

Hines held up his hands. "We spoke when Lisa Grant first went missing. We're on police business. If you give us a chance, we can show our badges."

Seth lowered his rifle. "Don't bother. I recognize you." His gaze lingered on Noah and his eyes narrowed.

"Mr. Bodell. Mr. Bodell," Hines raised his voice to gain the man's attention. "We need to speak to your nephew."

"What do you want to pin on Travis now? Am I goin' have to call my lawyer to get you to stop botherin' me? It's the middle of the night, for cripe's sake."

"We've a few questions for Travis." Hines shifted to look over Seth's shoulder into the house, but the man angled his body in front of the detective and blocked his view.

"Well, you came for nothin'. Travis is gone, and I don't know where or when he'll be back. I've nothin' more to say about the girl. You shouldn't be bangin' on doors at night. Show respect for people who need their sleep to work hard."

"Yeah, life on the force is a snooze," Noah answered. "When was the last time you spoke to your nephew?" Would the guy alibi Travis or let him hang?

Seth shot Noah a venomous glance. "How would I remember? I don't wear a watch or keep track of when we talk. Might have been breakfast yesterday."

"You're his uncle, and you're not worried about what he's doing at two in the morning?"

"I can't chain him to his bed. He sneaks out when I'm working. There's not much I can do."

"It's important we meet with him," Hines said.

"The cops already spoke to him plenty. Besides, Travis broke up with that girl before she disappeared. They broke up a month ago. I told you this before."

"That's strange," Noah said, "because two students reported them together at the mall food court the last afternoon she was seen."

"Must have been someone else," Seth snarled.

"We need your help," Hines said. "Lisa Grant's been missing for almost three days."

"Me help Travis' ex? She's poison, just like the woman she lives with. She treats my nephew like he isn't fit to take out their garbage. Go ask her."

"Who?" Noah asked.

"Teagan Raynes, she was always tellin' Lisa to dump Travis and get herself another boyfriend."

"I'm sure her advice bothered you." Noah imagined the anger and words Seth would spew at Teagan. "Enough for you to threaten her."

"What?" His eyes popped wide. "If she said that, she's lyin'."

"Yeah, and if I find out you're lying, I'm bringing you down to the station. Got it, Bodell? I don't like liars. Stay away from Teagan Raynes."

"I don't want nothin' to do with her, and Travis was done with the Grant girl before she disappeared. He was the one hurt. He's sensitive."

"We want to hear it from Travis," Noah insisted. "We can come in and wait for him."

"No use waitin'. I don't know where he's gone or when he'll be back. He's been missin' for over a day now."

Noah sidestepped as his irritation rose. The guy was unbelievable.

"I've nothin' else to say. I can't yack all night about Travis' schedule. I'm a workin' man." Seth began to close the door.

"Mr. Bodell, what do you think happened to Lisa Grant?" Hines moved toward the shrinking opening.

Seth paused. "Lisa went out with a boy she thought was better than Travis and he did somethin' to her. She learned her lesson. Too late."

"Who would hurt her?" Noah yelled to Seth as he began to shut the door.

Seth paused. "Maybe it was you. Everyone knows about how you went rogue." He slammed the door.

"Well, he's a charmer," Noah said as they turned to leave. "Remind me to send him a happy birthday card."

"He didn't like your unsmiling face, Cassidy."

"I never smile on the job."

"Exactly." Hines waited until they reached the bottom of the steps to speak again. "The guy's a loose cannon. He's also a pretty big guy. He could easily fling Lisa over his shoulder and carry her once he tied her up or knocked her out."

"Agreed," Noah said, "but someone smaller and pointing a gun could have taken her, too."

"True." Hines sighed. "Did you notice Seth said Lisa and Travis broke up a month ago, and Teagan Raynes stated they were together until the day she disappeared?"

"Bodell will say whatever helps his nephew appear innocent and causes him the least grief. We've got to find the two summer school students to confirm or deny the food court story." Noah unlocked his car.

"Paul's working on their contact info. We'll check with him. Besides, I doubt Travis went far. He'll come back for a meal, clothes, or money."

"Good idea. We'll watch his house for the next day or two. Who's telling the chief, so he'll give us his waste of manpower speech?"

"You've been away for a week. I vote for you, Cassidy."

"Right. At the end of our stakeout, we'll find out Travis never left his bedroom but was hiding in the closet. I've a better idea. Let's head home and get some sleep. We're meeting with the chief at seven a.m., and I'm sending a couple of our best men over to the Raynes to look in the daylight for signs of the intruders. If we hit the sheets now, we can catch three to four hours." His bed would feel great right now.

"Works for me. Maybe Chelsea will think she dreamed I left during the night."

"As long as she's not dreaming about the priest from the movie."

"I'll wake her and help her forget him."

"TMI, Hines."

Shortly before seven a.m., Noah and Hines walked into the chief's office for their private meeting. He'd hold another conference in the squad room in an hour with the rest of the team, but preferred to meet beforehand with his lead detectives. The calendar above their boss' head reminded Noah the teen vanished three days ago.

Teagan's hoarse voice floated into his mind. "She's out there in trouble, not far from home. Why can't I find her?"

The chief cleared his throat. "Well?"

Noah focused and updated the boss on Teagan's night caller and that two of their best were at her house to investigate in the daylight. "I doubt we'll find a print, but if one shows, I'll let you know immediately."

"Bring in Travis Bodell. He's a key player in this case," the chief's order boomed across the room, grounding Noah in the present. "The boy didn't show up for his daily squawk at the station yesterday. If he's stalking Teagan Raynes and sending out possible death threats, we can't ignore him, no matter if he scribbled the slice poem for his sweet Grammy."

"We will, sir." Hines too out his phone for his notes. "I re-interviewed Travis' core teachers. They hadn't seen him produce any written assignments. If he uttered a word, they considered it an A plus day. Another teacher stated he would have given Travis a passing grade for turning in a blank paper with his initials."

"The kid was cruising through school on his path to bigger problems. Either way, I want Travis Bodell brought in. From where I sit, he had motive and opportunity. Dig up the truth about what happened when he and Lisa last met. Don't accept any of his mambie-pambie 'I don't remember' or 'didn't see her' answers."

"We should have the students who witnessed their fight located today," Hines said. "They can confirm the mall story."

"The men searching the river found nothing." The chief moved his unlit cigar to the other side of his mouth. "We'll hold off on dragging further from the village for now. Tomorrow evening you'll be at the Grant vigil along with the officers I've assigned. I'll make a statement to reassure the public we're working day and night to find both girls."

The chief snatched up a sheet. "I have the report on Lisa's phone. She sent twenty texts to Travis Bodell between July third and forth and called home twice from work. On July fifth, the phone was not in use. Any more on alibis?"

"I checked out the wife of the ill parishioner Father Matt was attending the night Lisa disappeared," Hines said. "She is in the early stages of dementia, and her memory isn't solid."

Noah jumped into the conversation. "And the holy card was mailed locally, though the trail dead-ended at the distribution center. Father Matt has access to holy cards but so does anyone with the Internet."

"Shake up the priest, too." The chief waved his cigar.

Noah fought the need to pace. Shaking up the priest sounded good to him. "Stacey Smith, the church secretary, can provide us with a detailed list of his appointments for the day."

The chief nodded. "Keep looking at the what, where, and when Lisa Grant disappeared."

"And I learned that Lucy Watson and Teagan Raynes were in AA," Noah said, "but she refused to give me her sponsor's name to be interviewed. I know there are at least two groups that meet in Hawick Falls, maybe more."

"I've got that one covered," Hines said with his feet stretched in front of him like he was ready for a nap.

"Someone in your family goes to the meetings?" the chief asked.

"No. They hold them in the St. Jude's Activity Center and since Teagan's a member of the parish, I'll bet she attends at the church."

"Father Matt's church?" Was Hines kidding? The priest was involved in every aspect of her life.

"That's the one," Hines confirmed.

"Go to the meeting. Interview the members. Go back to Jake Clark. Find out his story and his relationship to Lisa Grant." The chief waved his cigar in the air again. "Vic Taylor, an editor for the paper, is covering the Grant vigil tomorrow. Give me something positive to announce. We don't want the public to think we're sitting around like fence viewers." He threw a glance at the wall clock. "I have a briefing with Paul on the Meter Feeder gang in ten minutes. Too bad we've got to waste time chasing teenagers through the city." He tossed his cigar on his desk. "Go. Now."

At the chief's final order, Noah and Hines hustled out of his office.

"Am I wrong, or did the chief just instruct us to rile up every person of interest?" Hines mumbled to Noah.

"I'm glad we don't suspect a baseball team." Noah's phone buzzed, alerting him to the text from his men at Teagan's house. He read the message that they'd found nothing to indicate a trespasser had been on the grounds.

Noah agreed the men should return to the station. He pocketed his phone and filled in Hines.

Paul was at his desk as they entered the squad room. He held up a sticky note with a number and address. "I made contact with one of the All Saints students. I posted a picture of a pretty girl along with a fake name on a social media site. Then I sent a friend request in her name to one of the missing students. He accepted right away. I told him I hoped to transfer to All Saints and was looking for someone who went to the school. He took the bait. Our missing kid was more than happy to give me his cell number and his grandmother's address, where he's staying in Maine. I'm still working on the second student. He's on the Cape."

"Thanks, Paul, and good luck with the chief." Noah turned to Hines. "Let's visit Jake Clark. He doesn't work on Fridays. We should catch him at home for a quick Q and A."

Within minutes, Noah was driving toward Jake Clark's apartment in the village. He found a parking spot on a side street by the pea-green, four-story building. Small balconies crammed with chairs and tables decorated each level of the residences of the Park View Apartments.

"They should rename the place Barely Making It." Noah took in the facade's appearance.

"Too bad, the building was a hot commodity twenty years ago," Hines said. "The lodgings were converted into condos before the real estate collapse of 2008. Most of the people who live in them now are on the verge of falling from the middle into the financial abyss of poverty."

"Jake's home sure doesn't match his inflated ego." Noah cut the engine. The front of the edifice sat on the sidewalk's edge and offered tenants a scene of the busy street and a view of Pretty Park. "Guess Jake spends his money on Italian movies and not his living quarters." He pocketed his keys while Hines glanced in the side mirror and smoothed his red hair.

"The guy's a person of interest in a possible kidnapping, Hines. Are you expecting a date?"

"I need to look my best when I grill a suspect, gives me a sense of authority." He scanned the clapboard building. "Place must contain a rear exit. If we have to take him to the station in the future, I hope he's not a runner."

"The guy has a degree in dead languages. He didn't impress me as the kind who exercises or spends his day at the gym."

"He might be into Latin dancing." Hines smirked.

Noah grimaced at the weak joke. "I was wrong. Maybe he will invite you in for a beer and a book discussion."

"I'm pretty sure we don't read the same books." Hines gave his hair one last pat.

Noah's phone buzzed and the chief's voice barked in his ear when he answered.

"Cassidy, we had a hit and run near St. Jude's Church about twenty minutes ago. Victim's a woman, who's unconscious and at the hospital."

Teagan? Noah tightened his grip on his cell.

"The uniforms found a purse and wallet nearby with a license for Lucy Watson, Jake Clark's ex. I've got men working on contacting family. We have a clerk from the hardware store across the street. He reported hearing a car speed up followed by a scream. When he looked out the window, he saw a white vehicle fleeing the scene. An officer has confirmed acceleration marks before the hit, looks deliberate. Bring Clark in."

"Will do, chief." What was Lucy Watson doing in Hawick Falls?

"I wanted to keep her name out of the press, but a driver passing by called the radio station and gave them details. The newscaster hopped on it and somehow identified Miss Watson. He's including her accident in the station's news report." The chief ended the conversation.

Noah explained to Hines the change in their assignment while they entered the building. In the hall was a series of mounted mailboxes and intercom buzzers to allow people access through the next locked door.

Noah pressed the button for the teacher's third floor apartment. A woman holding a baby came into the foyer.

She glanced at Noah ringing Jake's bell. "He's not home."

"Do you know where he is?" Hines asked peering at her child. "Cute baby."

"Thanks." She smiled at Hines.

"You were about to tell us where Jake Clark is," Noah reminded her.

She jiggled the infant up and down. "He's at a meeting about that missing girl. He was her teacher."

Hines smiled at the infant and asked, "Did he tell you much about her?"

The mother shook her head. "Not really. He's upset because the girl might have run away. She has lots of problems. He told me he feels awful she's disappeared. He was trying to help her."

Noah exchanged a 'you've-got-to-be-kidding' glance with Hines.

The infant let out a wail, and the woman pulled out her key. "Sorry, my baby needs his bottle. Wish I could help. One girl vanishes in Hawick Falls you think she ran off. Two girls disappear and you wonder if a sex perv is running loose in the city. At least that's what they say in the paper. Makes me afraid to walk to the store." They disappeared through the inner door.

"She's got the last part right." Hines turned to Noah. "Any ideas where they'd hold the planning meeting for the vigil?"

"I have one and if that doesn't work, I have a second. Let's go and find out if Jake Clark took a detour to run down Lucy Watson."

Chapter 13

After the early morning search at her home, Teagan drove to the shooting range. Today was the only day the range opened early, and she hadn't wanted to miss the opportunity to sharpen her rusty skills. On her way back, she'd spied at least five purple bows around trees and telephone poles. "Yesss."

She arrived home six minutes before the planning meeting.

Now seated in her kitchen, she looked over the small committee. At the head of the table, Matt was discussing the schedule. The two elderly volunteers, a husband and wife, nodded their gray heads in unison to Matt's suggestions, but Teagan didn't hear a thing. She sat at the opposite end in Lisa's seat.

The teen loved to tilt the chair back on its hind legs and yell, "Ladies and gentleman, my first balancing act."

That was Lisa. She couldn't resist teasing or irritating others.

Teagan's mind leaped to images of the teenager wandering the streets of an unfamiliar city, and then to Lisa bound with duct tape, locked in a closet, and begging for help.

Nausea crawled up Teagan's throat. Get through the meeting. This is for Lisa. She forced herself to take in Matt's low spoken words and shut out the image.

He held up his notes. "I'll speak first about Lisa's disappearance."

Trying to concentrate, Teagan wrote the information on the notepad resting in front of her, and then continued to scribble her thoughts. *Lisa gone three days. Run away or abducted? Why would she leave home when she was going to be adopted? How? Who sent me the threat? Who'd kidnap her?*

She stopped writing. She'd call Noah and talk to him. The reassurance in his voice boosted her spirits. Her mind drifted to the last time they'd met. They stood together so close she could see the individual whiskers on his chin. She'd been so sure he was going to kiss her.

"Teagan?" Matt cleared his throat. "Teagan?"

She snapped her head up and found three pairs of eyes staring at her.

"Sorry, what did you say?" She put down her pen, and her cheeks flared with heat. What was wrong with her, letting her thoughts wander?

"Stacey will send a thank you to Muffy Mart for the candle donation, unless you feel it is your place."

The front doorbell's chimes interrupted her response. She started to rise, but Matt jumped to his feet. "I'll get it."

Jogger sprang from the side chair where Aunt Sophia always sat. The cat padded across the floor as she tailed Matt out of the room.

The elderly volunteers continued gaping at her. They'd already exchanged fleeting looks of disapproval with each other over a cat's presence at the kitchen table when they thought Teagan wasn't looking. Now, who knew what they were thinking about her?

"If you'll excuse me, I forgot something." *Like my mind.* She crossed the floor and slowed when she reached the living room. Matt's conversation carried from the hallway to her.

"He's not here. I'll call you if he shows up. You should check his apartment or his classroom."

Teagan walked into the hall as Jogger perched on the bottom step of the staircase. She paused beside Matt. Noah and his partner were standing in her doorway. Lack of sleep tightened Noah's face, but his gaze held the same assurance and grit that drew her to him. She wanted to run to him, invite him inside, and confess her fears. Then what would happen?

Nothing. He was on an investigation, not a social visit.

"Good morning, Miss Raynes," Detective Hines said with a

nod. "We're sorry to intrude, but it's imperative we speak to Jake Clark. Do you have an idea where he is?"

"I'm not sure. He was supposed to join us, but he doesn't like early meetings. I thought he skipped it to sleep in. Is something wrong?"

"We need him to answer a few questions," Noah said. "A car hit Lucy Watson this morning near Saint Jude's."

"Lucy came back to Hawick Falls? She was hit?" First Lisa, now Lucy. Teagan clutched Matt's arm. What was happening to everyone?

Matt patted her hand. "She's alive, Teagan."

She nodded and withdrew a step. Why would Lucy visit and not get in touch with her? Had she changed her mind and wanted to move home, but was hoping not to alert Jake?

"When was the last time you spoke to Miss Watson?" Noah's voice sliced through her spinning questions.

"We talked a couple of days ago. She works as a night auditor at a hotel and sleeps during the day. We don't communicate a lot. She never mentioned a visit. What happened? Who was the driver?"

"We haven't located the person involved yet," Hines answered. "It appears to be a hit and run."

"But she's okay?" Teagan inhaled deeply. *Hold it together.*

"I'm sure she'll be fine, Teagan," Matt said. "Keep the faith."

She nodded and bit her lip to silence a sob. Noah moved forward into the hall. They were almost in the same place hours ago. Suddenly, she could feel the touch of his fingertips on her face and the tingle of her skin. When he glanced toward her, she sidestepped away to put a few more feet between them. She had enough problems. Forget fantasizing about Noah Cassidy.

If his thoughts were on their previous encounter, he showed no signs.

"Does Jake usually skip meetings without contacting you?" Noah asked.

"He's a late riser when he's not working and sometimes oversleeps," Matt said. "It's not unusual, but he hoped to show for Lisa."

The detectives wanted to question him about Lucy's accident. What would happen next? Teagan's temple pounded. "He ran down Lucy?"

"We want to clear up a few details," Noah said. "When was the last time you spoke to him, Teagan?"

"The first day Lisa disappeared. He came over to offer me support. Where's Lucy now?" Teagan rubbed at the ache in her forehead.

"She's at the hospital," Hines announced.

"How badly was she hurt?" Teagan could hear the stress in her voice.

"I'm afraid it's serious," Noah said. "Do you or Father Matt know the names of her family members?"

Matt shook his head. "She has a brother, but they haven't spoken in years. I don't know any more."

Teagan would zip over to visit her friend. "Lucy told me the same about her brother. I have to go. Lucy shouldn't be alone. I have to see how she's doing. Matt, will you lock up?"

"I'll take you." Noah stepped forward to hustle her out of the house.

"I'll get my keys."

Teagan broke away from the group and heard the silence in the hallway when she raced upstairs. In her bedroom, she checked her purse for her weapon and scooped up her keys from the top of the bureau. Slinging her bag over her shoulder, she wound down the stairs. Matt met her on the bottom stair.

"You don't need a protective escort," the priest objected, turning as she passed him. "I can take you."

"It's police business, Father. Miss Raynes, you'll be safer with us."

The idea sounded excellent, especially if someone was driving around Hawick Falls running people down or abducting them.

Noah kept his iron clasp on her while he guided her out of the house and to his car in the driveway.

Detective Hines jumped into the rear seat.

"I didn't remind Matt to give my apologies to the volunteers in the kitchen." She unfastened her seatbelt.

"He'll figure it out." Noah keyed the ignition. "You can fill us in on Lucy's background."

No wonder he offered her a ride. Now he'd question her without interruptions, and she couldn't get over the feeling he wanted her away from Father Matt. The two acted like they were in competition for her time, but that made no sense. Forget them both. She had bigger problems.

Disappointment speared her as she buckled up. *Yesterday, I had a moment with Noah, but today it is business as usual.*

"Do you think Lucy wanted to get back together with Jake?" Noah asked without taking his eyes off the road.

"I don't. Their relationship was over long before she left him. They shared a place for six months, and she knew him for two before they moved into his apartment at the Park View. Lucy confided that they'd acted too quickly, and she wished they'd gone slower before they jumped into sharing a home."

"Was Jake violent?"

"Never. Lucy didn't tolerate violence. Besides, she did lots for him. Jake liked having her around."

"What did she do for him?" Hines asked from the rear.

"Kept him on a budget for one. Before Lucy, he didn't bother to pay his bills until final notice and ended up paying a lot of overdue charges."

"Would you say he enabled her when she drank?"

Would she betray Lucy if she discussed her drinking? Teagan shrugged, searching for a response and keeping her mind off Noah and his peering glances. "Lucy took responsibility for her problems."

"Sounds like an AA answer."

"You asked. I answered."

"Who else might hurt her?" Hines asked.

"Lucy is an easy-going person who liked everyone. I can't imagine someone deliberately hurting her. It must have been an accident." She tightened her hands together in her lap.

"What's going on with the vigil?" Noah asked. "Is Father Matt speaking for you?"

"I speak for myself. Matt will lead us in prayer and ask for Lisa's return, too."

"You're not taking my advice about hanging low?" Noah threw her a disapproving look.

"Detective Cassidy, a plea from Matt is not the same as a request from me. I must do it."

"She's right," Hines chimed in. "When the Linn girl went

missing, everyone wondered why her mother didn't attend a press conference. Taylor spoke, but the public expected her mom."

"Was she taking your advice, detective?" Teagan asked, feeling a touch of vindication.

"Kara's mother suffered a breakdown," Noah answered in a level tone. "She'd been hospitalized."

"I didn't know." A pang of guilt struck Teagan. She should have guessed. The woman always appeared broken in the pictures of her.

"You okay?" Noah's question tore her away from her musings.

"Better than others. Any chance you pinpointed where Lisa was when she vanished?"

"We've good news on the river. Nothing turned up there."

Another place she'd cross off her search list. They knew little more than before, and why would anyone hurt Lucy? She'd help anybody in trouble. "Why are you trying to connect Lucy's accident and Lisa's disappearance?"

"We're just searching for the truth," Hines told her as they drove north to the hospital.

They rode the next few miles in silence, and Teagan allowed herself to get lost in musings she kept stowed away in the back of her mind.

She was almost eight. Aunt Sophia had driven them to the hospital. They walked down the hall, where white-clothed people hurried past without a glimpse at them.

Her aunt slowed and pushed a door wide. "Go in, Teagan."

A woman with dirty, scraggly hair, and a gray face lay on the bed. Her open mouth gasped for air. Her cheeks were shriveled old apples. She looked like the witch in the fairy tale book.

Teagan backed away into Aunt Sophia, who was blocking her escape. She was trapped.

Noah slowed his car for the turn into the hospital, and Teagan's thoughts returned to the present. In the lot, Detective Hines jumped out and opened her door.

Teagan's throat constricted, shortening each of her breaths. She'd do this for Lucy, the woman who always lent a supportive shoulder. Besides, she had no rational reason to fear a hospital. Just a bad memory.

She walked between the detectives into the brick building and waited a few feet from the desk where Noah and Hines spoke to the receptionist.

Fighting off her anxiety, she glanced around the lobby to distract herself. Nothing resembled her past memories. *Relax.*

A man sat in the TV nook across from a couple. She did a double take. What was he doing here?

CHAPTER 14

"Seth Bodell, what are you doing at the hospital?" The words slipped past Teagan's lips before she could censure herself. But why was he here? Had he run down Lucy and was trolling for information on her condition?

Seth's lower lip turned under when recognition flared in his eyes. He got to his feet, and she became aware how large he was.

"You don't own the hospital, Teagan Raynes," he spit out.

Her already queasy stomach rumbled with nerves. Don't let him know. Stand your ground. He was up to something.

Noah stepped up on her right and Hines flanked her left. Their action buoyed and reassured her.

"Didn't your mother teach you how to speak to a lady?" Noah asked through gritted teeth.

Seth narrowed his eyes and shoved his fists into his pockets as though he was trying to hide evidence of his anger.

"We're looking for the driver who hit Lucy Watson this morning, which means I have a few questions for you." Noah stabbed his finger at Seth. "And your nephew."

"Me? I don't know nothin' about her. I didn't know it was hit and run. Cops like you are always trying to find someone to blame."

"I told him Lucy was here because of an accident."

Teagan turned toward the voice. Stacey Smith? The church's secretary glided to them with a white vase full of yellow flowers in her hands.

"Miss Smith." Noah's left eyebrow shot up in surprise. "What brings you here?"

Stacey patted her hair and sniffed the blossoms before answering. "Father phoned and asked me to check on Lucy for him. He had to finish up the details for the vigil at your house and couldn't come. I was tied up and asked Seth to help." She looked at Teagan. "Didn't you want Father Matt to wrap up the meeting after you ran off to the hospital?"

Her last words rubbed against Teagan's tolerance. Matt wouldn't complain she'd 'run off.' The bouquet in Stacey's hands caught Teagan's attention. "Are those from the altar? My aunt pays for those lilies from a fund she left."

Stacey shrugged. "They were on their way to the trash. I figured someone should enjoy them while they were still blooming." She held up the vase. "When Lucy wakes up, she'll see a happy color. Good idea, huh?"

"I'm afraid she's not napping," Hines told her.

"If you've all come to sit with Lucy, then there's no reason for me to stay." Seth grumbled and backed away from them.

"Just a minute." Noah blocked the man's direct path and forced him to halt. "Stay away from Teagan."

The defiant look in Seth's eyes set off an alarm in her head. At the information desk, the receptionist was staring at them.

"Seth should go," Teagan said, hoping to diffuse the situation.

Instead, Seth spit out, "Detective, you remember to stop accusin' my nephew of crimes when he's innocent. First you blame him for his ex-girlfriend disappearin', and now, you ask me questions like I did somethin' to Lucy."

"Who do you think ran Miss Watson down, Mr. Bodell?" Hines asked in a quiet voice, crowding closer to Seth.

He blinked several times. "I didn't know she was run down. Stacey just told me she had an accident. I thought she'd slipped and fallen. Besides, why ask me? Talk to her good friend." He pointed a finger at Teagan.

"Me?" She'd had enough of Seth Bodell's attitude. "As I recall you acted like you wanted to run me over when I was jogging to Muffy Mart."

"What are you talking about?" Noah asked, his mouth

tightening.

Teagan gestured to Seth. "He pulled up next to me on Main Street and accused me of setting the police on Travis while he revved his engine and waited for me to cross the road."

Seth ran a calloused hand over his face. "I was tellin' the truth. The cops were houndin' Travis."

"If I find out you've threatened Miss Raynes," Noah said in a low, deadly voice, "then you've committed a crime, and I'll haul you in."

She should have kept quiet. The scene was getting worse by the second.

"I was mad that the cops kept treatin' Travis like he did somethin' to Lisa." Seth flung his open palms upward. "She should know how it is. Lisa's missin' and now my nephew is too. I want to find him." He fisted his hands, and his expression returned to hostile.

Noah and Seth looked like they were about to start a fist fight in the hospital lobby.

"Noah." Teagan tugged on his arm to get his attention. "He was upset about Travis. I understand." She added, "Please."

Releasing a deep breath, Noah inched back. "Miss Raynes is more lenient than I am. Don't forget that you've used your one get-out-of-jail-free card. Now explain why you came to visit the victim of a hit and run when you aren't close friends."

"I came because Stacey said Father Matt was busy and I owed him a favor. I figured Lucy might need a ride to where she was stayin'. They told me at the desk her doctor would come down and talk to me in a few minutes." The man paled, but kept his chin up as though daring Noah to make good on his threat to take him into custody.

"Favor?" Hines asked.

"A personal one," Seth snapped. "I was short on my mortgage money last month. The church has a fund for hard times that can be loaned. I'm already workin' on payin' the cash back." Seth glanced at his watch. "I have to leave. I've got to search for Travis. He left, and he didn't leave a note. Why don't you go look for him instead of troublin' honest people?"

"Did you report him missing?" Hines asked.

"I told you when you came to my house in the middle of the

night. You didn't bother to listen to me because you only care about a girl who took off on her own and was bad news from the start."

Teagan had enough of his finger pointing. "She didn't run off and she wasn't bad news." Seth had his nerve badmouthing Lisa. "She's a bright, lost girl who deserves to be found."

"Mr. Bodell," Hines interrupted. "If you go to the station and fill out a report, a whole team of police will hunt for your nephew."

"So you lied when you said you were lookin' for him?" Seth demanded of Hines.

"Mr. Bodell, we'd love to find Travis and talk to him. You can help by going straight to the station from here and making and filing a formal statement. We are looking for Travis, but a formal statement makes an official paper trail."

"Seth," Stacey said, picking off the brown leaves on the stems of the flowers and acting oblivious to the tension in the group or the stares from people passing. "You should stop at the church office and ask Father to have the group looking for Lisa search for Travis, too. That's a good idea, huh?" Stacey tilted her head and nodded, confirming her own suggestion. "Since we're all gathered together, are we going to Lucy's room as a group or one by one?"

Was Stacey serious? Teagan resisted rolling her eyes. The secretary expected them to go to Lucy's room like they were friends at a party? How could Stacey be so clueless? Teagan became aware of the strangers watching them.

"I'll drive you, Mr. Bodell," Hines offered.

"Forget it." Seth stomped a few feet away before turning back to them. "I'm goin' to the church, where I'll get help findin' Travis and not because he's a criminal. Stacey you can give Father Matt a report about Lucy." Seth marched through the automatic doors.

The tension seemed to diffuse around Teagan.

Noah leaned toward her. "What was his relationship to Lucy?"

Teagan opened her mouth, hesitated and blurted. "Confidential."

"I got it," he said in a low voice. "AA."

Stacey put her hand up to the side of her mouth as though to confess a secret. "Seth's emotional because of his problems."

"I've never seen him anything but angry," Teagan blurted. Was

Stacey kidding? "That's his normal self. He'd live at the police station if people filed a report every time he lost it."

"What are his problems?" Noah asked Stacey.

"He's upset because Lisa and Travis took off together." She ran her aqua painted nails that matched her dress through her hair. "You understand, Teagan. You're a mess since Lisa disappeared. You've been crying a lot."

"Thanks, Stacey, for reminding me, and we've no proof that Lisa and Travis are together. He didn't disappear when she did."

"I didn't mean to insult you." Stacey laid a hand over her heart. "If you pick up eye drops at the drug store and use them, no one will know you've been crying a lot, and they won't look at you funny."

At least with Stacey and Seth around, Teagan didn't have time to fret over the memory of her mother's last hospital visit.

"We're not here for medical tips, Miss Smith," Noah said. "What makes you think Lisa and Travis ran off together?"

"Nothing in particular. I figured it out for myself. They were going out, and no adults approved of them dating. They solved it by running away." She flashed a smile. "Pretty smart, huh?"

"What's your relationship to Lucy Watson?" Noah persisted.

"I don't have relationships with women. I took her job after she left Hawick Falls. Lucy and I barely knew each other. I mean she trained me, but it was only five days. I came to the hospital today to help Father Matt."

"How can we contact her family?" Hines asked.

"Does she have one?" Stacey wrinkled her brow.

The buzz of a phone interrupted the group.

"It's mine." Hines fished his phone from his pocket and moved away from them.

"I'll check if Miss Watson's doctor is available soon," Noah said. "And no, we won't be going together to her room." He crossed to the receptionist, who then placed a call while Noah lingered in front of the curved desk.

Stacey filled the moment by discussing the need for makeup under the bright lights at the vigil. Teagan breathed a sigh of relief when Noah returned.

"Lucy's had a setback," he said, rejoining them, "and has been transferred to ICU. Her doctor's not allowing visitors at this time.

I'll drive you home, Teagan. Miss Smith, you must be needed at the church."

"Did the doctor say anything else about Lucy's condition?" Teagan asked, gripping her hands together.

Noah shook his head.

"Oh." Stacey pursed her red lips. "You're right. I've lots of work. With Lisa gone, I do everything in the office. I tried to talk Father into hiring someone part time, but he wants to wait for Lisa. He thought he'd help me, but the planning meetings, the searches, and vigil have eaten up his free moments." She tapped Teagan on the arm. "Don't worry about the microphone for your speech. The media expert will get it working soon, and the boxes of candles are counted and ready to be handed out by the volunteers."

Teagan's throat tightened with her effort to keep her response civil while her friend was upstairs, maybe dying. "Father Matt reviewed the schedule with me earlier. I'm set."

"Good. I've spent tons of my time on the ceremony, I'd hate for you to be confused." Stacey's lips drew upward in a fake smile. "I'd better get back to work since, as you reminded us, detective, no one's at the church office but me. Teagan, remember if you need anything, I'm there for you. I'll drop these flowers off at the desk, and someone can bring them up to Lucy." After exchanging a few words with the receptionist, she set the vase on the desktop. With a wave to them, Stacey disappeared through the sliding glass doors.

"I hope Lucy recovers soon," Teagan said to give herself a moment to cool after Stacey had wound up her emotions.

"Does Stacey stand in often for Father Matt?" Noah asked.

"She never has before, and I prefer not to talk about her since she always rubs me wrong." Teagan glanced toward the stairs. "I hate to leave Lucy. She should be with friends." Maybe Teagan could sneak into her room and see how Lucy was for herself. "Do you think whoever hit her will come to the hospital to hurt her again?"

"Lucy's monitored twenty-four seven by her physician and security. Don't worry." His voice softened. "I'll give your name to her doctor. You'll be one of the first allowed to visit."

"Thank you, and good luck finding her brother. Lucy hasn't seen him in years. She really didn't have anyone. It's why she didn't leave Jake sooner. She didn't want to be alone."

"What about Travis? Were he and Lucy friends?"

"Lucy did have a soft spot for Travis. She used to lecture me that I should give him a break because his life wasn't easy. She thought Seth had a good side too. That was Lucy. Why would anyone hit her?"

"Seems Lucy was the one who needed the break," Noah said.

Detective Hines returned and Noah filled him in on Lucy's condition before asking Teagan, "Where does Travis hang out?"

"Lisa mentioned a hunting store he'd visited in Maine, but I wouldn't call it a place he went frequently. Most of the time, they hung at our house. I figured it was better than the streets."

"If Seth threatens you—"

"I've never considered him dangerous. He yells a lot to let off steam."

"Call me if he threatens you. You know I bet Seth will never report his nephew missing because he knows where he's hiding."

"I don't understand Seth at all," she confessed.

"Let's hope he's not expecting the family award for best uncle." He held out his hand.

She reached out to grab it, and lines of confusion crossed his face. Yikes, he was gesturing for her to go before him.

She spun around to exit and hide her embarrassment. What was wrong with her? This wasn't one of her daydreams about Noah. Teagan hurried to the lot while the detectives shadowed her.

CHAPTER 15

Lisa dreamed of sweaty, cold glasses of water and opening her mouth under a faucet. The stream flowed down her throbbing throat and like magic soothed the aches in her sore body. She smacked her dry, cracked lips and pictured the sun breaking away from the clouds and ending the blackness that wrapped around and smothered her.

At the sound of a slam, she tensed. He was back. Her stomach growled. Last time, he'd given her half a sandwich and two sips from a plastic bottle. How long had she been here? She was starving. Tears burned her eyes.

Please, God, help me. I'm sorry for my sins. I promise. No way will I do them again. Just let me out of here. I'll do good. Help others. Become another Mother Teresa. Yes, I've broken the rules. But I'll change.

But would God save her? The times she lied, refused to do as her foster parents asked, or did the opposite to prove they couldn't make her, piled up on her conscience. She'd said mean things to kids at school and laughed at them. Yes, they were cruel first, but Father Matt said it didn't matter who started the problem. Weirder, she'd tried at All Saints to be a nice girl. She didn't argue with her teachers, did she? No. She just expressed her opinion and did her work Look what happened to her.

Her belly cramped with fear. She had to figure how to get out of wherever she was.

Teagan! Teagan would search for her. She was stubborn and didn't quit. At least, that's what she told Lisa when Aunt Sophia died. She promised to adopt Lisa because it was never too late for family. That's when Teagan confessed her secret. Everywhere Teagan went—online, shopping or around Hawick Falls—she looked for her mother. It didn't matter she'd disappeared twenty years ago.

On the other side of the wall, the girl begged. Her words slurred together by panic and terror.

Lisa shook and tears spilled over her cheeks. She didn't have to imagine what was happening. She knew. Forget food. Listening, picturing, and knowing what was going on killed her little by little.

"Please, please, no. Stop." The girl's pleas turned into shrieks.

Lisa had to drown out the girl or go crazy. She recited nursery rhymes one after the other. Her voice grew louder and louder, but she still heard the cries of pain. They were in her head, in her brain pumping the girl's horror through Lisa's bloodstream.

I will be strong, strong, strong, stay strong, Lisa chanted. The monster was playing music.

Another terror chomped through her mantra and ripped apart her small amount of courage.

She was next.

CHAPTER 16

The next morning, Noah and Hines met with the chief in his office for their daily meeting. Dressed in his crisp white shirt and navy blue tie, the boss stood by the portable whiteboard near his desk. The suspects were listed in red marker across the shiny surface. He fixed his stare on Noah, who was speaking.

"We came up with zilch when we questioned the AA members after we went to the hospital. They acted like they'd be branded and lynched as traitors for revealing a name from their group. But I talked on the phone to the kid from Jake Clark's summer class. He confirmed the fight between Travis and Lisa at the food court. Hines and I spoke to the manager where they bought lunch. He reported Travis kicked a chair on his way out, but otherwise, it was a loud verbal, not physical, disagreement."

Noah handed the chief a copy of Travis' note and explained how Clark found it. "Our expert verified the handwriting belonged to the boy."

The chief added the info under Travis' name before turning to Noah and Hines. "Travis is our main suspect. Today, we're adding three search dogs from out of state. I've alerted Miss Raynes. They'll start at her house in an hour."

Teagan's face surfaced in Noah's thoughts. Lines of worry had collected at the corner of her full lips. She'd tugged her hair back in a ponytail which accented the pain in her large dark eyes.

"Noah."

He refocused on his boss, who was staring at him, judging his attention. "Yes, sir."

"You'll report to me on the day's search. On the Lucy Watson investigation, no paint chips found at the scene of the hit and run. The car must have clipped her instead of running over her. A team is recreating the accident today. Right now, the acceleration marks left behind suggest Miss Watson was the driver's target."

Noah put a mental checkmark next to Jake.

"What do you have, Hines?" the chief asked.

"Sir, Jake Clark, Lucy Watson's former boyfriend, drives the same color vehicle seen fleeing after the hit."

The chief's marker squeaked on the board as he wrote white car/hit and run under Jake's name.

"We can work on connecting the crime to Jake Clark, which shouldn't be too hard," Noah added.

The chief glanced at his watch. "I'd say yes, except Jake Clark reported his vehicle stolen at eight forty-seven a.m. yesterday. He said it was missing from its designated spot when he went to drive to a vigil meeting."

Hines scratched his head. "Someone swiped his car. That's his alibi?"

"The guy's lying." Noah blew out a breath of frustration. "We tried three times to find him, and he was never home. I bet he spent the day ditching the vehicle." Did the Latin teacher believe they'd fall for his story?

The chief fisted his hands. "Unless we can prove different, he was looking for his car. Keep searching for a link between Lucy Watson and Lisa Grant's disappearance. Too many of the same players are crossing over in the two cases."

"She hasn't regained consciousness, sir," Hines said.

"Stay on it. What else do you have?"

"Teagan Raynes let on that Seth Bodell threatened her the day we found Lisa's phone at Muffy Mart," Noah said. "Bodell said she'd be sorry for setting the police on Travis. She didn't report him because she thought he was just blowing off steam, which she described as his normal behavior."

"Maintain the pressure on him, but keep Raynes away from Bodell." The chief added the new fact under Seth's name.

"What about Lisa's boyfriend, Travis?" Hines asked. "She didn't call him the night she disappeared. Is that because she was with him?"

"No contact with Travis could support the theory Lisa was mad at him," Noah noted.

"Maybe she was so angry she ran away," Hines said.

The chief's voice boomed across the room. "I've put out a BOLO for Travis Bodell. He's already hiding, which means he's ahead of us. I don't like it."

"If the kid's in Hawick Falls, we'll get him, sir," Hines said.

Noah rose and walked to the window. The more they talked about the cases, the more he wanted to get out and question everyone involved. He'd start with Jake Clark and the fake theft of his car. The man continued to irritate him even when he wasn't near him.

"Go back to the school and the Latin teacher's neighborhood," the chief ordered. "Find him. Make the teacher and boyfriend account for every second since Lisa Grant disappeared."

Noah recognized his boss was reaching the end of the meeting as he pinpointed their last steps. Adrenaline rushed through him.

The chief stabbed his finger in the air. "Go. You're wasting manpower sitting here."

Hines and Cassidy sped out of the office.

As they exited into the hall, Hines turned to Noah. "Do you think Jake did something to Lisa Grant and Lucy Mills?"

"I wish I knew."

"At the hospital, you came on strong with Bodell." Hines was rubbing his chin and looking at Noah as though he were a suspect.

"He's lying to us. I'm sure he knows where Travis is." Admitting that he was irritated with the man's treatment of Teagan didn't seem to justify his reaction to Bodell. Noah took off down the hall before his partner questioned him more.

Hines kept up with him, not willing to let him off the hook. "You seemed more upset about what was happening between him and Miss Raynes than Seth lying about our primary suspect."

"Did I?" He shrugged while he replayed the scene in his mind.

Hines's phone rang. "It's Chelsea," he said, checking his cell. He walked a few feet away from Noah.

Paul waved Noah to his desk in the squad room. "Did you see

the paper?" He didn't wait for Noah to reply before holding up the front page.

A picture of the chief wearing a crown frowned back at Noah. "The boss must love this new one. Listen." Paul read the print. "The Merry Men have been passing out pictures labeling the Hawick Falls Chief of Police as Prince John."

"I bet he'd hit delete on this image if he could."

"You know what's worse?" Paul lowered his voice. "The chief's first name is John. I doubt he's seen it since he hasn't yelled at me today." Paul's phone buzzed and the young man's face whitened. "It must be him."

"Watch out for the dungeon, Paul." Noah left him holding the phone two inches from his ear.

Outside, he hopped into his car. The clock in his head ticked reminding him to hurry and find Lisa Grant before it was too late.

CHAPTER 17

Teagan re-counted the candles she found in the church's last pew. Muffy's had donated two hundred. She had no idea how many people would show up, but that seemed to be enough. She'd posted a reminder on the Bring Lisa Home page, where readers responded with prayers and words of encouragement. At least the page was a success, reminding everyone not to forget Lisa.

In about twenty minutes, she'd be in front of the crowd. Once she stepped onto the podium, she'd scan every face for Lisa, Travis, and as always, her mother. Maybe a listener would step forward to tell them where Lisa had gone. One person was all they needed.

Okay, she'd lost count of the candles, again. *Don't think about faces or the news Noah Cassidy would bring about today's search. Noah.*

She fumbled and dropped a candle on the aisle's wine-colored carpet. Scooping it up, her thoughts returned to today's hunt. It had taken a lot of restraint not to tail after the dogs, but Noah had promised to let her know the outcome as soon as they finished. Why hadn't he called yet? She'd been waiting hours for the results. He'd sent a cruiser over to follow her to the church with word that he was tied up and couldn't take her himself. The new outside lightings installations had served as a distraction this morning. She needed something to keep her calm now.

Concentrate on the vigil.

The building held the scent of wax and the flowers that the community was dropping off near the shrine for Lisa on the church's front steps. The odors and Matt's voice testing the mic drifted through the open stained glass windows. Inside, the fading light matched the soft glow from the hanging pendants.

A loud screech of feedback from the microphone sent a quiver through her. She covered her ears for a second then relaxed and pulled her speech from the pocket of her black skirt. She'd memorized the words, but she wasn't about to rely on her recall when she faced the crowd and the emotion of the evening.

A damp breeze carrying the promise of rain blew into the building. The meteorologist had predicted a shower. Was Lisa somewhere dry? Was it possible Jake or Seth had abducted her or that she'd gone off with Travis? Maybe a stranger had taken her, but Travis had been stalking around her house at night. He'd have been with Lisa if they took off together, wouldn't he?

The tight band around her chest warned her to slow her thoughts, and the need for sleep burned her eyes. She directed her attention to the head of the aisle, where the shadows had fallen over the altar's cross.

Please, God, bring Lisa home safe.

Her phone rang from her pocket, where she'd stuffed it along with her St. Jude's medal. Lisa? "Hello?"

Deep breaths carried from the receiver into her ear and turned into panting louder and louder.

"Eew." Another sick person. This was the third one today. Was there a website for sickos with her contact info written on it? She hit the end button and pocketed the phone with a shiver of repulsion. She'd have changed her number except then Lisa wouldn't know the new one.

A shadow moved in the corner by the altar. Someone was lurking, watching her. She cleared her throat and called out, "Hello? Lisa?"

Stacey stepped out of the darkness. "No, it's me. What are you doing?"

"Why were you standing there?" The young woman was beyond strange.

"I was wondering what you're doing to the candles." She glanced at the empty boxes on the table. "I told you I've assigned people to pass them out to the crowd. You don't need to bother counting or whatever you're doing. I can add." Her high heels tapped across the wooden floor until she hit the aisle carpet. She stopped to frown at Teagan in a dying beam of light.

Teagan felt like the kid caught sneaking the money from the poor box. "I needed to stay busy. Didn't Muffy Mart donate two hundred? I only counted a hundred."

"Are you sure?" Stacey shrugged. "I must have left a few boxes in the basement. I'll look in a minute after I see if the mic is working out front. Did you hear that noise? Father Matt needs my help."

As she spoke, another screech of the microphone sent goose bumps up Teagan's arms. "The mic seems to be winning."

Stacey held up an index finger. "I'll be right back. Don't worry. You've enough problems thinking about Lisa and what horrible things are happening to her."

"Thanks, Stacey," Teagan managed through gritted teeth. Hopefully, the woman didn't aspire to become a counselor.

Stacey headed out the double oak doors and silence returned to the church. Now what should she do? She glanced around until her gaze landed back on the candle boxes. I'll check.

She marched through the open fire doors, into the entryway and to the top of the basement stairs on her right. The muffled sounds of voices from outside confirmed people were assembling. She wound downward. A window at the top of the stairway threw light over the narrow passageway. Her footsteps echoed in the stairwell.

At the base of the staircase, she veered to her left and into the open dark hall. Eager to banish the dimness, she flipped the switch on the wall. Overhead fluorescent lights flickered to life over the yellowed-linoleum.

She peered at the vacant space. The muffled sounds of loud music poured through the first floor windows, reminding Teagan of long-ago events. When she was little, the basement hummed with the excitement of socials from suppers, high school dances, to religious classes. Long tables and fold up chairs had furnished the room where adults and children laughed and enjoyed the functions. Now the congregation had abandoned the below ground level room in favor of the newer Activity Center built a few feet from the church.

Her thoughts drifted back to her current problem. No signs of the white boxes in here. Teagan snapped off the lights and headed into the hallway. To her right was a closet. The door was slightly ajar. Aha, the missing candles must be in the storage. Teagan flicked the switch and walked inside.

Half-empty shelves were marked for the different liturgical seasons. Scattered boxes sat on the metal case. Stacey wasn't tall. The candles would most likely be on the bottom. Teagan crouched.

Her phone rang. She jumped up and hit her knee on a shelf. Pain shot through her. She closed her eyes and waited for the ache to fade. Finally, she dug her cell out of her pocket. The ring ended. It was probably her obscene caller, or it could be Noah, or possibly Lisa. Teagan pulled up the last call history. Unknown. Yeah, she'd missed a good one.

No sooner had she set the cell phone on a shelf than the buzz signaled a text message. Her heart thumped loudly in her chest. What if it was Lisa, hurt and unable to speak, only breathe and Teagan had hung up on her last time?

She closed her eyes. Then she read the text. Cepi corpus.

A quiver of fear shot through her. *Okay, be strong. Don't panic.* Latin, but she'd figure out this one. Corpus Christi meant Body of Christ. So corpus meant body. Cepi meant— I've got the body.

Oh, my God. Had her texter found Lisa's...body? Her phone fell to the floor.

The door slammed shut. She lunged for the knob. Locked. The light went out.

CHAPTER 18

The vigil. Her speech! Cepi corpus. She had to get out. *St. Jude, help me.* Teagan banged on the door. "Open up! Hello. Hello."

She stopped and listened. Whoever locked her in might be on the other side, laughing or worse. With the music playing, would anyone hear her?

Wait, she had her phone. She'd be fine. Slowing her breathing, she scooped up her cell. The backlight and the strong signal eased her anxiety. She'd call Noah. She brought up his number and pushed the button.

The rings seemed to last forever. Her hand shook and the closed room grew hot and suffocating while she waited for him to answer. Sweat rolled off her face. It was like an oven in here. At a sound from the hallway, she froze then pressed her ear to the wood to listen. Was someone out there? "Hel-lo?"

The door swung wide and light from the hall hit her eyes while she staggered back before recovering her balance.

Stacey stood in the doorway, frowning at her. "Teagan? What are you doing in the closet? With the light off?" She swept a gaze over the small area as though she expected to find another person or stolen goods.

Noah's voicemail was speaking. Teagan disconnected. "I was searching for the rest of the candles. You said they were downstairs."

"Yeah, I meant in a kitchen cabinet, not this stuffy, old closet.

You know the room off the basement activities' room."

Teagan had to stop herself from running out. She needed a little dignity in front of Stacey. "Did you close the door and turn off the light?"

"Of course I didn't shut you in the dark. In fact, I was looking for you because the vigil is starting soon. The volunteers grabbed the candles from upstairs." Stacey frowned at her. "You're lucky I saw the open door to the downstairs and checked. You think I locked you inside on purpose?" She pouted her lips and lifted a perfectly shaped eyebrow.

"I didn't imagine being stuck in the storage area, Stacey." Teagan stepped out and peeked into the multipurpose room. No one could hide in the empty space. "Did you pass anyone on the steps?"

"No. The door's tricky. You have to lift and turn the knob at the same time." She demoed for Teagan with a click of the handle. "Voila! I bet when I opened the main door to come into the church, it caused a draft and shut you in the closet."

Teagan fanned her face, trying to recover her cool, literally. She'd freaked out over nothing.

"These antique buildings have lots of quirks." Stacey hit the closet switch a couple of times without results. "The bulb must have burned out. The light's about a hundred years old. We don't have time to fix it, Teagan. Let's go. The volunteers are passing out the last box to the crowd. Father Matt didn't want to welcome everyone until you were on standby."

Stacey crossed the hallway with Teagan at her side. "Father asked me to bring you to the platform. I thought you were by the pews where I told you to wait."

"We were short on the candles. I was trying to find them."

"I have it under control. I'm sure the missing boxes are in the kitchen. I'll run and get them." Stacey stopped in front of the open doorway to the multipurpose room and shook her finger at Teagan. "Don't move a foot." Stacey's sandals echoed in the empty space until she disappeared in the rear.

Teagan couldn't resist. She flipped the closet switch again without results. The bulb must have burnt out. She'd been paranoid. Good thing she hadn't reached Noah.

"Is Travis outside?" she asked Stacey as she sped back with a large plastic bag.

"I didn't see him. Come on. I have the candles." She hooked her arm through Teagan's, and they climbed upward together. "That cute Detective Cassidy is here," Stacey said in a stage whisper. "He asked about you, too. I found out the other detective is married."

"You mentioned Detective Cassidy's family was in a boating accident." Why had she brought it up again? Stacey would probably give her a smug answer.

Instead, the secretary slowed her step and leaned closer. "I already told you most of what I know. The rumor was the detective threatened to kill the driver, a young man, who hit and killed his wife, child, and father and almost did. But the man had no proof of being terrorized, and no charges were brought against Detective Cassidy. The driver went to jail for involuntary manslaughter, but a lot of people said Cassidy's a powder keg and should have known better since he works for the law."

She'd expected a story about an argument or a fistfight, but not attempted murder.

Her aunt's scolding voice popped into her mind. Gossiping at Lisa's vigil? And with Stacey!

When they reached the upstairs, the oak door was open and the sounds of outside had grown louder. Ignoring her conscience, she peeked out at the gathering. Stars and a full moon lit up the sky. A crowd filled the front green and stretched from the steps, past the sidewalk to the Main Street curb. The sound of a guitarist played in the background. People fixed their gazes to the right of the church where the speakers' platform was setup. Portable lights shone on the stage.

"I'll let Father Matt know you're ready. Don't move." The door swung shut behind her.

She should give her speech a final read. Teagan grabbed her purse from the last pew and slipped her phone inside as Noah entered the church. He was dressed in gray with his badge clipped to his belt. A surge of relief and excitement pumped through her and shoved aside the doubts she'd had about him. She resisted the urge to throw herself against him and soak up the strength he exuded.

"You're a tough woman to find. Did you call me a few seconds ago?"

"Yes, I've something to tell you, but first, what about the search updates?"

"I have one for you, but it can wait."

Her heart skipped a beat. She looked into his face, trying to judge if it was good or bad news. "You found Lisa?"

"Why don't we discuss the latest after the vigil?"

"I'm ready." She curled her fingers into her palm, bracing herself.

"The dogs tracked Lisa from your house to Pretty Park and back to Park View Street. The scent ended there. We now believe Lisa snuck out, went to the park, and got into a vehicle the night she disappeared, Teagan. Kara Linn went missing in the same area."

Pretty Park, where the happy laughing brides had their pictures taken on their wedding day was now the scene of abduction and terror.

"Has she ever hitchhiked?"

"Not to my knowledge. And Travis doesn't own a car, but I guess he could have borrowed his uncle's truck and picked her up." Who else would give her a ride? "Jake Clark lives on Park View. Have you talked to him?"

"We'll be re-interviewing him. We're also exploring the possibility Travis got a loaner from his uncle, who isn't cooperating at the moment."

"I've no idea why she'd be at the park." None of it made sense.

The tap of heels announced Stacey's return. She slowed at the sight of them. Only then did Teagan realize how close she and Noah stood to each other. One deep breath and they'd touch.

Stacey gave them a curious look and pasted on her usual smile. "Father Matt is ready for you. I think he snuck a cigarette while he was waiting."

"What do you know a priest with a bad habit."

"Hello, Detective." Stacey tilted her head and smiled. "Has Teagan told you she locked herself in the basement storage? She's lucky I went downstairs or she'd still be in there. You could say I saved the day or the vigil, right, Teagan?"

Noah shifted and touched Teagan's hand briefly.

Stacey's gaze dipped to their hands and up to their faces with renewed interest.

"Is that what happened to you?" he asked Teagan in a concerned voice.

"Yes and no." Should she admit the door was stuck? She'd look like a dummy, but she didn't want to talk about her latest cell phone text until Stacey left. "I had my St. Jude medal with me. He's the saint who helps when we're lost and all is hopeless."

Stacey rolled her eyes. "You weren't lost or hopeless. I found you."

He shook his head. "Is your medal some kind of rabbit's foot?"

"Not exactly. My aunt gave it to me when I first arrived." She should have kept quiet. Noah wasn't into saints.

Stacey shook her head. "We're going to need St. Jude if you don't get on the stage soon."

"I want to speak to you in private." Teagan managed to say before Stacey stepped forward and angled herself between them.

"You two can chat later, Teagan. Let's go."

"After the vigil?" she asked Noah, ignoring Stacey's tugs on her arm.

"You can't miss me. I'll be standing behind you. We'll continue our conversation when you finish."

Stacey led her outdoors. The gathering was larger than she expected, spilling out into the sidewalk by the street. She scanned it, but most of the solemn faces belonged to strangers. One of them could be a kidnapper.

CHAPTER 19

Stacey and Noah lingered near her. The chief of police sat on the stage with a man Teagan recognized as FBI. Matt stood at the mic. He threw her a nod of encouragement, and then asked for the crowd to bow their heads for a moment of silence. Only the sound of cars passing broke the quiet.

Teagan couldn't restrain herself from skimming over the throng one more time. Seth Bodell had positioned himself in the second row behind the media. Unlike the others, Seth's head was not bent, and he met her gaze with a scowl. A chill shot through her. Why was Seth always angry? Was he still claiming his nephew had disappeared and blaming her, or was it a trick to hide the truth that Travis had something to do with Lisa's disappearance?

Matt began speaking again in his low, somber voice. Someone brushed against her elbow, and she looked up to find Noah beside her.

"Doing all right?" He sent her a searching look.

She nodded. The music ended, and Matt introduced her. She targeted the spot in front of the microphones and headed to it. Lights glared in her eyes. She squinted to look beyond the press lamps, but her audience was a sea of strangers. Had one of them come to watch her beg over what he'd done to Lisa?

Doesn't matter. Speak to Lisa.

Teagan squared her shoulders, but her nerves seemed to revolt. Her mind went blank. No. She couldn't mess up.

"Lisa, please come home," Teagan forced the plea out of her dry mouth. "We love and miss you. I want us to celebrate your birthday together the way we planned. Call and let me know you're safe. To anyone who has her—" Teagan gulped a breath. *If you have her, are you watching me and enjoying my pain? No. Don't go there. This might be my only chance to reach Lisa's abductor.*

"If you have Lisa, please keep her out of harm's way and let her return to us. Thank you." She turned away as tears rolled down her cheeks. At least she'd gotten through her speech, although she'd skipped most of what she'd practiced all day. Unnerved, she climbed down the steps to retreat to the church and take a few minutes to compose herself.

"Miss Raynes. Miss Raynes," a man yelled to her.

Her throat clogged with a multitude of emotions: fear, sadness and hope.

On the stage, Matt introduced the police chief who would update them on the progress of the search.

"Miss Raynes." A man wearing a press pass lanyard dodged in front of her. "I'm Vic Taylor, an editor for the Hawick Falls Citizen."

He was bald, fortyish and dressed in a blue short sleeved shirt and tan pants, not much taller than Teagan.

"I've been writing pieces about my missing niece, Kara Linn. She was last seen in April. You can read my print column in the paper or my blog if you need more information."

"I'm sorry about Kara, but I can't talk at the moment. Excuse me." She ducked around him, but he cut in front of her again, using his square, broad build to stop her.

"Let me be clear. I want to bring both girls home." He pushed wire rimmed glasses up on his nose. "We should band together. Women get more sympathy and air time. My sister..." His lower lip quivered. "She's too upset to help."

"Miss Raynes is finished speaking to the public." Noah was next to her, a scowl on his face. "Sir, step behind the line for the media."

"He wants to discuss his niece, Kara, Noah."

"This is not the place. Too risky. We don't know who's in the crowd." When Vic Taylor didn't move, Noah waved an arm, and two uniformed men flanked Mr. Taylor.

Taylor raised his hands. "I'm leaving. I don't need armed guards."

Noah gripped Teagan's elbow and rushed her forward.

"Call me at the paper, Miss Raynes," Vic yelled. "We must join forces to uncover who took our girls."

Before she could answer, Noah escorted her up the church steps. He shut the doors and then steered her into the center aisle, where he faced her. "Are you okay?"

"Give me a second to unwind." She became aware of their solitude and the stress from the past few minutes eased from her.

She inhaled once more the odor of candle wax and the sweet fragrance of roses that floated through the open windows. Night had fallen and the pendant lights glowed like candles over their heads.

"Want to sit?" Concern lowered his voice.

She shook her head and tried not to cry. What was wrong with her? "If someone took Lisa, would he or she listen and bring her back?"

"We videoed everyone who came tonight and we'll review it. You can relax. No one will bother you while I'm here."

His powerful stare made her self-conscious, but she was unable to glance away, and she felt the warmth of a blush.

She fumbled for words as a new tension filled the air. "I'm...fine." What would he say if she told him the truth? She wasn't fine. She was a mess who barely remembered the speech she'd practiced and forgot the notes in her pocket. Worse, she was thinking how attracted she was to him when every thought should be devoted to Lisa, a girl who had seemingly vanished off the Earth.

What kind of selfish person was she? More tears burned her eyes. Guilt, regrets, and the urge to be closer to him grew inside her until she was unsure what to say or do. So her feet stayed glued to the floor.

She blinked and focused on the shadow of blond stubble on his jaw and the scent of his soap.

"I have officers posted outside the building. You're safe." He leaned toward her. Her heart thudded faster against her ribs. He brushed his knuckles across hers cheek, causing her skin to tingle, and she welcomed the realization. He was going to kiss her, here in the church. Sacrilegious. But the thrill of anticipation spiraled through her.

Teagan's body warmed, aching for his touch. His thumb skimmed her lower lip as he stepped closer, ending the distance between them. Slowly. Slowly, as though he wanted to give her a chance to turn away, say no.

She held her breath until their bodies met, and then he wrapped his arms around her. Heat radiated off him, merging into her when he kissed her.

She shut off the weak voice that whispered, *wrong*, and became aware of the hollow of his throat, the roughness of his chin against her skin, and the increased pressure on her lips until she opened her mouth. The voice in her head tried once more to warn her to stop, but the light play of his tongue against hers urged her to taste more.

The building, the background drone of voices outside and the entire night faded away. For one memorable moment, no more pain, no suffering. The world was only about them.

She tightened her arms around him, wanting to hold on forever.

Sirens shrieked in the distance. Their wails grew louder and stronger as though they were meant for her, screaming she'd entered dangerous territory.

"Fire." Noah pulled away. "They're coming closer." He was already ahead of her, walking into the vestibule. She ran across the aisle and entryway to stand beside him on the front steps. On the street, two red engines approached and raced past the vigil with their alarms blaring.

The throng in front of the platform was a sea of flickering light. She hooked a strand of hair behind her ear to give herself a second to compose her thoughts.

"The blaze is close." Noah pointed to the south end of the village where smoke billowed into the air. His phone buzzed. He paced a few yards from her and answered. She fought the urge to join him. She didn't want him to leave her side. Her craving for him still hummed in her blood.

Don't think about the kiss. Teagan focused on the gathering of town people, media, and police. The flames of the candles illuminated people's features with an eerie glow. Nowhere did she find a face that matched Lisa or her mother's.

Seth was gone, but in the middle of the mass stood Jake Clark. He was staring at the street along with many of the others, following the engines until their taillights vanished.

Even from the distance of fifty feet, she recognized the apprehension in his stiff body when he turned and their gazes met. He whirled around to the sidewalk and worked his way through the mass of people to exit.

Noah pocketed his phone and returned. "We need to go. Where's your car?"

"I parked in the rear lot. Noah, Jake is out there. Did you want to speak to him?"

"I do. Where is he?" He snapped his attention to the pack of people.

"He headed away from the vigil." She pointed in the direction. "He's probably gone.

Seth was out there, too, wearing his usual scowl."

"Don't worry. I'll get you an escort. Wait a second." He ran down the church steps to his men standing at the bottom.

On the stage, the FBI consultant was discussing the five-mile radius that had been searched and asking for any tip, large or small. Teagan ducked inside the church and grabbed her purse. She paused to stare at the center of the aisle where she and Noah had kissed. One moment gone forever. She hurried back to him.

"Let's go, and stay beside me." He turned on his heel.

"I want to tell you something." She caught his wrist and dropped it when he faced her with a question in his eyes.

"Someone sent me a text when I was stuck in the basement." She dug out her phone and scrolled to the message.

Noah looked over her shoulder at the screen. "Latin again? Did you figure it out?"

"I think it says 'I have the body'."

"Right, that's the literal translation. The phrase has a legal meaning too, but if it's a threat, I'd go with your interpretation."

"I guess the texter wanted to make sure I was able to translate it."

Noah's phone buzzed. She started to move away to give him privacy, but he hooked his arm around her waist and tugged her to his side. Surprised, she glanced up at him. He was listening to the caller and not paying attention to her.

He hung up and released her. "*I'll* drive you home."

"I don't want to leave my car here." The idea of being stranded filled her with another fear.

"Hand over your keys, and I'll assign an officer to bring your vehicle to your house."

The pressure of his hand on her arm alerted her he wouldn't stand around discussing it. She passed him the key ring.

"Come with me." He steered her inside the church and to the exit at the other end of the building, where they exited.

Father Matt's closing prayer carried over the bent heads of the gathering. The odor of ashes and soot choked the night sky.

Noah paused. "Where's your car?"

A mass of vehicles parked at odd angles filled the rear parking lot. Anyone could hide behind an auto, or truck, spring out, and attack her. Teagan's teeth began to chatter with stress. She pressed her lips together and pointed toward her hybrid a few feet away.

Noah spoke to an officer, who suddenly appeared, and passed him her key along with her address. Noah guided Teagan to his vehicle parked behind the stage. He opened the passenger door, and she slid inside.

In the closed quarters, the smell of smoke clung to her clothing and to her hair. She angled her head to glimpse the dark cloud rising skyward. The woods below the mountains must be burning.

Noah climbed into the driver's seat. He gripped the steering wheel in a white-knuckle clench. They rode in silence until they reached her house, where he parked in her driveway. He shifted and looked beyond her out her window. "Teagan, remember the dogs tracked both Kara and Lisa into Pretty Park? Our new theory is that someone is hunting girls at the park."

CHAPTER 20

Teagan focused her attention on the shadow of the smoke spiraling past the mountains. The rest of his words became lost as fear grew in her mind.

The gray cloud billowed higher and higher and disappeared into the heavens, but not before they marked the spot. The woods at Pretty Park were on fire. Was the clue to bringing Lisa home going up in smoke?

Noah escorted Teagan into her home. "I have to go to the fire. I'll need your cell before I leave. The techies will work on tracing your last call."

He held up his hand when she started to protest. "We'll pick up another one when I get back."

"Never mind. I'll use Aunt Sophia's phone." Hers was still in service. "I'll give you her number." She plugged her aunt's digits into his cell when he passed it to her. "When will you return mine?" Not that she was up for chatting or texting, but what if a miracle happened and Lisa called her phone? At least the tap was still on her phone and all calls recorded.

"Depends on backlog at the lab, but we'll hope for forty-eight hours."

Jogger appeared in the hall and meowed at them until Teagan bent and patted the cat. "You'll keep me company, right?"

"I'm not reassured." Noah muttered. "Remember, no one enters." He reached for the doorknob and hesitated.

"What is it?" Had he more to report?

"I'll check the house first."

"I'm starting to feel OCD about my locks."

"You can never be too careful. I'll do a walkthrough. Wait until I'm finished to enter." He marched into the living room.

She turned her attention to the outside and the stray ashes that blew her way. The longer she watched the smoke, the more her anxiety built.

"All clear," he said, coming back into the hall.

"Noah, if the dogs found traces of Lisa at the park, she might have gone back to hide in the woods." Teagan rubbed her arms that were chilled and whispered, "I pray she's safe and not in the area that's burning. Please, go look for her."

"I'm sorry, Teagan, but there's no guarantee Lisa is still at the park. The dogs didn't track her returning."

"I understand, but we have to investigate every possibility."

"You sound like a detective." He pulled her to him and gave her a kiss that seared her lips. "Don't go anywhere."

She stood savoring the moment, watching him leave. Should she pinch herself? After years of dreaming about Noah Cassidy, he was with her, kissing and touching her. But were his feelings for her genuine? People reacted strangely during periods of high emotion, and his job had to be stressful, and what about Stacey's story about his temper? How well did she know him?

She pictured Aunt Sophia's disapproving face. *Focus on Lisa, not a temporary crush.*

Teagan sat on the sofa and removed her .38 Special from her purse. She laid it on the coffee table within reach. Now all she needed was her car.

She jumped up and crossed to the hall and swung the door open. The odor of thick smoke greeted her. How bad was the blaze?

A picture of Lisa surrounded by a wall of flames sprang to life in Teagan's mind. She spun around and ran to the TV. Grabbing the remote, she clicked the on button.

The local newscaster was reading from the prompter. "A five-alarm fire is currently destroying the woods in the south end of Pretty Park. At this time, no injuries are reported, but the firefighters are still attempting to contain the inferno. This section of the recreational area is popular with joggers, walkers, and nature lovers."

Once the bulletin was over, she muted the sound and put on the shopping channel. The familiar blonde hostess was pitching a tea pot that fit over a mug and allowed the steaming water to drain into the cup through a bottom sieve.

Teagan glanced out the window to the street. Where was her car? "You can't even trust the police to deliver on time."

Restless, she found Aunt Sophia's phone in her bedroom and plugged it in downstairs before she pushed the power button. An alert popped up on the screen that she had ten messages. This was how your life ended, a bunch of unanswered emails on your cell.

Don't let this be Lisa's ending, too. She hit Matt's number, and he answered immediately.

"Teagan, are you using your aunt's phone? Her ID came up on mine."

"I needed a temporary replacement."

"Where are you? Stacey told me you left the vigil with the detective."

"I'm safe at home. Matt, Pretty Park's on fire and Lisa was there before she disappeared."

"What do you mean? She went to the park the morning she vanished?"

"I don't know the time she disappeared." Teagan looked out the front window. No signs of her vehicle. "The search dogs followed Lisa's scent to and out of the park. Then they lost it."

Headlights emerged from the dark. The driver slowed as he approached. Her car!

"Matt, I've got to go. Thank you for your help tonight."

"Take care, Teagan. I'm here if you need me."

"Thanks." She dropped the phone on the cushion, headed to her entryway, and stepped onto the step.

As the vehicle drew near, her spirits sank. It wasn't hers. An unfamiliar blue compact slowed and turned into her drive.

Teagan fought the urge to duck back inside. What if it was an officer with news of Lisa? Her hand tightened on the knob.

A man climbed out of the auto as the light above the garage flashed on and spotlighted her visitor. It was Vic Taylor.

He halted by her walkway. "Miss Raynes? It's me, Kara Linn's uncle."

"I remember you." He probably hoped for an interview. "I don't have any updates for the press."

"I understand. If you'd give me a few minutes to talk on a personal level, I'd be grateful." He started toward her and paused. "Is the detective inside?"

"Detective Cassidy? No. If you want to join me for another vigil, contact Father Matt at the church."

"I want to fill you in on what I know about my niece, Kara. It might help with your search for Lisa Grant and forgive me for coming to your house. I looked up your address since I wondered if Lisa lived in the same neighborhood as Kara." He moved closer when she didn't object.

A small wave of excitement rushed through her until her suspicious side kicked in. "Have you shared what you learned with the police?"

He walked to the steps. "I have, but a fresh pair of eyes and ears often sees and hears what others don't."

Stay locked inside, Noah's voice reminded her.

"Miss Raynes, you'll find it interesting. I promise."

The memory of his sad face at the vigil rolled into her thoughts and ended her indecision. She stepped forward. But what if she was wrong and the guy was her invisible stalker? "You can tell me here. I'm expecting an officer to arrive any second with my car."

"I won't take long." He glanced at the debris floating in the air and wiped his perspiring face with a handkerchief.

He looked like he could use a cool drink. *Don't trust anyone, even harmless looking people.* She tossed the idea aside.

"If you're uneasy, we can talk under the light." He eased down onto the top step and blotted the sweat on his forehead. "Excuse me, I need to sit. Tonight took a lot out of me. I imagine you, too." He fisted his hand around his handkerchief." You can watch for the police while I talk."

She nodded, but kept two feet between them. He gave her a smile that she didn't feel comfortable returning.

"I'd hoped to speak to you earlier, but Detective Cassidy was playing offensive lineman. Then I drove to the park, but the police have blocked access within half a mile."

"What did you find out?" The sooner he told her, the sooner

he'd leave.

"First, thanks for seeing me. I know how tough it is. Each morning you pray for the strength to make it through the day. At the end of the day, you pray to make it through the night."

He said the right words. "Do you have an idea where Kara is, Mr. Taylor?"

"I've been conducting my own investigation. My niece has been gone for three months. During that time, I've pulled up the background of every missing girl and sex pedophile in the six-oh-three area code. I can recite them for you."

"No need." His rambling and odd expressions made her nervous. Never mind Noah's last warning that a predator was hunting girls in the park added to her jitters. "And you discovered what?"

"I didn't learn much on the Internet. Instead, I started spending hours at the park since she was last seen there walking her dog. I watched traffic, wrote down the plates of vehicles that visited frequently. Most of the cars I've ruled out. I've ascertained, however, there's a bunch of high school kids who hang out in the woods and fancy themselves as a group of Robin Hoods."

Now he was onto something. "I've heard of them. Lisa could be hiding with them."

"My belief is the same. Kara might have joined them. She had an unrealistic romantic idea about life. I'm afraid she was meeting a boy at Pretty Park when she disappeared. Maybe he was part of the group. The cops claimed they questioned her friends and searched her electronics. No signs of a boyfriend surfaced." Behind his thick lenses, Taylor's eyes widened. "What about Lisa? Did she have a boyfriend who might be in the band?"

"Travis didn't belong to any group, but search dogs tracked Lisa into Pretty Park. I'm hoping she's holed up in the vicinity, possibly with her boyfriend. I'd grounded her for a week before her disappearance. Lisa might be trying to punish me by not coming home." Would she ever return? Had the worst already happened to her? An unexpected wave of grief hit Teagan. She turned her face away and blinked back the tears.

Vic rose and put his arms around her, holding in her a tight embrace that cut off her breath. "I'm sorry." Strong cologne similar to the kind worn by grandfathers floated around him.

Her senses jumped to alert as his sweaty body heat seeped into her and his hand moved lower. Was he expressing sympathy or something else? She broke free of him and stepped nearer the door, ready to escape inside.

The awareness of her deliberate act flickered in his eyes.

"I don't need pity, Mr. Taylor. I want leads to bring Lisa home."

"That's why I came. Let me finish." He wet his lips and continued. "I've heard the teenagers in the park referred to as the Merry Men. They'd probably like a girl or two in their group."

"Lisa might be with them." Was she alive and nearby? But then why didn't the search dogs locate her?

"I'm trying to determine if the Merry Men existed when my niece went missing," Vic said. "Kara is a young, impressionable girl. Though it's tough to believe she'd stay in the woods through rainstorms and our recent heat wave when she has a bed and shelter close by. But I suppose it's not unthinkable that Kara and Lisa might be camping in the woods."

Lisa living outside didn't fit her profile either. None of her clothing was missing from her room. And the girl complained when the temperature sank to sixty degrees or a fly buzzed near her head.

"I'm at the point where I must grasp every possibility. I wanted to know if the police are looking into this teenage group any further."

"Why don't you go ask them?" It was a good way to finish the conversation and get Mr. Taylor on his way. The odd little man was a rabble-rouser, but was he also skilled at luring girls to take a ride with him?

He removed his glasses and began to polish the lenses with a handkerchief from his pocket. Vic was in no hurry.

"I've approached the police with different scenarios, from the UFO group that meets once a month to the chance my niece became a hooker on Times Square. They assure me they checked them out, but I've no proof they did. The longer Kara has been gone, the more I've increased the scope of what transpired with her."

"And you wanted me to do what?"

"You can ask the detective to interview this Robin Hood band.

The police don't listen to me anymore. Frankly, I'm surprised they haven't talked to these kids already. The paper has run several of my editorials on the loss of revenues caused by the teens feeding expired meters along with my blogs about Kara's disappearance."

Teagan kneaded the back of her neck, which was cramping with stress. "When Kara vanished, did the police search the park?"

"Three times. We had so many people, they linked hands and formed a human chain.

They walked the grounds and scoured the overgrown ball field, the boarded lookout tower on the hill, and the far end with the picnic tables."

"You know the park well." Well enough to kidnap a girl from it? What was wrong with her? The guy was in distress and seeking help, or was he? She could still feel the dampness from his body pressed against her. She concealed a shudder.

Time to remind Mr. Taylor that she wouldn't be alone. "Thank you for filling me in. I'll have to go inside and call the officer who has my car. He should have been here by now."

"I should leave, too." Taylor pointed over his shoulder toward the smoke. "I may be able to learn something from the cops controlling the traffic by the fire."

"Good idea." Headlights shone on the street and the vehicle slowed for her driveway.

"My officer has arrived."

A cruiser followed behind and waited at the curb while the driver of her car climbed out. The officer was set with a ride back to the station.

Vic Taylor's phone began to buzz. "Excuse me." He pulled his cell from his pocket. "Might be a text about the blaze."

The patrolman spotted her in the light. Teagan waved to him and turned her attention to Vic who was reading his cell's screen.

"There's a possibility of a death at the park," he said, pocketing his phone.

"Dea—" The word stuck in her tight throat.

"Could I bother you for a drink before I go? My throat is dry."

"Okay." She whirled around and trotted into the kitchen. She needed a moment to collect herself. The news of a possible fatality spun in her head. Was it Lisa? She filled a glass from the tap when she sensed him behind her. "Mr. Taylor?" She swung around to find him a foot away and taking in the sight of the appliances like he'd never seen a stove or refrigerator.

"I was going to bring you the water." She shoved it at him.

"No need. This room reminds me of my grandmother's house." He accepted the drink and gulped it down as his Adam's apple bobbed up and down. "Thanks. I hope you'll speak to the detective and encourage him to check out what I've told you."

She nodded and led him to the front hall while keeping him within her vision. "Before you go, Mr. Taylor, do you know who died at the park?"

"I have no idea."

She opened the door, and he sped by her. Relief surged through her.

After locking up, she retreated to the living room. Jogger's snores from the footstool filled the house's quiet. The past few minutes with Vic Taylor had been odd and disturbing.

Now what? Picking up her cell from the coffee table, she hit Noah's number and hung up before it rang. When she heard the knock on the door, she ran to it.

A patrolman greeted her. "I waited for your company to leave." He handed over her keys.

"Officer, could you stay outside the house for a little while just until I'm sure Mr. Taylor won't come back?"

"That was Vic Taylor?" The young officer's brown eyes widened. "He's the one who wrote in the newspaper about the police not doing their job."

"You got it."

"No problem, Miss Raynes."

She returned to the TV and unmuted the channel. Today, the familiar sales host didn't bring her comfort. If only this feeling that someone was out there watching her would go away.

The swing of the clock's pendulum ticked one word: *A-lone. A-lone. A-lone.*

CHAPTER 21

"Looks like we located Jake Clark's car," Hines told Noah as they met below the tennis courts at Pretty Park. "Two firefighters found it while scouting the area for containment. The license plates are gone, but the body is in decent shape. I gave it a perusal, but nothing else."

Noah swatted at an ember floating through the air near his shirt. He blinked his smarting eyes. The wind blew the worst of the smoke away from the jogging path. "Is it too early to ask the fire chief if the inferno is arson?"

"He can give us his professional opinion. Got your flashlight, Cassidy?"

Noah held up his Police Force 7,000,000, which was used both as a stun gun or a torch. "With a possible arsonist and abductions, it's time for the big boy. We won't require flares."

"And if I get zapped with that, I'd feel like lightning struck me. My flashlight will be enough."

They crossed the main running route and trudged up the trail with Hines in the lead. Noah tramped past two officers stationed at the bottom of the slope where the streetlights ended.

"I posted a couple more men further up the hill," Hines said over his shoulder and turned on his beam. Fifteen feet into the woods, he stopped before the white auto that blocked the rest of their trek. Hines beamed his light over the car.

Noah approached for a closer look. Mud caked the sides. A

fresh dent marred the front of the hood. Was it caused by hitting Lucy Watson? Paint scratches marked the body. "I'm surprised they could get it this far up on the narrow track. And it's backed in."

"Might have been easier to back with rear-wheel drive," Hines said.

"Scratched the coat to hockey hell." Noah leaned down to examine the tire tracks. "It's jammed in here with a log underneath the front axle. You're right, the model seems like a match for Jake Clark's missing vehicle." Noah straightened. "My guess, whoever abandoned the auto stuck it on the hill for us to discover. Maybe the same person set the fire to draw us here."

"I'm sending the VIN number." Hines punched in the digits on his cell as he spoke. "I vote Clark abandoned his compact to confirm his alibi. Ready to look in the trunk?"

"Hines, you're making my day." Opening trunks was like unwrapping a surprise package. You never knew what was inside. "We should check with the chief. We might need a search warrant though we could argue an abandoned car near a fire in a public park is suspicious and dangerous."

"The chief would cut off our heads if a judge threw out evidence inside because we didn't follow procedure."

Noah's wall of protection slid upward, leaving a smaller slice of optimism. "Maybe the arsonist stole the car and left the blow torch that started our inferno in the trunk." He walked on the edge of the path, dodging the overhanging tree branches. "Not that I'm greedy. A can of gas and matches would be a good find, too."

He stopped at the car's rear. A stained cloth hung out of the trunk and over the license plate. "Hines, is that blood on the rag?" Noah dug in his pocket for latex gloves and tugged them on.

"Looks like a matter of life or death," Hines confirmed. "We better pry open the boot."

Noah crouched for a closer view. "Forget the crowbar. It's open. An uneasy sensation rippled through him. This was too easy.

He couldn't get over the convenience of the unlocked trunk that seemed flagged for them.

Had someone set them up? Was someone watching them, smiling at his or her cleverness at what they were about to find? Thick trees grew close to the dirt trail, hiding them from anyone who wasn't near. No one could see them.

Teagan's last text jumped to the front of his mind.

"I got the body," whispered in his ear as he flung the lid wide.

CHAPTER 22

Teagan woke determined not to let Lisa's disappearance and a stalker steal her life. She spent the afternoon at the school's summer workshop on Best Reading Strategies to keep her mind occupied, and pretended she felt normal. She arrived late to avoid questions and braced herself during the break to accept the sympathies and questions of the other teachers. At home, she flipped through the pages of notes and hoped by opening day, she'd be able to absorb the methods and teach them.

She called the hospital and was connected to Lucy's nurse, who told her that the doctor would allow visitors, even though, Lucy remained unconscious. The rain poured down the rest of the day while she worked on the Remember Lisa Page and expanded her list of stores to contact about putting up Lisa's flyer.

By evening, humid air trapped the smog that rolled across the yard. Teagan hoped Noah wasn't driving around tonight. Thank goodness for the two fans she'd found in the attic. They kept the bedroom livable.

She glanced at the clock on her nightstand. It was almost midnight, and she hadn't heard a word from Noah since the afternoon. At least the news reported the fire was out at the park.

She picked up her aunt's phone lying next to the book she'd been attempting to read. The quiet in the house yanked on her nerves. Her thumb hovered over Noah's number plugged into the contact list.

Jogger sprang off the spread and sat near the bed meowing at Teagan.

"You can't be hungry, can you?" Her stomach felt like she'd consumed rust remover. Just the thought of a trip to the kitchen made her queasy. If only she could sleep, maybe she'd wake fit and hungry.

She opened the door, and Jogger raced from the room. The empty house lay beyond. Closing the door, she stared at Noah's number, and debated calling him again. She just wanted to hear his voice.

A piercing screech broke the hush. Teagan spun around, dropping her phone. Was that horrible noise Jogger? Unable to move, she waited, straining to hear another sound. The shriek had come from downstairs.

But nobody was there to hurt her cat. Her stomach cramped. *Do something.*

She scooped up her phone and pocketed it. On unsteady legs, she crossed to the bureau and picked up her .38 Special. Gripping the unloaded weapon, she peeked into the hall.

The nightlights burned in the empty corridor. She wet her lips and in a loud whisper called her pet. Leaning forward, she listened for the pad of the cat's paws or a meow. The silence in the house roared in her ears.

She crept to the stairs. No sign of Jogger in the hall. Maybe she smacked into furniture in the dark. No. Cats can see in the night. Maybe she had a heart attack and was lying on the floor dying. The idea pushed Teagan forward. She stole down the steps, her mouth went dry. Halfway, she paused again. The grandfather clock chimed the hour.

The familiar musical ding reassured her. She was overreacting. Lowering her gun, she walked into the living room and snapped on the light. The space looked the same as usual except no Jogger on the footrest. The cat must be in the kitchen.

She whirled around and scanned the furniture and bookcase. She could have sworn the cat's cry came from the living room. Where was Jogger? Teagan's head throbbed with worry and alarm. She'd become a paranoid flake cake.

Massaging her forehead, she entered the kitchen and froze. Someone was in Lisa's chair. No, couldn't be.

Sweat popped out on Teagan's forehead.

As she inched forward, the small functioning part of her brain warned the almost human figure was too small to be Lisa. What or who was at the table? Teagan halted. An oblong, faceless head rested on a midsection. Stumps protruded from where arms would go. Legs without feet jutted from the lower portion of the trunk. The entire form was encased in a dark brown shell. A rancid odor of something burnt permeated the room. As Teagan struggled to make sense of the scene, a worm wriggled out of a hole, a hole where an eye should be. The pieces whirled in her mind and fell together. A burnt human corpse sat in Lisa's chair.

She gasped. Nausea rushed up her throat. She darted to the sink and vomited. No. No.

Reeling with shock, she wiped her mouth with a shaking hand and stumbled into the living room.

Noah. He'd come. She fished out her phone and blubbered her fears the minute he answered.

"Slow down, Teagan," he said. "Try again. What happened?"

She swallowed, and forced a string of words out of her tight throat and answered his questions with yes or no. Finally, he spoke the magic phrase. "I'm on my way. I'll alert my men. In the meantime, I'll contact dispatch for the patrol. I bet they're closer than I am. Stay on the line with me."

She couldn't stop the tears that flooded down her cheeks while she waited. In five minutes, the patrol officers identified themselves to her, and she let them inside. Six minutes later, Noah and Detective Hines arrived followed by a team of men. They invaded her home with the sense of urgency in their footsteps. At the sight of Noah, she wiped away the tears and retold her story in a more coherent voice until she reached the part about the worm.

He captured her hands, which were in constant motion, in his large ones and guided her to the sofa. "Sit. We'll find who did this. Don't worry."

He gave her time to regain her composure, and then he and Detective Hines took her statement. When she finished, he reassured her that he and Hines would take care of everything.

"Where's Jogger?"

"She's safe under your couch. I guess she won't be supervising. Stay here. I'll keep you up to date.

While the techies snapped pictures, wrote measurements, and videoed her nightmare, the big question kept running in her mind. Was it Lisa?

The techies and uniformed men and women threw her glances on their way through to search her house. She couldn't focus or think of anything else. It felt like two eternities before Noah sat next to her and said something about the unidentified burned body in her kitchen.

How could this happen? She sagged against the cushion and tried but failed to imagine Lisa coming in the front door.

Hours later, people drifted out the door. The police were leaving. Was it morning? Was Noah going?

"Stay," she whispered when he approached and before he announced he was leaving.

He sat beside her and covered her hand with his. They sat in the silence. She was too exhausted to speak, but all she needed was Noah next to her. For the first time in hours, she closed her eyes.

She fell into a restless slumber haunted by giant worms and Lisa screaming she was on fire. Teagan stirred and touched a body. She jumped up with a gasp to find a startled Noah drawing his weapon.

"I'm sorry," she blurted while her mind fast-forwarded through memories of her night. "I fell asleep and had a nightmare. What time is it?" She glanced at the window and rubbed her eyes.

"Still night." He holstered his gun and then tugged her down next to him.

She burrowed closer to his large form and asked the important question. "Do you need to leave?"

"I sent in a quick update to the chief when we finished. We can rest a little longer."

She closed her eyes. Maybe she would just sit here. At the touch against her shoulder, she tilted her head up to Noah standing in front of her. Had she fallen asleep again? She rubbed her eyes and asked, "What time is it?"

"It's nearly six." He ran a hand over his shadowed jaw. "I should go home, shower, and change before my meeting. Did you sleep?"

She worked her fingers through her uncombed hair. "I'd call it passing out. I wonder where Jogger's hiding."

"After everyone left, Jogger claimed your bed. I'd bet she's still enjoying a catnap upstairs."

"I'm glad someone can catch a few winks." She pointed toward the kitchen, and her throat tightened. "Is the—"

"Gone. Someone broke the lock on your back door. The locksmith will be here this afternoon to take care of it. I've hooked up a temporary bolt for now that will keep you safe until he arrives."

"Thanks." The numbness that protected her when she woke was fading. She walked to the window and peeked outside. Streaks of light lit the sky above the rooftops. A beautiful bright day was ahead, but her life was filled with revulsion and darkness.

Noah's car sat alone in the driveway, unlike the previous evening when it was packed with cruisers and the Major Crime Van. "The neighbors must be wondering what happened to the neighborhood."

She wrapped her arms around herself and shivered over the memory of the brown encrusted human. She had to stop thinking, remembering or she'd be ill again.

At least Noah had stayed with her. The idea sent a quiver of pleasure through her until she recalled the smoke that had filled the air yesterday.

"Noah, I didn't comprehend much last night. What happened at Pretty Park? Is the fire out?"

"You were in shock. Sit, first."

Oh, oh, this sounded ominous. She sat next to him.

"Lots went on yesterday. A portion of the park's woods burned before the blaze was extinguished, but the firefighters stopped the fire from spreading up the mountains. We found Jake's car hidden on a wooded trail near the main jogging path."

"Jake must be glad to have his car back. Did you find out who stole it?"

"Not yet, and we're working on informing him. We'll process the vehicle first for blood, hair, fibers."

She nodded and locked her fingers together in her lap to keep her hands still.

"I don't like leaving you by yourself." His eyes reflected worry and concern.

She fought the urge to lean against him and pour out the horror from her night again, but the man had enough going on in his life without absorbing her problems over and over. "I know what happened to your family."

"What?" He shook his head and frowned.

Why had she blurted out that information? "I'm sorry." Her face heated. "Stacey told me about the boat accident before the vigil. I had to tell you. It's been on my mind." She rose and paced in front of him. "I keep hearing Aunt Sophia's voice telling me to stop being a gossip."

"I doubt you heard your aunt saying that."

Now she'd have to explain talking to her aunt, a dead person.

"If she did speak," he continued, "she would have told you everyone in Hawick Falls already discussed the accident a year ago. It's old news, except for people with long memories."

"How awful." Everyone gossiped about him? If Noah had threatened the man who killed his family, it was likely to have hit the city's popular rumor mills. Maybe Stacey's story had been the truth and not an exaggerated tale. "I won't bring it up again, unless you want to discuss it."

"We'll gossip about my family when we have more time. Believe me. It could take days." Noah gestured toward the window. "I believe your company has arrived and I can go."

Outside, a blue cruiser parked at the curb in front of her house.

"I talked with the chief," Noah said. "He agreed you shouldn't be left in your house alone. If you need anything, the officer will take care of it. Paul is on duty today." Noah rose. "No more surprise guests at the dinner table."

"Does Paul do windows, too?" she asked, hoping to lighten the dark expression on his face.

"He might." Noah kissed the top of her head. "I'll come by later. Call if you need me."

She followed him to the door. "What happened to the...body?"

"Gone for postmortem exam. We already have Lisa's DNA to determine if there's a match. I talked to the chief, and he's pushing the lab to fast track the results. We should have the outcome in a couple of days."

The charred figure from her nightmare could be Lisa, but who put her there?

"Take care, Teagan." He touched her shoulder in a quick yet

intimate gesture.

She wanted to lean into him and kiss like they had in the church to bring back a moment when she wasn't filled with sadness or revulsion.

As though reading her mind, he dropped a feather light kiss on her lips. Well, he didn't quite read her thoughts. Maybe their private moments were just distractions to keep him sane while on a tough case. Wasn't she doing the same?

"Remember, Paul is outside. Why don't you consider moving out of you house for a while?" he asked.

The memory hurtled into her mind. Mom plunked her on their sleeping bag and pointed a finger at her, "Don't let anyone take our spot. It's our home tonight. Scream if anyone tells you to move. Got it, baby? I'll be right back."

"Teagan?"

She looked at Noah who stood with his brows raised, waiting for my answer.

"No one scares me into leaving my home."

"Call if you change your mind and let me know." He turned on his heel to exit, but whirled back around to give her a toe-curling kiss that left her nerves jumping and her brain racing. "I've wanted to do that since I arrived last night."

He left before she regained her senses.

She managed a wave as he drove away.

Closing the door, she allowed her worries to seep back into her thoughts. *God, keep Noah safe and don't let the DNA be a match.*

CHAPTER 23

The rest of the day passed without word from Noah. Well, he had a job to do, and it wasn't taking care of her. Teagan spent the morning composing and posting her daily blog about Lisa and writing thank you notes to friends and volunteers. She avoided the kitchen after one glance at the empty room.

Before supper, Bennie from Village Hardware arrived. While he installed her new lock, he listened to her condensed story about her break-in with comments about the old days when no one locked their doors. He assured Teagan that the new security device was rated number one in defeating burglars. After he left, she'd debated calling Noah, but decided to believe that no news meant another day of Lisa being alive. She clicked on the TV to blot out the thoughts running rampant in her mind and created little purple bows to hang on the bushes outside.

The next morning, her phone rang at nine a.m. She answered on the first ring. Noah's voice was tense as he explained he wanted to come over and update her. Was he saving the worst to deliver in person? Maybe she was imagining things. She could win a blue ribbon for creating ghastly case scenarios in her head.

The clock ticked down the minutes until Noah arrived. On the footrest, Jogger yawned and fell back asleep. The park's blaze had made the front-page headlines for the last couple of days. Teagan reread the newspaper article about the fire and listened to the drone of the fan she'd placed by the chair.

A paragraph in the local news section reported the police had located a missing vehicle at the park. Nothing else was mentioned about Jake's car or the charred body in her kitchen.

Vic Taylor's piece was absent from the daily edition. Had he been too involved in the hunt for his niece to write? Teagan strode back and forth past the window until she recognized Noah's car headed toward her driveway. A cruiser tailed him and pulled up in front of the patrolman on duty. The shifts were changing. She'd brought the last officer snacks and drinks, which he'd accepted with polite thanks and a smile. The guy must be super bored and probably speculating on what he'd done to deserve the job of staring at her house.

Now she flew to the hall. Jogger scampered into the entryway and sat by her feet. She threw open the door and ate up the sight of Noah. Shadows under his eyes suggested he was functioning on little rest; although, his white shirt and navy pants carried the fresh scent of laundry soap and were wrinkle free.

"Morning, Jogger," he said when the cat meowed. He scanned Teagan. "You look better."

She ran a hand over her black skirt. "Thought I'd dress up a bit. It helps lift my mood." She'd managed a few hours of sleep between dreams of bodies burning and worms crawling in her cabinets. "Come in." She turned and walked into the living room with him at her heels. "Would you like coffee?"

"Thanks, I already drank my hourly quota of two cups. We should sit."

She perched on the edge of the sofa cushion and locked her cold, clammy hands together.

He sat beside her and left a sliver of space between their knees. "I brought pictures of the items from Jake Clark's trunk. Are you up to looking at them today?"

Not really, she wanted to say, but she'd fake it. "Ready."

He pulled his phone from his pocket, scrolled downward, and then held out the image.

The picture was of a white T-shirt. "It's similar to Lisa's. I can't be one hundred percent certain it's hers."

With a few clicks, he produced a picture of denim cut-shorts. The mended slit on the left leg left her with no doubt. "They're Lisa's. I sewed the rip." She pointed to the spot. Teagan sank against the back of the sofa and blinked away the tears. Something bad had happened to Lisa. *Please, God, let her be alive.*

"I'm sorry," he said. "Are you up to one more?"

Nodding, she wiped her eyes and leaned forward. A picture of a bra and a pair of panties popped onto the screen. "I'm not positive they're Lisa's."

He clicked off his cell and a large dose of stress flowed away. She cleared her throat and asked the big question. "Have you heard the results on the DNA from the remains in my kitchen?"

"Not yet. First, we're trying to determine if the remains were male or female."

Hope rolled upward and her chest expanded, until the image of Lisa's shorts popped into her head. Worries spiraled through her mind and drowned out Noah's voice. She caught the terms forensics and genetic code.

When he finished, she searched for a response and used the most obvious. "So it might be tough to ID the remains."

"If a fragment of the victim's dental work exists, it's easy. For now, we have a few questions for Jake about the clothing in his trunk. We'll be talking with him today. The chief and the mayor are pushing for a break and his car might be our lead."

"Do you think Lisa hid in the woods, found the stolen car and ditched her shorts and shirt in it? Wait, Lisa took Jake's car. She knows where he parks. Then she was trapped in the fire and lost her things?" But how to explain what she was wearing now and how she started Jake's vehicle.

"It's a hypothesis."

His noncommittal tone wasn't encouraging. "Maybe the night I saw Travis outside my house, he was searching for a way to enter and snatch a few of Lisa's clothes. When he couldn't get inside, he bought her a top and shorts at a thrift store or borrowed some." That meant Lisa was alive for sure.

Skepticism and then sympathy glittered in his eyes. "We don't know yet, Teagan. I'd appreciate you keeping quiet about your vigil text and the garments we found. Personally, I believe the thief ditched the car with Lisa's belongings in the woods for us to find."

"You think she was kidnapped, and her kidnapper taunted the police with her clothes?"

"Again, it's a theory, not a certainty."

"Sounds like someone is watching our every move." Her throat burned from the fear rising upward. She had to talk of something else or become ill. "Vic Taylor stopped by the night of the vigil."

"Vic Taylor came to your house?"

"He arrived after you left for the fire. He thinks the girls joined the teenage Robin Hood group at Pretty Park. I didn't mention him sooner because I was distracted by the burned body in Lisa's chair." She linked and unlinked her fingers while she pictured the fried corpse before she rambled onward. "Vic Taylor wants the police to investigate the Robin Hood boys."

"Teagan, the teens are already under investigation. You shouldn't have spoken to him. Take no chances should be your motto. Next time, send him away and call me if he won't leave."

"Will do. Do you think the kids who hang out in the woods set them on fire or Jake was involved in the arson?"

"I don't have the answers. Trust no one, even Kara Linn's uncle." The intensity of his gaze pounded her until she broke eye contact.

"I'm suspicious of most people, and Mr. Taylor is kind of creepy. Don't worry. I'm done talking to him." She recalled the man's embrace. Had she misread him? No, it wasn't only his physical touch that creeped her out. He'd been trailing her the night of the vigil to her house and inside.

"Noah, when Vic was here, he followed me inside for a drink of water. While he was here, he kept looking around. He claimed the place reminded him of his grandmother's, but what if he was planning where to leave the…remains." What if he had killed and burned his niece? Her hands and legs began to shake. She clasped her palms and knees together to keep them still.

"I'll talk to Mr. Taylor."

Noah's steel voice wasn't reassuring. "Could Vic Taylor have put Kara in my kitchen?" She wet her dry lips and focused on Noah's face to blot out more images and questions.

"We'll arrest him if he did. Whoever took the girls hasn't made a mistake, yet. I'm hoping we'll get a lead from the victim at your table, as terrible as it is to imagine."

Teagan nodded and glanced out the window at a young couple walking past the house. The girl was laughing and playfully shoved at the boy. Strange that people could smile and be happy.

She didn't know if she'd ever laugh again. "Sometimes, I feel like an awful person, and today is one of them. I've been praying the remains are anyone but Lisa."

He rose and pulled her to her feet.

"*Teagan*," he said in a low voice. "You're not bad. You're normal." He slid his hands to her elbows.

Her skin tingled from his touch, and the intimate way he said her name reminded her of the last kiss they'd shared.

"You care about Lisa. It's natural to want her to be alive." He tugged her to him and tightened his hold.

She inhaled the clean fragrance of his soap and toothpaste. The urge to kiss him and drive away the grief that held her prisoner cheered her onward. She wanted to be a normal person, not a woman filled with sadness and fear, spending hours worrying until her head and stomach hurt. He slackened his grip, and she sensed he was about to release her. No, she had to hold onto him for one more moment.

Rising up on tiptoes, she brushed her lips against his. Surprised flickered over his face. The button of his shirt pressed against her chest. Then his mouth opened and his heat melted into hers. The world of pain drifted away.

His hand cupped her breast, and he nibbled at her chin.

The front doorbell buzzed.

They'd leave when she didn't answer. She tightened her arms around his shoulders. Desire clawed at her.

"Teagan?"

The voice registered in her mind. Matt! He stood a yard from them. His open jaw and his eyes bright with shock warned he understood what he'd interrupted.

There was no one she wanted to see less at this moment. She should have paid attention to his ring. She broke free from Noah's grip. "Ma...at," she stumbled over his name. Her cheeks burned with embarrassment.

"Father," Noah acknowledged, seeming unfazed, almost defiant.

Matt recovered before she did. "I rang the bell." He pinpointed his gaze on Noah and frowned.

"I've so much to tell you," she blurted to cover her awkwardness and added another two feet of distance between herself and Noah.

"Did you find Lisa?" Matt asked her.

Noah's phone began to ring while Jogger leaped down from her perch to twine herself around Teagan's legs. She picked up the cat and held her against her chest. The sound of her pet purring soothed Teagan's frazzled nerves.

"Excuse me." Noah turned away with his cell against his ear.

She had to say something. "Matt, the police located Jake's stolen car at the park yesterday, and someone put a burned body at my kitchen table."

"What? A body was here, inside your home?" His eyes widened. "Lisa?"

"We have to wait for forensic results." She bent her face over Jogger, trying to hold onto her composure.

"You should have called me, Teagan."

"The police came."

Jogger jumped free as Noah walked back toward them. He stopped and watched them from across the room.

She didn't have time for whatever was bothering him about Matt.

Was Matt wondering why she and Noah were kissing when they'd found a person's remains? How did she explain the comfort and attraction she felt when she was with him? Life was more confusing each second.

"I've got to go, Teagan," Noah told her. "I'll brief you later if I learn anything. Maybe I need to speak to Paul about who comes into your house."

"Matt is always welcome." Almost always.

"Paul's father is a deacon in the church. He knows me."

"Any chance you'll search for the Robin Hood group?" Teagan asked, sensing a no win contest between the men brewing, "It's a wild guess, but maybe Lisa joined their band."

"We investigate every possibility. If you'll excuse me, I'm off." Noah compressed his lips and nodded at the priest as he passed him.

An uncomfortable silence fell between her and Matt. What should she say? Forgive me, Father, for I have sinned? No, she hadn't sinned. Why did she feel like she'd committed the worst kind of crime and sin?

"I couldn't sleep and knew you've been having the same problem. Since the last time we spoke was the vigil, I drove over. With the cruiser and the detective's car parked out front, I thought you were getting more bad news and might need support."

"I appreciate your concern." Except when I'm kissing Noah.

"I didn't realize you and the detective were…close, Teagan."

"It just happened." She twisted her hands together. That wasn't exactly true.

"I'm worried about you. You're stressed from your aunt's death, adjusting to life in Hawick Falls again, and Lisa's disappearance. It's easy to get caught up in a relationship that you wouldn't seek under normal conditions."

"What's wrong with the detective?"

"Your mind isn't clear when you're upset. You could regret your actions later when your days return to normal."

Regrets? She imagined Noah's arms around her, and the gleam in his eyes when he wanted her. No, she wasn't sorry or sad about their kiss. And she'd kissed him first. If he was using her, she was using him, too. "I'm fine, Matt. Don't fret."

He laid his hand on her shoulder. The warmth from his palm seeped through the fabric. "You've had your ups and downs, especially when you were younger. I always hoped you'd meet a steady, stable man to give you what you deserve. A detective lives a life of irregular hours. Often, he deals with people at their lowest points round the clock."

"I'm sure he must find rewards in his job, and I'd describe your day as similar."

"I don't have a family. Teagan, Detective Cassidy may be the most talented investigator in Hawick Falls, but he grew up in a troubled home and carries a great deal of anger. I've never been into gossip, but you should consider the facts. His parents left him to raise himself and I suspect he bears scars from their abandonment. He's learned to use threats to get results instead of reason and compromise. I'm sorry, but it's common knowledge in Hawick Falls since his father drank too much and told their problems to anyone who would listen. I don't believe Noah Cassidy is the type of person you'd date under normal circumstances."

Matt was mistaken about Noah. "I've seen only good in him.

Besides, each of us has faults."

"I'm not arguing that you date only perfect men because there are none. I'm saying step back until Lisa is found, and your life is stable. That's all. If Noah Cassidy has changed, then I'm happy to be wrong."

She barely caught his last piece of advice. Her mind whirled with questions about Noah's 'troubled home'. Was she gravitating to a man who'd never commit? Was this what attracted her to him?

Matt was waiting for her response. She searched for an honest answer. "I don't want to mess up my life either."

The tension in his shoulders eased. It was rare that she argued with him, if ever.

"Your aunt would be proud of you," he said in his low even voice. "You've grown a lot from the little girl who lived on the street. Just consider what you've always imagined for your future. I trust you'll do right."

Matt didn't approve of Noah. His meaning was plain. "I have good news for a change. I called the hospital yesterday. Lucy's doctor will allow a few visitors to stop by and talk to her."

"She's regained consciousness? The rosary group will take full credit."

"Not yet. Her physician subscribes to the theory that his patients can hear you when they're unconscious, which means we're allowed into her room, but she won't be talking. I planned on visiting today. Do you want to come with me?"

He shook his head. "I've got the Coffee Chat in an hour. We meet early to accommodate people going to work, and I'm booked the rest of the day. This was the only time I could squeeze in to stop by. And I promise in the future to call beforehand."

"I appreciate your concern. Oh, did anyone turn in a St. Jude's medal at the vigil? I can't find mine and wanted to loan it to Lucy. I thought it was in my purse, but no such luck."

"None of the parishioners brought a medal to the rectory, but I can get you a new one."

"Aunt Sophia gave me the medal when I first arrived. I'm a little sentimental about it. But I might take you up on another if mine doesn't show up."

"Why don't I ask Stacey to go with you to visit Lucy?"

"She has lots to do in the office without Lisa's help." Teagan swung her purse over her shoulder. "I won't be alone. My escort will be with me." She pointed out the window at the patrol car. "Detective Cassidy asked his chief to have an officer posted at my house after the last threat. I'm sure Paul wouldn't mind a change of scenery."

"What do you mean? You received another holy card with a warning?"

"I received a text while at the vigil." Too late, she remembered giving her word to keep this piece of information secret.

"What did it say?"

"The same as the first," she hedged.

"I'm canceling the Coffee Chat."

"No. Consider the officer in the cruiser carries a gun. I'll be fine."

Matt locked onto her gaze. "If anything happened to you—"

"Don't worry. If a person kidnapped Lisa and Kara Linn, he's into young girls. I'm ancient, and I bet the holy card warning was from Travis, wherever he is. Travis needs you, not me. He's probably wandering around searching for food and shelter."

"I'm going to call Seth later this morning and organize a search for the boy."

"I appreciate your concern, Matt." She reached up and kissed his cheek to let him know how much she cared.

"Especially since I'm not dogging your steps," he added. "Why don't you come to the Chat? We serve baked goods, and I'm guessing you haven't eaten. Then you can go visit Lucy. Bring your new escort along."

"You've convinced me. Besides, I'm trying to have a life and find Lisa. I'll be ready in a second once I explain to the officer he'll be getting free food and coffee."

At the Activity Center, Teagan accepted people's sympathy and concerns about Lisa. Many offered to volunteer in searches or vigils. Officer Paul drank and ate, but maintained a distance from the group.

It was late morning when she ducked out of the meeting with the patrolman tailing her. Hospital security had set up a chair outside Lucy's door and Paul settled into it to wait for her.

Keeping the memory of her mother's hospital stay locked away, she entered her friend's room.

Lucy lay in the bed with wires attaching her to a monitor.

Teagan relaxed her shoulders and wandered closer. "Hi, Lucy, it's me. I've missed you. When you're better, we'll go shopping and buy lots of chocolates."

The soft music playing and the buzz of the machine filled the quiet. The vase of yellow lilies sat on the cabinet on the other side of the bed. Had Stacey delivered them? A beam of sunshine glinted off something in the leaves. What was that? She shoved aside the stems of the bouquet and found a silver chain wrapped around two stalks. Teagan pulled it out. A heart dangled from the middle link. Lisa's bracelet! Teagan turned over the pendant. What was the rust-colored stain on the back?

She held the jewelry closer, and her mind spun. Blood!

Teagan's legs wobbled. The wristlet fell to the floor. She closed her eyes and fought the wave of nausea sweeping over her.

At the swish of the door opening, she rested her foot over the bracelet and faced the newcomer.

CHAPTER 24

A loud noise woke Lisa. She lay listening, too sore and sick to move. Go away. Go away. Come again no other day.

No wire, chains, or handcuffs imprisoned her, but she didn't budge a muscle. If she just kept her eyes closed, she wouldn't see the monster who invaded and controlled her mind. The monster who would strangle her until she passed out, and then bring her back to life for more torture.

"Lisa. Lisa."

Her foster mother was scolding her. Which one? Was it morning? She couldn't sit up. She was trapped in a hole, a pit that stunk of sweat, piss, and filth.

Ashes to ashes. Soon she'd join the surrounding dirt. Had the other girl joined it? Lisa hadn't heard her crying for a while.

A chill waved over her. Her throat hurt. Her body ached everywhere.

"Lisa. Lisa."

The voice grew louder. Who was calling her? "Aunt Sophia? I'm in here," Lisa rasped. She scooted downward and slammed her feet against the door until queasiness overcame her.

She waited out the need to barf. No, Aunt Sophia died. Maybe someone else was looking for her. If only Travis had loved her.

At night, she'd put the key under the angel in the backyard and he'd sneak down to the cellar where they'd meet. Teagan would be sound asleep. When they were fighting, she kept the key and the door locked. But when they were happy, they'd sit on the old wicker two-seater and make out. That's where they first had sex and he claimed to love her.

Why hadn't he? Lisa blinked at the tears while the voice whispered her name.

It was Aunt Sophia again, except now she wanted Lisa to join her.

No. She wasn't going to heaven. A sharp pain stabbed her chest. She was sick because of the monster man.

She hated him. The next time he came for her, she'd resist. Whatever he did for punishment was better than remembering those gross, painful things he did to her.

The music was playing. He was here.

I'm dying in this hole. Please, God, help me escape.

The door swung open. He dragged her out of the chamber by her heels. She blinked against the light. The monster shoved her forward. She fell against the torture table. Catching herself on the edge, she leaned against the edge, waiting for her agony to begin.

She tensed and turned her head. A shadow in the corner shifted.

She squinted at a shape. She wet her cracked lips and croaked, "Help."

Had she imagined the movement? No. She wasn't crazy, yet. But what if the creature in the dark wasn't human? The silhouette was too big for rats. The girl? Yes. He was making the girl watch them.

CHAPTER 25

At the moment, Noah would cast a vote for Jake Clark as best professional liar. He stared at the man on the other side of the table for facial tells. Hines, sitting next to him in the bare, beige-walled room, was doing the same.

From his pocket, Jake produced a list of phone numbers and names. "I called each of these people, trying to find my vehicle the day it went missing. I'm sure you can verify my timetable with them."

Noah scanned the paper and set it aside. "You carry this around?"

"No, when Officer Hines—"

"Detective Hines," Noah corrected.

Jake frowned and continued. "When I was asked to come to the station because you found my car, I decided to arrive prepared. I'm not a backwoodsman who's unfamiliar with the law. You're looking for someone to pin a crime on. I brought evidence. I'm not the one who hit Lucy. My car was stolen, and I couldn't have done it."

"You last saw your vehicle in the evening," Hines said, "when you parked in the lot behind your apartment building?"

Jake nodded.

"We talked to the people where you live," Hines said. "None of them can vouch you were at your place the night your car disappeared. In fact, your upstairs neighbor remembers the evening your vehicle vanished as one of the most restful nights he's spent in a long time. He usually can't sleep because the music you play comes through his bedroom floor."

"That resident has his evenings confused. I don't socialize with him, and we've never discussed my schedule." Jake shook his head. "Besides, how does my being or not being home the night before Lucy was hit prove I'm responsible for her accident the next morning?"

"You might have been out with her." Noah began to pace the room.

Jake kept his eyes on Noah, but he didn't respond.

"The teenager from apartment 6C told us your car wasn't in its spot when he rolled in around eleven forty-five p.m. His space is beside yours."

"Then the thief stole my car during the night. Really, detectives. Where's your proof and where's my vehicle? I'm ready to leave."

The man thought he was the president of MENSA and they were the clueless police. "It's like this, Jakie." Noah grabbed the file off the table. "We received a call from a hotel outside the village. They watched the news and recognized the woman in the hit and run as their guest." Noah threw the credit card receipt from the folder in front of Jake. "The desk clerk looked at Lucy's picture and confirmed she spent the night."

"What's that got to do with me? That's not my bill."

"You went to see her and stayed overnight. Probably offered to take her out for breakfast, but you argued or things didn't go the way you'd hoped. So you dropped her off on the street, told her you were going to park, and then meet her. Instead you ran her down."

"Preposterous. I didn't know she was in Hawick Falls. Why would I risk my life for someone who wasn't interested in me?"

"You said it. She wasn't into you anymore. Revenge is ugly." Noah flattened his palms on the table and leaned into Jake's face. "We're going to search through your car, electronics, and apartment. Then we'll subpoena your neighbors and co-workers. We won't stop until we find the truth."

"I've told you the truth."

Noah dragged out a chair and sat. "Tell us what you keep in

your trunk."

Jake's brows knit together. "You'll find the usual tire and jack. I rarely use either."

"Then explain why we found these articles of clothing in the boot of your vehicle." Noah swiped the pictures on his phone and showed one after the other to him.

Jake shook his head. "I don't wear or carry bras or panties in my trunk." He snapped his head upward and stared into Noah's face. "What's this about? What are you accusing me of doing?"

"The clothing belongs to Lisa Grant. Where is she?"

Under the table, Jake's leg shook. "Whoever stole my car is framing me. I don't have anything of Lisa Grant's, and I have no idea where she is." His body sagged in the chair. "Have you run out of people to accuse?"

"Evidence points to you. We've found no proof your car was stolen."

"Okay, I feel stupid but I kept a copy of my keys on a ring under my hood with a magnet. I'd locked myself out of my apartment enough that I thought this was the answer. Obviously, I used them, and someone watched me, and then helped him or herself. The thief did a good job of making me look like a fool." Jake put his head in his hands.

Too easy to respond to that remark, Noah thought.

"Who can vouch for the key under your hood?" Hines asked.

Jake shrugged. "No one. I didn't advertise the fact."

Seconds ticked by in silence.

"Mr. Clark," Hines prodded.

Jake's shoulders straightened, and he sat upright in his seat. "Offi—" He raised his palm before Hines could correct him. "Detectives, let's cut to the finale. I'll take a lie detector test to prove my innocence. My lawyer will work out the details with you."

Noah exchanged a glance with Hines.

"Okay, call your attorney to come down to the station." Hines nodded toward the door. "We'll wait outside the room while you speak to your attorney."

"I prefer to speak in the privacy of my home, where I'm free to discuss the injustices of the cases you're trying to build against me. I assume I'm not under arrest since you haven't read me my rights?"

"You're not," Hines said.

Noah felt the meeting coming to a fast ending.

"Gentlemen." Jake rose and shoved in his chair. "We're done until future notice from my legal representative."

"One more thing." Noah reached into his file and handed papers to Jake. "In case you haven't guessed we've search warrants for your car, home and electronics. Happy reading."

After Jake stalked from the station, Noah and Hines joined the chief in his office. He agreed chances were slim Jake Clark and his lawyer would show up. "Waking the judge to get the papers issued did not put me on his friends list. Let's hope we find something. I've sent the detectives working on Kara Linn's case over to Jake's place. I'll join them when we finish. I want a solid case. We'll proceed with today's plan and find Travis Bodell for questioning."

The chief held up search warrants from the top of his desk. "Don't worry. I've a big job for you both. Paul hit pay dirt. The second student, who witnessed the altercation between Lisa and Travis, provided us with the threat we needed. Seems this student ran into Lisa's boyfriend outside the mall, where Travis ranted to him and threatened to use a knife on the Grant girl. We've a signed statement. Take your team to Seth Bodell's property. Look for anything that can be used as a weapon. If the kid ran off with Lisa Grant, he probably took some clothes or belongings with him. If he abducted her, then we're looking for Lisa or her remains."

Slash. Slash. The words echoed in Noah's mind.

"We'll also sweep the beach on the west side of the lake," the chief said. "We've a tip the Meter Feeders are meeting there around eleven. Since it's a recreational area, we'll pick them up for violating curfew. I'm tired of kids using our city facilities like their own personal playground. Let's see how merry the band is once we lock them in holding. Now get on to Bodell's. The warrants are for the house, grounds, and electronics. Find Lisa Grant or bring in Travis or both."

"Yes, sir," they chorused.

"Christmas in July," Noah said, once they left the chief's office. "After we brief the men, Hines, you ride shotgun."

Forty minutes later, Noah, Hines, and two cruisers pulled up to the Bodell's residence. A shirtless Seth was in his yard cutting wood. Music from an old boom box blared across the grounds.

Noah climbed out of his car and took in the front of the barn that sat twenty feet from the small house. A collection of deer antlers decorated the building, reminders of Travis and Seth's hunting abilities.

Hines perched his sunglasses on his nose. "From his stacks of cordwood he must expect a bad winter with plenty of customers."

"Can't wait to make his day better." Noah sauntered toward the man.

The team hung near their cruisers ready to go.

Seth shut off the chainsaw and music. He met their approach with a glare and hands fisted by his waist. "What are you doin' in my yard?" He wiped the sweat from his brow and sneered at the uniformed men. "This looks like you're arrestin' me," he growled at the detectives. "I've got work to do. I can't go with you."

Hines handed over the legal documents and informed him of the searches.

"The girl and Travis aren't here." Seth ripped the paper from Hines' hand and kicked a rock near his foot. "This is BS. I'm goin' to get my lawyer. Don't touch my stuff or I'll sue you." He stamped to his truck and hopped inside. A cloud of dust filled the air as he bolted.

"I think he should work on his customer service skills." Noah turned and gave the signal to disperse. The officers jumped into action, putting on their gloves and shoe coverings. He directed the teams to note recently dug earth, fire pits, and out buildings on the land.

Noah and Hines marched to the house with a couple of techies. Noah prayed they'd get a break today. Tick tock, said the clock in his head, reminding him days were passing for Lisa Grant. Travis had to be the link to finding her. How far could the kid have gone?

In the living room, mismatched furniture and a large mounted screen told them the home hadn't been updated in decades, except for the addition of the television. Empty takeout boxes littered the kitchen counter. The computer sat on the table. The techies set to work there. Two small bedrooms contained space for a cot and a dresser. One bathroom with towels thrown over the shower curtain rod completed the decor.

Noah and Hines began in what appeared to be Travis' bedroom based on an English textbook on the bureau. A crumpled sheet revealed someone had slept in the bed. Hines went through the drawers while Noah started with the closet.

Piles of jeans, school pants, and shirts were heaped on the floor. Noah pawed through them. "The kid didn't believe in wasting energy hanging up his clothes."

Hines nodded and went back to his search for a few seconds before stating, "Interesting." He held out a packet of condoms.

"I'm glad Travis wasn't planning on having a mini him."

Hines returned to sorting through T-shirts until he pulled out a plastic baggy stuffed between the shirts. "I hit the jackpot again. He has enough for a few joints."

"Wonder if he's coming back for it." Noah sorted through jean pockets while Hines bagged and labeled his discoveries.

At the bottom of the first mound, Noah dug out a white box. He blew out a whistle when he opened it to find a set of carving knives.

"Travis had a little fetish?" Hines asked.

"I doubt he was using these to carve a family dinner. Doesn't prove he killed anyone though. One blade is missing. Travis could be armed."

"I found something else." Hines held out a silver bowl with the initial R etched into the side. "Family heirloom?"

"R for Raynes?" Noah asked. "I don't think Sophia or Teagan would gift Travis with dinnerware."

"He must have gifted himself. Another business for the Bodell men? We'll check this one out for sure." Noah took a picture of the dish.

After an hour of hunting through the house, barn, and woodpile, Hines and Noah joined their men in searching the fields.

After twenty minutes, Noah finished walking around a copse of trees and hiked into a field. Bodell's property ended in ten feet. At stone wall marked the boundary. Beyond the wall, the ground had been plowed for a garden, but it was now overgrown. No signs of the rhubarb or strawberry plants that refused to die once planted. Strange place to grow your veggies. No road led to it and the plot was a distance from a house. He scanned his map.

The land belonged to an eighty-three-year-old woman who was currently in a nursing home. He bet something illegal had been grown here and his second hunch was that Seth had taken advantage of his neighbor's absence to farm the banned crops. He'd probably moved his plantings to another spot to avoid detection. Since Noah's warrant didn't include this parcel, he'd let the narcs know and leave the problem to them.

Noah's phone buzzed. He pulled up a text from Teagan.

I'm okay. Sitting with Lucy at the hospital. No change in condition. Found Lisa's bracelet in flowers in the room.

Why did a woman in a coma have the teenager's jewelry? Was it another kind of threat?

He called Paul. The officer confirmed he was outside Miss Watson's door and just spoken to Miss Raynes, who was safe and still visiting her friend.

Noah hung up and texted Teagan. On my way.

CHAPTER 26

Noah raced for the hospital and Teagan. She said she was fine, but until he saw for himself, he wouldn't trust the message. He didn't stop for the elevator, but took the stairs two at a time. On Lucy's floor, he found Paul leaning against the desk of the nurse's station, oogling a young RN.

The officer's smile vanished, and he snapped upright when he spotted Noah's stern expression. "Detective Cassidy. You're here? Any news?"

"Why did you leave your post?" Without waiting for an answer, Noah turned to the nurse. "What's the number for Lucy Watson?"

"She's in—"

"301," Paul finished. "I can see her door from here." His voice rang with confidence, but his eyes flickered with concern.

"Go to your position, Officer."

"Yes, sir. I was picking up the paper and going right back." Paul gripped the newspaper in his hand and returned to sit.

Noah crossed the floor and entered the room. Stacey Smith hovered over Lucy. He wheeled to a stop. Why was she here?

She broke into a smile of recognition. "Detective, hello."

Movement on the other side of the bed snagged his attention. Sitting in the corner was Teagan. Next to her, stood the night table with the vase of yellow flowers.

"Detective Cassidy came to visit." Stacey patted the pasty hand of the comatose dark-haired Lucy Watson. She reminded Noah of

Snow White.

"Maybe he has good news about arresting the driver who hit you." Stacey looked up at him. "Do you, detective?"

"I'm afraid not." He walked around the bed to join Teagan and faced Stacey. "Did you bring the flowers upstairs?"

"Me?" She raised one shoulder in a half shrug. "I left them at the desk downstairs, remember? I don't know who brought them up, but Lucy enjoys them, don't you?"

"Lucy's nurse thinks a volunteer carried them upstairs." Teagan was clasping her hands tightly together on top of her purse as she spoke to him. "Thanks for coming, Noah."

"Are you okay?"

"I always am. I've been waiting to hear Lucy's prognosis from her doctor. The nurse informed me he'd be available soon. That was over an hour ago."

"I told Teagan that Lucy can understand every word we say. Can't you?" Stacey smiled into the immobile woman's face.

"Let's speak in the hallway so we don't disturb Lucy with our talking." Noah waited for Teagan to rise. He wished they were far away from Stacey, who was protesting their conversation wouldn't bother the motionless patient.

When Noah ignored her, Stacey bent to Lucy's ear. "They don't want us to hear them. I still hope it's good news." Stacey tilted her head to the side and watched them cross the white floor. "From their faces, I'd guess the detective has bad news. I hope no one else is missing or been run over by a car."

"Miss Smith." Noah nodded at Stacey as they exited.

"Come back soon," she called to them.

Noah clenched his jaw and let the door swing shut after him. Paul glanced up at him, but Noah ignored him to guide Teagan to the end of the corridor away from the hub of the floor's activity.

They stopped in front of a window that overlooked the parking lot. She leaned against the fawn-colored wall as though she needed support. He wanted to put his arms around her but here was not the place.

"Did—" they said at the same time.

"You first." She gestured to him.

"The chief met with a judge and procured search warrants for Jake's apartment based on your ID of Lisa's clothes in his trunk.

Sorry, nothing turned up."

"I guess I should be happy."

"I've more. Hines and I searched the Bodell home and property. No evidence of Lisa 's presence, but I wondered if this bowl looks familiar." He pulled up the picture on his phone.

Teagan blinked at the image. "Where did you find my aunt's fruit dish?"

"In Travis's bureau. I looked on Craigslist before I came and found it for sale. I'd say Travis was making money selling at least one of your possessions, maybe more. The night you saw him, he might have been planning to rob you. Maybe he saw you upstairs and changed his mind."

She blew out a breath. "I bet the bowl was tucked in one of the barrels or trunks in the cellar. What else can happen today?"

"You found Lisa's bracelet in Lucy's room?"

"The bracelet was hidden in the pot of lilies on her bed stand. It's the same bouquet Stacey brought to the hospital for her."

"And Stacey happens to visit Lucy."

"Stacey denied putting a card, gift, or message with the flowers." Teagan's face paled. "I think the heart has blood spatter on it.

"What?"

"I slipped the jewelry in my purse when Stacey got water for the bouquet." Teagan pulled out the tissue-wrapped chain and pendant. "I did my best to protect it, but why put the bracelet in the flowers?"

"Might have been to get rid of it and to try and freak someone out." He held the pendent in his palm and unfolded the covering.

Teagan shuddered. "Tell me I'm overreacting and the brownish-red stain is paint on the silver heart."

"I'll assign a man to watch the security video and note who handled the flower pot. The lab will confirm the rest for us."

"Confirm if the stain belongs to," she gulped, "Lisa."

He sensed her stress level rising. "Let's go outside for a walk."

She pushed away from the wall. Now that he'd seen her, relief was pouring through him, along with the urge to comfort and reassure her. The nurses and Paul tossed glances at them as they passed.

When they reached the safe distance of the elevators, Noah

debated telling Teagan that if Seth kidnapped Lisa, he might use her to settle a criminal debt. Teagan might be right. Lisa was alive, but in another life, the girl would never survive long. He couldn't float the idea unless he had proof. "I wish I had a better report."

"I hope Travis and Lisa haven't gotten into something they can't handle."

"There's a good chance Travis is armed with a knife. So if you run into him, keep on running and call 9-1-1."

"I wish this would end." She rubbed her forehead.

"You should go home. I'll take you." At least they'd get a little time together if he drove her.

She shook her head. "I have my car. Besides, today we got a lead. The person who put the bracelet in the flowers must have seen Lisa. She always wore it."

"We'll find out," he said as they waited before the elevator. "I'll get the hospital's security videos."

At the ding, the doors slid open and they stepped inside for the ride to the lobby. Teagan glanced at the numbers changing on the panel as they glided downward. "Talking to Stacey and worrying about Lucy have sapped my energy."

They headed to the walkway in front of the hospital, and Teagan picked up the conversation. "I'm surprised Stacey hasn't gone back to work; though, she hoped to get an update from Lucy's doctor to bring to Matt."

As they strolled along the sidewalk, the heat and humidity enveloped them. He guided her to the shade on the side of the building where they were alone. The fragrance of the cut lawn permeated the air. Lines tugged at her mouth as he put his arms around her.

He skimmed his palm over her blouse and curled his fingers over her hip, enjoying her curves and her firm breasts. She wrapped her arms around him and rested her chin against his chest. The urge to be with her, enjoy more of her, consumed him. He wanted to take her somewhere, to escape from their problems and be together. Seize the moment, he told himself and focused on the expression of longing in her brown eyes to block out the sound of the traffic floating across the air toward them.

She raised her face to him. Her lips parted, inviting him to taste them.

The whisper of shoes against the blades of grass warned him. He swung around to the fist coming at him and ducked to the side, taking Teagan with him. The crunch of bones hitting against the brick wall was followed by a howl.

Noah released Teagan, drew his gun and leveled it on Vic Taylor. "Don't move."

Vic stood shaking his hand with reddening knuckles that had come into contact with the solid building instead of Noah's chin. Vic's lower lip jutted out with distaste, and his face reddened with rage. "Is this how you search for my niece, Cassidy? Miss Raynes, is this how you show concern for Lisa?"

"I've had enough of you." Noah took a menacing step toward Taylor

"Don't. Please." Teagan gripped his arm and tugged at him to stop.

"Afraid, Cassidy?" Vic taunted.

Teagan pushed forward. "Of course he's not. What's wrong with you?" She demanded.

Vic inched a safe distance from them while he eyed the gun still in Noah's hands.

"Why did you try to hit Detective Cassidy?" Teagan shook her finger at him. "He wasn't doing anything to you."

"Nothing is what he's doing to find Kara. How can you forget Lisa?" The man spit out the accusation.

"I never forget her. Ever."

Noah's anger ebbed at the sight of Teagan, the tiger. Then it was time to take charge. "I'll handle him now."

Their gazes connected and he saw her silently pleading to let Taylor go, not cause a scene. He hesitated and then stepped back. "Taylor, you owe Miss Raynes and me an apology." Noah kept his weapon trained on Taylor to make it easier for him to pay attention. "I always work a case by the book. I suggest you leave before I change my mind and arrest you for attempted assault. You can thank Teagan for my decision to let you go."

"Miss Raynes, be careful." The man shifted his gaze over the grounds as though afraid or hoping someone was watching. "Detective Cassidy, You haven't fooled me. You're no more searching for my niece than the groundhog looks for his shadow. Lies. Miss Raynes, the man is using you. Think about it. Would he be interested in you if you weren't always around while he looked for your foster teen? You're a convenient distraction." He spun around on his heel and fled.

Noah holstered his gun. "The man's certifiable."

"I guess we all act strangely under severe stress." She glanced away from him and bit her lip.

"Are you okay?"

"Yeah, I'll just go home and hope I don't run into Taylor anywhere else."

"I'll call Paul to follow you. He's on duty until six tonight. Then another officer will take over for him. Taylor won't get near you." Noah dug out his cell phone and spoke to the officer.

She clutched her keys in her fist. "If you'd arrested Vic, he'd have made himself look like the victim and crucified you in his blog."

She was telling the truth. Taylor had the attention of many in Hawick Falls with his controversial posts, and Noah didn't need the notoriety of the editor's piece pointed at him. They crossed the lot to her vehicle. Once they reached it, he checked her car for unwanted passengers. At least he was satisfied nobody was hiding inside to ambush her.

"Noah, what was Vic Taylor doing at the hospital?" she asked as he held her door.

"I could give you several theories, but I'd vote for following one or both of us."

CHAPTER 27

Teagan sat up on the sofa and rubbed her eyes. Daylight had fled long ago and the darkness had taken over the house, except for the outside light filtering in through the living room window.

She'd fallen asleep. Fragments of dreams spun in her head and ended with Vic Taylor's snarling face. All afternoon she'd been unable to shake the feeling of someone watching her. Was it Taylor? Had he followed her to the hospital, home, everywhere?

She turned on the lamp and shut the book she'd tried to read. A fragment of her last dream burst into her mind. A blood-spotted heart dangled around the neck of a burned corpse.

"No!" Jumping up, she paced the floor until the image faded.

She glanced at the clock. It was almost eleven. Jogger meowed from the threshold between the living room and the kitchen. The cat was overdue for her supper. "Tuna delight dinner, coming up."

She crossed to her pet who ran for the refrigerator in the dark room. The motion detector light flashed on in the backyard and spilled through the window above the sink.

Teagan froze. What was that? Her thoughts leaped, searching for a reason for the light. Had Travis returned? What about the creep who left the burned body at her table. No, it was probably a neighbor's dog who'd escaped outside.

She angled to the side of the window but only caught the edge of a blur of black. Could it be Travis? Just to be sure, she whirled around, scrambled to the coffee table, and grabbed her gun.

Perspiration dripped from her chin as she crept across the floor and cracked the kitchen door enough to slip into the mud room. In a few more steps, she'd be able to peek out the screen door. She'd prove to herself she was overreacting, or catch whoever treated her home like a graveyard.

The last thought filled her with anger. Stuffing her hand in her pocket, she hit the number for the duty officer sitting in front of her house. His phone rang.

Who the heck was in her yard? Why didn't the officer answer? Turning the knob, she pushed the door open a slit for a better view, and peeked out across the grass.

CHAPTER 28

Five feet from her, a person was bent over the bulkhead. He was twisting something in the keyhole. He was trying to break inside, and he could be in her house in a few seconds. She'd had enough. Anger poured through her, boiling her blood, and clouding her brain. She shoved her cell in her pocket. Leveling the barrel of her weapon on the target, she blinked at the sweat dripping into her eyes and shouted, "Stop or I'll shoot."

The man straightened and his eyes widened as he turned to her. He was about five-seven, wore a torn T-shirt, work gloves, and sweatpants. The overhead lamp illuminated his white hair. He shot a glance toward the woods before his gaze returned to land on Teagan's gun.

She held the weapon steady with her clammy hands. At least he was afraid of her. He looked about forty; although, the few teeth he showed when he licked his lips gave him the appearance of someone older. His dirt-stained sweatpants and top hung from his thin form.

Tightening her two-handed grip, she demanded, "What are you doing in my backyard?"

He retreated a step.

"Do you know Lisa?"

He remained mute.

Maybe if he was hungry and she fed him, he'd talk to her. "Do you want to eat? You can have milk or juice. Would you like that?"

A strange glow gleamed in his eyes. He wasn't quite right, Teagan realized. A shiver of fear passed over her. "If you wait a minute, I'll bring you a snack."

The white-haired man whirled around and sprinted to the trees.

"Stop! Do you know Lisa? Did she send you for something?"

The sound of his feet crashing through the bushes faded and disappeared.

"Miss Raynes? Miss Raynes?" the officer's voice spoke from her cell in her pocket.

****

Noah had joined his team for the raid on the beach, but Teagan's call changed his plans. He wasn't sad to miss the night's foray.

Teagan. His desire for her ate at him no matter where he was. She was always on his mind and blotting out thoughts of her had become an hourly challenge.

He cleared his departure with the chief and headed away from the water. The sting was in less than twenty minutes, but he doubted he'd make it in time to round up the soon-to-be-un-merry men. The chief, Hines, and the rest of the uniforms would handle the action.

Paul had been excited to join the group tonight and hand over his surveillance duty at Teagan's to another newbie officer. First, Noah would have a few words with this officer about his surveillance techniques. Teagan had been reluctant to discuss the man's failure to investigate when her security light had flashed on in the rear yard.

The quiet of the night and the dark homes in the village gave him a feeling of being alone in the world. On Teagan's street, her outside light blazed in the blackness. He drew up beside the cruiser and signaled the patrolman to open his window.

The guy was sweating and avoiding eye contact with him. He reported nothing unusual until Teagan knocked on his window and asked if he'd seen a white-haired man run across her yard.

"I don't have a view of the rear exit or the woods behind the building that the intruder used to enter and escape from the property," the officer said, rubbing a hand over his eyes.

The officer's guilty expression revealed the truth. Noah would bet the man fell asleep. "A good cop stakes out all entrances and stays on top of the situation no matter how mind-numbing. Remember this in the future. Your career depends on your wakefulness."

"Yes, sir, I secured the point of entry used by the suspect and inspected and found no signs of tampering with the homeowner's locks."

Noah nodded and hit the gas. He turned into Teagan's driveway. More reprimands could wait.

She opened up before he pressed the bell. He didn't say a word, simply pulled her inside, took her in his arms, and kicked the door shut. He'd wanted to do this since she called him.

"Are you hurt?" he asked, conscious of the tightness in her body.

"A little scared," she muttered against his chest.

"I'm glad you're okay." He released her and stepped away. "What happened? Tell me."

"I fell asleep on the couch." She gestured to the other room. "I woke up and found a man about forty with long white-hair trying to break into the cellar."

"How was he dressed?"

He wore a baggy T-shirt, sweatpants, and gloves to break into my house."

"Doesn't sound like we'll find prints."

"I guess the new lock held. I hope he doesn't come back." She ran her hands through her hair.

"I thought he might have seen Lisa and know where she is." Her eyes widened with hope. "It's a wild idea. I imagined she sent him here for food."

"He came for something." She was reaching for proof that Lisa was alive.

"I'll look around outside first." Noah put on the latex gloves for his search. He crossed to the bulkhead and shone his penlight on the lock. No signs of tampering. The guy was either a professional or had no idea how to break the lock. He scanned the grounds and returned inside to check the cellar.

The wooden stairs creaked as he made his way into the

basement. Noah walked back to the center of the cellar. The furniture and trunks seemed untouched. The last barrel lay on its side with clothes and plates scattered on the cement floor. He counted the boxes by the settee. Hadn't the pile been higher?

The sound of light footsteps on the stairs broke his attention.

Teagan approached and stopped a few feet from him. "See anything important?"

"No, but tomorrow after my men will investigate."

"I never spent much time down here." She moved around, scanned the concrete floor, and finally shook her head. "I'm glad I changed my locks."

"It's time to go high tech, Teagan." How professional was this white-haired man? Noah slid his arm over her shoulders, and they walked together to the stairs where he stepped aside for her to go first.

She sank onto the chair at the table, and he sat in the chair beside her. "Now that he's gone, I'll admit he looked frightened, hungry, and dirty. He had the odor of the homeless. Even from the rear steps I caught a whiff of a body denied soap, water, or deodorants for too long." She wrinkled her nose. "I remember it well.",

"Any possibility, he was a friend of Travis Bodell?"

"I never saw them together. Why?"

"They both were wandering in your backyard." Noah's phone buzzed. A text from Hines popped up on his cell's screen.

In position.

Noah texted back. Good mojo.

"My team will be out in the morning. You know the drill. I'll take you to a hotel for the night, and don't argue about leaving. You can come back when it's safe. I'll let the patrolman know he's off duty. Do you need to pack a bag?"

"I'll call Matt. He offered—"

"No."

She startled and he realized how loudly he'd spoken.

"Don't bother the priest. I have a better idea." Forty-five minutes later, Noah walked into the station and into the chief's office where Hines was already seated.

"Nice of you to join us, detective. What happened with the break-in at Teagan Raynes' house?"

"A homeless man was attempting to break into Miss Raynes' home. He escaped. I secured the home and found no evidence of tampering with the lock. Miss Raynes is at a friend's place for now. I'm interested in the fact that Travis Bodell took one of Miss Raynes' silver bowls to sell from the basement, and maybe this guy was interested, too. He chose the cellar for entrance. Travis was fencing his on the web."

"We'll look for a connection at the pawn shops and online." The chief tapped his fingertips on his desk. "We brought in six teenagers tonight, four males and two females, from the sweep. We're in the process of separating them for questioning. Remember, if they ask for a parent to be present during the interview, we oblige. Otherwise," he closed his hand into a fist, "apply pressure."

"Sir, what happened with the search at the Clark residence?" Noah asked.

"We found nothing to connect Grant and Clark. The men took some fibers and combs, but we're shooting in the dark there. Go interview the kids."

Noah and Hines rose when someone knocked on the door. The chief signaled for them to sit before he barked, "Come in."

Paul entered, swallowed, and glanced around. "Sir, I have good news."

"Spit it out."

"The blond boy we're holding knows something about Lisa Grant."

The chief scowled. "Did he tell you?"

"No." Paul gulped. "He wants the charges against him dropped in exchange for his information."

The three men swapped raised brows of surprise.

"Is his father a lawyer?" Hines asked.

"Maybe his old man gets arrested a lot and taught his son the ropes," Noah added.

"I d-don't know," Paul stuttered.

"Ignore them," the chief ordered. "Hines and Cassidy suffer from a case of weak humor. Put the boy in the room across from my office."

"Yes, sir." Paul turned and left.

"I'd let the Meter Feeder kid stew awhile, but since we'd like a couple of hours sleep, find out now if he's telling the truth." The chief gestured for them both to leave.

Outside the boss' door, Hines turned to Noah. "I'd hoped to go home to Chelsea tonight. It's not looking good."

"Don't worry. She won't be lonely."

CHAPTER 29

Teagan sipped her tea while Chelsea Hines placed warmed muffins on a plate and slid into the chair across the table.

The last thing Teagan wanted was food. The strange gleam in the white-haired man's eyes kept flashing in her mind. Her home was no longer a safe haven.

Chelsea picked off a piece of the baked goods and dropped it on her plate. "If you change your mind and feel hungry, grab a bite. You know who's likes to cook? Noah. He used to work at a grill when he attended Granite Edge College. He's invited us to dinner a few times. Lasagna is his specialty."

"I'm not much of a cook. The microwave is my best friend."

Chelsea put her muffin on the saucer in front of her. "Denny should be home soon. A lot has been going on with his case, but he doesn't talk about it. Sometimes I worry we'll run out of things to say to each other because his life is his work."

"Must be nerve-racking never knowing what's happening with him."

"He can tell me a little." Chelsea fell silent, and then bit her lip. "I'm sorry. You're under much more stress than I am."

"It's been tough, but I work on keeping the faith that Lisa will come home soon." She rarely added the word soon, but tonight it sounded right. "I appreciate you letting me stay at your place this late at night. You're not a social worker, are you?"

"Me? No. I manage a dental office, boring stuff. And Noah's

never brought anyone here."

"I guess most people have family nearby that they crash with."

"Consider me your adopted cousin." Chelsea gave Teagan a wide smile. "Wait." She left the room and returned in a few minutes. "Here's my card. I had them made up as a joke since Denny had some, but turns out I use them. Call my cell whenever you like, and you have the best detectives looking for Lisa. I'm biased, but it's true. If anyone can find her, they will." Chelsea's card could be useful and why reject an offer of friendship? "I'll put your number in my phone now."

Her hostess beamed while Teagan plugged in the digits before pocketing her cell. She was a pretty woman when she smiled.

Chelsea ran a finger over the rim of her mug. "I'm sorry, but I'm a nosey person. You might as well know. Can I be blunt?"

"Do you mean about Lisa's disappearance?"

"Ah, no, I was wondering if you've known Noah for long."

Teagan shrugged. Guess it was normal for Chelsea to speculate since Noah dropped Teagan, a complete stranger, off when everyone was asleep. "We went to camp together when we were kids, but we didn't hang out. He was a counselor, and I was a lowly camper."

Chelsea folded her arms on the table and leaned forward on them. "Teagan, I was watching out the window. I saw you and Noah kiss before you came inside."

"Oh." Teagan felt her cheeks warm. They'd kissed several times, reluctant to part. What should she say? How good a friend was this woman to Noah? She'd gotten out of bed and opened her home because Noah called and told her Teagan needed a place.

Chelsea reached across the tabletop and patted her hand. "I apologize if I embarrassed you. I was just surprised and glad. Noah deserves to be happy. I've been trying to match him up with friends, but he's a challenge. His family's deaths were traumatic. He seems hard, but he's not. I remember him as gentle with his wife and child, and he loves Denny, though he'd rather be shot than admit it."

She knew Noah's family.

A cell phone rang. "Denny." Chelsea jumped up from her seat. "Excuse me."

Teagan glanced at the kitchen. The compact room contained a

table and chairs for four. Did Noah sit in one of these seats when he visited? Once the case ended, they'd have no reason to see each other. He would go the way of other men in her life, and Chelsea would invite more friends to dine with them and Noah.

The idea sent a wave of disappointment through her, but she'd adjust. She always did. People came and went. She was beginning to fear Matt was right about waiting until the investigation wrapped to examine her feelings for Noah, if he was still around.

Her thirst vanished. She picked up her cup and poured the tea down the sink's drain.

Chelsea could fill her in on Noah's wife and child. *No, don't open the door.* She didn't need to hear how much he loved his dead wife.

Her hostess' slippers shuffled against the tiled floor. "Denny is hung up for another hour at the station. I didn't get a chance to mention you're here. I hope he doesn't wake you when he comes home. He usually doesn't work this late."

"Don't worry about it. In fact, if you don't mind, I'm going to bed now."

Chelsea tilted her head and scrutinized her. "I bet you're tired. Let me show you where we keep the towels." She led the way to the linen closet by the bathroom.

Teagan followed her. "Have you and Denny been together long?"

"We met through a friend when Denny first joined the force. He proposed three months later and told me he'd been waiting. He was afraid I'd think it was too soon, but I knew right away he was the one. We said our vows at Christmas. Law Enforcement has a high divorce rate, but we'll prove them wrong. We've been married ten years already."

"I'm sure you will." A decade seemed forever to Teagan.

Chelsea pulled out a towel and washcloth and gave her a tour of the two-bedroom condo. "You won't get lost." She flashed a warm smile when they'd finished. The woman was easy to be around.

Teagan's guard slipped. She should ask how long Noah had been married. Right? It would fit into the conversation. She glanced at the leather furniture in the living room, pretending to be interested in it while she debated how desperate she'd look to ask questions about him.

"I leave for work at eight. Do you need a ride?"

Teagan refocused her thoughts. "Noah will pick me up tomorrow."

"Of course, he will. The thermostat for the AC is near the bed. You can control the temperature for your room."

"Chelsea." Teagan waited until her hostess turned to her, and then hugged her. "Thank you for your kindness. I appreciate it."

"You're welcome. You must visit again and bring Noah." She winked and Teagan felt an instant bond with her.

A few minutes later, Teagan slipped into the twin bed. She lay listening to the drone of the air conditioner. Sleep, she wished she'd experience it. Lying in the strange place reminded her of her first months at Aunt Sophia's. Whenever her mother had visited, Teagan would ask to leave with her.

"Soon," her mom always answered. "I've got to find someone to hire me. Then I'll rent us a big house, and you'll have one of those beds with lace over the top."

Teagan tossed on her side. No use torturing herself. Even when she was little, she doubted her mother would follow through with her word. She'd broken too many promises, but Teagan never expected her to disappear.

Aunt Sophia held a memorial after two years of searching because a counselor recommended the ceremony to bring closure. At least it gave Teagan a response when anyone asked where her mother lived.

Forget her. Tomorrow, Teagan was going home where she belonged, and she wasn't running away again. She was done sleeping in unfamiliar places like a homeless child. Pulling the sheet to her chin, she pictured the gleam in Noah's eyes when he bent to kiss her. She'd hold onto the memory to get through another night.

CHAPTER 30

The kid swept his blond hair out of his acne-marked forehead and smirked across the interview table at Noah and Hines.

Hines glanced up from the notes on his tablet. "Hugh Smith. Nice name. You have information about Lisa Grant?"

Hugh slouched in his chair. "I might if you're not pressing charges against me."

Noah moved from the wall, where he'd paused to observe. The punk wanted to play cop and lawyer games? Let's play. "Spit out where Lisa is, or you'll be accessory to kidnapping."

"What?" The kid's eyes popped wide. "I saw her at the park." He swallowed and sat upright. "I'm not saying any more until you agree to let me go."

"Listen, kid." Noah smacked his palms down on the tabletop and leaned into his face. "A girl could die while you pretend to be a big shot. Tell us what you know."

Hugh's lip quivered. Hines cleared his throat, a signal for Noah to back off. He straightened and waited for his partner to speak.

"Hugh, we appreciate your offer of help. Truth is, trading for a person's life is a little unequal in your case and unethical."

"I was afraid you'd think I had something to do with her disappearance. My parents will kill me if they find out I'm a member of the Robin Hood Men. My father's a bully. I'll be grounded for life." The kid's defensive tone suggested he'd already recovered from Noah's harsh words. "Besides, fair is fair. I give you what I know and you give me a pass."

"Enlighten us," Noah said, pacing while he kept his gaze on the teen. "We know you were at the park where you claimed, to what, run into Lisa?"

"Okay, my friends and I used to meet there before the fire. That night I ran late for our meeting because..." The kid wet his lips and glanced away from them for a second. "Because I was late. I saw her when I was walking on the narrow path in the woods." He folded his arms over his chest.

Something wasn't quite right with the kid's story.

"Don't leave anything out," Hines said. "Your dad might be upset, but in the end, you'll be a hero for providing the lead to Lisa."

Hugh hunched his shoulders and remained mute.

Noah stopped in front of their reluctant witness. Dealers used one or two of the wooded paths to sell their drugs. The police would make arrests, and then in a few months, the illegal deals started again. Noah had a hunch about the kid's reluctance. "You were late that night because you were up to no good. Getting high before your get together, Hugh? Is that why you weren't on time? Maybe we need to look a little closer at you, and then talk with your father."

"I didn't do anything wrong." The kid shifted with discomfort. "Okay. I'll help you, but don't tell my parents about the park meetings."

"Who's the leader of your group? Cause if you happen to mention a few facts about the Meter Feeders—"

"We prefer Robin Hood's Men."

"Sure you do," Noah reassured. "Now if you give us the dirt on both, we'll forget your little detour at the park and the fact you withheld evidence about Lisa Grant. Otherwise, if anything happens to her, you'll be the first person we arrest."

"What? No way. He's lying. Isn't he?" The teen turned to Hines. "He can't do that. I never helped anyone hurt her."

Hines motioned his hand up and down. "All right. All right. Talk. After, we'll let you go home, and your parents will be none the wiser."

Hugh sat silent for a few minutes then nodded. "Basil is the leader, not me."

"That's a surprise." Noah dragged out a chair to sit next to Hines.

"Is Basil the tall, dark-haired boy with the ponytail?" Hines asked.

"Yeah, that's him. Plugging the expired meters and our meetings were his ideas."

Noah tapped his fingers on the table. "What do you have on the missing girl?"

"I can leave as soon as I tell you?"

"You got it." Hines signaled for him to continue.

"The day after the Fourth, the Robin Hoods planned to meet in our usual spot and time at the park. We changed to the lake after the fire. That night, I ran late like I said. I cut through the woods near the hiking path. That's when I saw her."

"Who?" Hines asked.

"Lisa Grant. She was standing at the bottom of the hill not too far from the tennis court."

"How close were you?" Hines asked.

He shrugged. "Close enough. I didn't know who she was, but after the posters went up around the city, I recognized her."

Hines sat back in his seat. "Are you enrolled at All Saints?"

Hugh ran his index finger over and over a dent in the table and shook his head. "I go to public school. But it was her. I got a good look."

"Did you let anyone know you'd seen her?" Noah asked

"No. I figured you guys would find her."

The selfish kid deserved to be locked up. Noah was glad he wasn't closer to him.

"What was she doing?" Hines asked.

"She must have been waiting for someone, and then Albino Man came."

Noah exchanged a glance with Hines who shook his head.

"Who's Albino Man?" Noah asked, a bad feeling eating at his gut. "Another kid?"

Hugh blew out a breath of disbelief. "The old guy with long white hair who hangs around the park. He's about five-six, thin, and always wears the same T-shirt and sweat pants. He can't talk. Ask him anything and he just makes sounds that make no sense."

Albino Man sounded like Teagan's intruder. "Where's he

live?"

Hugh shrugged. "In the park, I guess. Once I saw him near the pizza shop."

"Is he part of your group?" Hines asked.

"Nah, he's about sixty. I've heard a couple of different theories about him. Some people say he had a stroke. Others blame his problems on PTSD from fighting in the Mid-East or another place with lots of bullets and bombs."

"What happened to Albino Man and Lisa?" Noah pressed. "Did they talk?"

"No. She started jogging down the path toward the street, and he took off after her."

"Was he chasing her?"

"He went after her. I watched until they reached the curve. Then they were out of sight. She was ahead though. I doubt he'd catch her. He doesn't run fast. When they disappeared, I went to join the guys. I never saw her again." He glanced from Noah to Hines. "Are we done?"

"How many minutes did you watch her?" Hines asked.

"Less than five."

Had the kid made up the story to get himself released? "What's the albino's full name?"

"I don't know. We dubbed him Albino Man because of his hair. No one calls him anything else. Are we done?" Hugh put one foot out ready to leap from his chair.

"We'll need you to describe the man to the sketch artist," Noah told him.

The kid tilted his head to the ceiling and moaned. "Why did I bother to talk to you?"

"Because you're trying to avoid jail and your parents finding out what you've been doing while they looked the other way," Noah said.

Hugh straightened. "Can I go home now and speak to the artist tomorrow? My parents will be worried." He flicked a peek at his watch. "I don't usually stay out this late. Really, my dad's going to be bull."

"Maybe you should have worried about that before you joined the group." Noah followed Hines from the room while their witness sat groaning.

They entered the chief's office and reported the latest on Lisa Grant.

"Albino Man sounds like the guy who broke into Teagan's house," Noah said when they'd given their summary of the interview. "He might lead us to Lisa, if our source was truthful."

"The patrol covering Pretty Park will bring him in. It's near midnight. He might be sleeping or hiding, but we'll find him. Let's hope he didn't move out since the fire." The chief sat forward in his leather chair. "Let Hugh call his parents, and release him when they come in. While he's waiting, he can scroll through our mug shots and talk to the sketch artist tomorrow. I'm sure his dad and mom will have plenty to say to me about their precious son ending up at the station. Cassidy and Hines, go home. I need you fresh in the morning."

"Hugh might not be reliable," Noah said, "and this Albino Man might have nothing to do with Lisa Grant."

"That's why we work with evidence, Cassidy. If the patrol can't locate him at the park, we'll search the usual places the homeless hang out."

"Hope he's a late riser. What time is our meeting?" Noah asked before his boss scowled over his sarcasm.

"I've an early briefing with the mayor. We'll meet at nine thirty sharp when I'm done with my meeting at the mayor's office. Leave before I change my mind and have you explain the facts to Hugh's parents."

The men exited. "I'll meet you for breakfast," Noah told Hines as they reached their cars.

"You're buying?"

"Nope. I'm stopping by for your guest, Teagan Raynes. Chelsea agreed to take her in for the night."

"You brought Teagan to our apartment? I'm not sure that was a good idea, Noah, on lots of levels." Hines shook his head and frowned. "Forget breakfast. I want to eat with my wife."

His reaction was the opposite of what Noah would have predicted. "I can get Teagan right now. Why wait?"

"Forget it. Chelsea would throw me out." He jumped into his car and slammed the door.

He was mad. His partner was never angry. "Hines! Hines!"

"Tomorrow," he shouted through his window and drove off.

What was going on with him?

****

Teagan called Matt before dawn and gave him the Hines's address. Matt always rose before the sun. So there was no need to worry about waking him. She left a note for Chelsea on her table. Next, she texted Noah that she had a ride and breathed a sigh of relief when she fastened her seatbelt in the old Rambler.

"Thanks for coming, Matt."

"Are you going to explain why you spent the night away from your house?" he asked as they merged into the street.

"A homeless man tried to break in to my place last night. He couldn't get inside because I'd changed the locks. I frightened him, and he ran away."

"When did this happen?"

As usual Matt spoke in his even tone, but his pinched mouth clued Teagan in on his disapproval.

"He showed up close to ten or eleven. Luckily, he ran off and Detective Cassidy showed up to investigate."

"Detective Cassidy bought you here?"

"Yes. His partner's wife let me crash, which was kind of her since it was late."

"What about the officer at your house?"

"He showed up after the man ran."

Teagan, you can't go home." He pulled to side, stamped on the brake, and shifted into park.

Now she had to diffuse this situation. "I'll be fine. I'll call the locksmith as soon as he opens. Before he dropped me off, Detective Cassidy told me the DNA test results come in today on the remains found in my kitchen. The lab pushed the tests up. I'm nervous about those and want to be home when they arrive. Please, don't add to my stress."

"I can find you another place to stay with privacy. Lots of people would like to help."

"I'm not letting anyone drive me from my house." She clenched her jaw and forced herself to relax.

"Keep the idea in mind." He pulled out onto the road. They rode in silence a few minutes before Matt spoke again. "I'll look around before I leave."

"I appreciate your concern."

Matt frowned over the wheel. "Teagan, have you considered the changes you'll have to make when Lisa returns?"

"What do you mean?"

"The girl will need counseling and what's going on with you and the detective?"

Teagan's moment of peace deflated a notch. "I'm aware of a couple of therapists Lisa might agree to see. Getting her to open up about whatever has happened will be tough."

"And the detective?" he persisted.

She shifted with discomfort. She'd rather skip this part of the conversation than talk about her dating life with him. "I'm sure you're aware, Matt, that long-term relationships are not my specialty."

"That's the reason I'm worried. Please, take your time to think about the possibilities and consequences. Your aunt was proud of you, Teagan, and your accomplishments. She'd want a man that matched your character and morals."

"Detective Cassidy doesn't lack either one."

"Don't mistake his temper for spirit. He could be dangerous under extreme pressure. You know I don't like to listen to gossip, but since your well-being is at stake, I tend to pay more attention."

"What did you hear, Matt?" Was it the same story Stacey told her?

He shook his head. "Not much, but consider Detective Cassidy entered a profession where he deals with violence. Many people choose a path because it's the type of life that is familiar."

"Not everyone."

"I understand, but promise me you'll go slow and learn more about him." He stared straight ahead at the empty road.

She didn't have a clue where she stood with Noah on a personal level, never mind getting more involved. Her feelings had progressed from teenage crush into something else. She was still sorting out where her emotions were headed, and Matt's questions were making her uneasy.

When she didn't respond, he added, "Your aunt wouldn't want you living in a home where people sneak inside in the middle of the night. This is the second break-in."

"Attempted break-in," she interjected.

"The correction doesn't give me comfort. Your latest intruder might also be responsible for abducting Lisa from her bed. It's happened to other girls. Be safe and move out."

"I'm adding a better grade of security to the house. Cross me off your list of parishioners needing your help. Matt, Aunt Sophia wouldn't run away, and I won't either."

"It's being smart, and don't put your aunt on a pedestal. No one can live up to an idolized version. Sophia was not perfect. We all have facades to our personality. You're remembering her good side."

His voice sounded flat as he drove from the intersection. He probably gave the pedestal speech to others.

"It's hard to measure up to her."

He turned into her drive and threw the car into park. "I'm ready to go in."

They climbed out as Noah's car swerved into her driveway. He was out of his vehicle with a slam. Disapproval radiated from his stern expression. His hands were jammed into his pockets, and tension seemed to roll off his rigid shoulders as he walked to her. "Teagan, you were supposed to wait for me this morning."

"I didn't want you to waste time driving me around when you're busy solving Lisa's case."

"You're a piece of the case, not a waste. Father Matt, didn't know you ran a taxi service."

"Teagan needed me, and I was about to walk her into the house. I wanted to be sure she was safe. Since you're here, I'll leave. Teagan, we'll talk later." He returned to his vehicle in silence.

As soon as Matt headed down the street, Noah faced her. "Let's sit down. I have some news."

Her hopes rose at his last words, but another part of her nose dived. She was a piece of the case. At least she now understood where she stood with Noah Cassidy.

CHAPTER 31

Noah filled Teagan in on her homeless man and announced he had arranged for Bennie from Village Hardware to arrive at her house before he opened his store.

No sooner had Noah told her about Bennie than her arrived. As usual, he was a wealth of knowledge about the local buzz in Hawick Falls and demonstrated a strong skill in his ability to talk while he worked on installing new technology. He finished the job and set off to work in world record time.

Teagan shut the door and returned to Noah in the living room. Her conversation with Matt had stirred up questions she'd kept in the back of her mind that now refused to be quiet. But she couldn't ask Noah where they stood in their relationship when he was in the middle of an investigation, could she? Of course not, she reassured herself and eased down on the sofa beside him.

He set the mug on the coffee table and stretched his legs in front of him. "I should head to the station soon."

"Thanks for staying and the update on the case. I'm disappointed and relieved that nothing turned up at Jake's home."

"He's still a person of interest. Watch yourself around him."

"I will." She held up her aunt's cell. "I can't believe the technology. Imagine. I can see the person on my step by looking at my phone's screen. And speaking of phones, what's the status on mine?"

"It'll take another day or two. Your calls on your cell are being forwarded to your aunt's and taped. I stayed for other reasons besides locks."

He was going to lecture her on leaving the Hines home again. She folded her hands in her lap, ready for the talk.

He tapped his fingertips on his thigh. "You seem to think he possesses special powers and depend on his opinions."

"He's a sensible person who cares about me."

"Maybe he does care, Teagan, but you're a smart woman. You don't need him to tell you what to do."

"I like to have his advice, but I make my own decisions."

"Think about it. You have to admit, the priest couldn't protect you if someone attacked you when you entered the house. What would he do, hit the intruder with holy water?" Noah stretched his arm over the back of the couch. "I like you, Teagan and worry about you."

What did he mean by like? She groped for an answer and uttered the first answer to enter her mind. "I like you, too."

Her admission came out as trite and empty. She'd tried too hard not to sound infatuated or whatever she felt. He sat staring at her. This was awkward.

"I have a bias against priests. I admit it." He expelled a breath. "A priest molested my father when he was young. His offender was never punished, but I often wondered if my old man would have been different if it hadn't happened."

She laid her hand on his arm. "Noah, you can't blame Father Matt for another's crime. You're a detective. You understand."

"Maybe it would be easier if I hadn't grown up listening to my father's ranting about how the church ruined his life. I will try, though, to be more reasonable in the future."

Noah's confession explained a lot about his attitude toward Matt. "And I'll try to depend on him less."

"Deal." He grabbed his phone from his pocket. "Last reason I'm here. I have the DNA results from the remains."

"I thought I'd have to wait until the afternoon. Where are they? How long have you had them?"

"The chief emailed them to me." He handed her his cell. "Read it."

In one second, she'd know if Lisa was dead or alive. Her hand shook as she looked down at the screen filled with sentences. The sentences went into her head, but made little sense in her keyed-up state. Halfway through the report, she started over and stopped. "Just tell me." Mentally, she braced. "I'm ready."

"The burned skeleton found in your kitchen wasn't Lisa."

Relief lifted her spirits and then she crashed. She put her hands over her face. Tears leaked out and ran through her fingers and across her cheeks.

"Teagan?"

"Don't know...why...I'm crying." Words jammed in her throat. "San—"

"The DNA confirmed Kara was the match." He hooked his arm around her shoulder and she leaned against him.

She rested her palms against his chest and felt the steady beat of his heart.

"It's okay," he whispered in a tense voice. "We'll get the person who hurt her."

"You have to find him," she muttered.

"I promise." He passed her his handkerchief.

She wiped her eyes and faced him. "Any news about the flowers and bracelet in Lucy's room?"

"We interviewed Stacey again, but she's sticking with her story about leaving the flowers on the main floor. We questioned the hospital staff. None of them saw or remember the plant, except the receptionist in the lobby and the aide who brought the flowerpot upstairs to Lucy's room after clearing it with the head nurse. None of the staff noticed anything in the pot. Video surveillance confirmed Stacey, the receptionist and aide were the only ones that handled the pot of flowers in the hospital."

"If the plant sat on the church altar," Teagan said, "anyone could have hidden the jewelry in the leaves." She wiped her eyes, but more tears poured down her face. "This is one never ending nightmare."

His breath brushed her cheek, and the warmth of his body seeped through her blouse. She sank further into the sturdiness and strength of his arms. If only she could stay this way forever.

He held her until she gained control and began to release her.

"Don't." She clutched at the sleeve of his familiar gray shirt. She wanted to hold on, just for a few more seconds, to suspend the terror in her life. The roller coaster of grief over the death of one girl and the desperate hope for another rose and fell with the swing of the pendulum. When she was with Noah, she felt brief periods of normalcy and hope.

He cupped her chin and tilted it upward until their gazes locked. A powerful slam, hot and steamy, hit her. Every nerve in her body erupted with need. "I want you to stay."

He threaded his fingers through hers, and pulled her to her feet. Her heart skipped, and then started to race. "We can say good night unless…"

His meaning obvious, she shook her head, and squeezed his hand. Her actions seemed to release his hunger. His kiss was long and deep, and his insistent tongue drove away coherent thoughts. His hand skimmed down over her hip and rested on her waistband. Then he released her and turning, he guided her into the hall. At the stairs, he waited for her to go first. Anticipation raced through her as she led him up the steps to her room.

At her bedroom, she paused and a distant voice whispered, "Mistake."

He reached past her and opened the door

Excitement purred in her blood and nerves yanked on her confidence. But this was the man who stood by her when life crashed. He wasn't a mistake.

She walked inside and paused by her bed. She'd one last chance to change her mind, or turn away. Or, she could fold her arms around him and show him how much she craved to be with him.

His mouth covered hers, and her thoughts scattered and disappeared. They eased onto the mattress, his heart thudding against hers. She kissed his forehead and his strong jaw before skimming her palms over his back to his waist. Her pulse slammed erratically as his hot kisses trailed over her chin into the hollow of her neck.

Her hands trembled as she slid them beneath his shirt and felt the heat of his skin against hers. His mouth continued to coax and caress her until she wanted to rip her clothes off.

Instead, his fingers worked down to her blouse, pants, bra and panties, undoing the fastenings and freeing her of their confines. She kicked them away, and the promise in his eyes took away her breath and urged her onward.

Her lips followed a path downward, kissing his chest as she

unfastened his shirt, his pants, and anything between them. He tossed his clothing aside, and their arms and legs tangled together as she found herself drowning in the taste and the scent of him.

From nowhere the warning whispered once more. *He could be dangerous.*

Noah whispered in her ear, "I want you, Teagan. I want y—"

His heat flowed through her and sensations swamped her, but his words of passion ended the doubts.

CHAPTER 32

Teagan's head rested against Noah's chest. His arm lay over her. He kissed her forehead. "I think I can breathe normally again."

"You have a true talent." She lay snuggled against him while her heartbeat returned to normal and sighed in contentment.

In the dimness, she became aware of how he filled her bed, and how their clothes were spread across the floor where they'd flung them. Her mind flashed to the images of Lisa's clothes in Jake's trunk.

"Ah, should I be jealous of the boy staring at me from your bulletin board?" Noah asked.

"Only if you're planning a trip back to my high school past." She propped a pillow against the headboard and leaned against it.

"You look serious," he said, skimming his glance over her.

"Sorry, my mind automatically returns to Lisa."

"What were you thinking about her?"

"Don't judge me, but sometimes, I wonder if my mother is alive and kidnapped her."

He pushed his pillow up beside hers and relaxed against it. "Why would your mother take Lisa and not contact you?"

"I imagine lots of reasons. She was mad at my aunt for keeping me and kidnapping Lisa might be her way of getting revenge. Maybe my mom's senile and thinks Lisa is me." Teagan shook her head when he raised one brow at her. "Sorry, they're silly scenarios, I know."

He cupped her chin in his hand and looked into her eyes. "Most of them sound like you wished she brought you back home."

"Wow, that's Freudian." She snuggled next to him. "I admit a shrink could have fun with my family dynamics. I don't understand many things about my mother." Okay, she sounded pathetic. "None of my ideas make sense. Worse, instead of being happy my aunt adopted me, I was always assessing my actions. I didn't want to disappoint her. I was afraid she'd send me away if I failed. I'd no idea where I'd go, but I grew up with that irrational fear."

He smoothed her hair from her face. His gentle touch sent waves of aching through her. She wasn't sure if it was for him, her missing mom or the little homeless girl she'd been.

"My mother abandoned my dad and me for life in Vermont. My fantasies were wilder than yours. I did learn she passed away."

She tilted her head up to him. "I'm sorry about the rest of your family, Noah."

He hesitated as though censoring what he'd say. "Thanks."

"Can you talk about it?"

"The facts are seared into my brain. My old man had bought a new boat and wanted to take us for a ride. As usual, I had to work. My dad wouldn't cancel because he said I should be the one to give. It was true. I never stopped working. But I was stubborn and so was he. June, my wife, tried to keep the peace by going with Kimmy."

"Your daughter."

"Yes. Also on the lake was a thirty-two-year-old who was out to impress his girlfriend and her two friends with his new cigarette boat."

"Cigarette?"

"It's a powerboat designed for racing. You can probably guess what happened. The guy couldn't handle the speed. He plowed into my dad, June, and my little girl."

Noah stopped talking and clenched his teeth. A spasm of sorrow crossed his face.

Unable to find the words to comfort him, she bent and kissed him.

He wet his lips and continued. "I took a leave, and even after three months, I had trouble coping. Hines and Chelsea were a big help. The worst part, the guy ended up with just a broken leg. His passengers were fine."

"I don't know how you stood it. My life has been a nightmare trying to hold it together while Lisa is gone. You're working and functioning every day." She pushed herself up.

"I understand." He squeezed her hand. "Therapists call doing my job progress." He grimaced. "Lots of days I wondered if I'd ever feel normal again. I'm not the forgive and forget type. I was filled with rage for everyone, especially the guy who destroyed my life. No one could talk to me and expect a civil answer. On the first anniversary of the accident, I paid the scumbag a visit. He hadn't gone to trial yet, thanks to delays by his lawyer. That evening while he was out on bail, I broke into his house and threatened to kill him."

A knot formed in her throat. She lay still, afraid the truth would be too much for her to handle. His muscles had grown taut beneath her. "But you didn't."

"Hines and the chief tracked me down. They interrupted us. Looking back, the person they saved was me."

"If someone had killed the people I love, I don't know how I'd react."

Noah shook his head. "I do. You'd yell at him and then pray for both of you."

"I didn't pray for Vic Taylor." She hadn't thought of him. "What happened after the chief and Hines saved you?"

"They read me the riot act and threatened to arrest me. My career would have ended there. The threat worked. Two months later, the guy went to jail and I went to counseling as I'd promised the chief. Word leaked out, and I had to fight to prove myself on the force. When the second anniversary of my family's death rolled around this month, the old rumor resurfaced and it seemed like people were waiting for me to suffer a breakdown. But I held it together. Maybe the therapy turned me around, or maybe it was my family. I had to straighten out for them, even if they were gone. I know it makes little sense, but I couldn't be the crazy dad and husband. I couldn't let the chief and Hines down either."

"I understand." Teagan attempted to picture Noah with a therapist, talking about his feelings.

"If you want me to go now, then I will. I should get back on the job. The bad guys don't take time off."

She rolled on her side and faced him. The question lingered in his blue eyes.

"Don't go," she said. "Stay for a bit."

He smiled and tugged her onto his chest. She laid her ear over his heart, listening to its beat in the quiet. Soon, he'd be gone to continue searching for Lisa. But for the moment, his presence kept her nightmares away, and her hope strong that they felt something real for each other.

****

The clouds had thickened when Noah approached the front door to leave. His phone buzzed. "Text message." He dug out his cell and studied his screen.

"Is it about Lisa?" she asked, unable to wait.

"I'm afraid it was." He pocketed his phone. "The stain on her necklace—"

"It was Lisa's blood?"

"Yes. Teagan, has Seth or Jake been to your home?"

She fisted her hands at her sides as a chill shivered through her. "Seth did some jobs in the house for my aunt, and Jake came over for coffee with Lucy. Why?"

"You reported the burned body was in Lisa's chair. I wondered if either man had seen her sit there."

"It's possible," she agreed.

"I have to go." He kissed her goodbye and promised to call later. The grimness in his voice warned her he expected a tough day.

She sat in the living room and replayed the last hour. Noah's confession about his anger interrupted her musings about Lisa. A chill raced up her spine. Something worse was about to happen. She felt it, but what?

Her aunt's eyes stared at her from the frame on the mantle as though accusing her of giving up.

Okay, she needed to stay positive. A spot of blood didn't mean Lisa was dead. Restless, she leaped to her feet and walked into the kitchen. The morning paper lay on the tabletop where she'd left it earlier without a glance.

A picture of Noah and herself embracing on the hospital lawn stared up at her from the front page. The intimate expression on her face as she looked up at him confirmed the hug wasn't just a quick one exchanged between friends. "Great."

Under the bolded headline '**Missing Local Girl Forgotten**' was the caption: Is Detective Noah Cassidy a little too close to Lisa Grant's guardian?

She glimpsed the byline. Vic Taylor. She blew out a breath of disgust. Scanning the article, she absorbed Taylor's criticism and sarcasm about Noah offering support to the victim's family and getting something for his troubles. Letting out a mumble about stupid editors, she flipped to page two.

A photo of a Vic holding up a limp hand was next to his continued column. She read aloud. "I haven't been able to write my blog and weekly feature due to the injury sustained after my encounter with Detective Cassidy. The detective didn't appreciate my suggestion he should be working to find our missing girls instead of offering his brand of comfort to Miss Raynes."

What?

"One handed typing has slowed my production. I recently installed software to dictate and publish my writing."

Vic Taylor tried to hit Noah and now Vic was blaming him because his hand hurt? She had to warn Noah if it wasn't too late. Teagan grabbed her phone and pressed his number. The call went straight to voicemail.

Why didn't he answer? Her cell rang. The ID told her it was the local news anchor.

****

Noah stared at the picture of himself and Teagan on the front page of the *Hawick Falls Citizen*. Below their picture was the figure of Kara Linn's mother sobbing. Another image showed Taylor displaying an injured hand that he hinted Noah had caused.

He looked at Taylor's bruised and swollen fingers again. At least something good had happened. Noah read the editor's ramblings.

"The only reimbursement I wish for my pain is the return of the city's missing girls. Let's hope Detective Cassidy's actions are not an example of how our police department conducts searches for our lost children."

"Well?" the chief asked Noah in a voice that always meant he was super pissed. "What do you have to say for yourself?"

"I was comforting Teagan Raynes, sir. She was upset her friend, Lucy Watson, was in the hospital. Taylor should be consoling his sister over the news of Kara Linn's death instead of spreading rumors."

"I'm aware of the facts, Cassidy."

Noah scanned the title of Vic Taylor's daily entry. He'd captioned the image of Teagan and himself '**Too Close for Comfort**'. Beneath the image of Kara Linn's mom he'd written, '**No Comfort for the Forgotten**'.

Clearly, Mr. Taylor had decided to exploit Noah's moment with Teagan. "Chief, Taylor is angry and aimed his fury at me. I never touched him."

The chief slammed his laptop shut.

That wasn't reassuring. "Taylor is blaming the department for his niece's death and wrote the piece to hurt law enforcement."

"The mayor has seen the paper. He called to discuss an investigation into the implication you attacked an innocent civilian, Cassidy."

"I'd be put on desk duty until I was cleared, which I will be. Why waste my days? We can't function without every man working full and overtime on the Grant case." Noah held onto his temper with effort.

"A little obsessed with yourself, Cassidy?" the chief asked, his cigar in the corner of his mouth. "I convinced the mayor I'd discuss the situation with you and he agreed. The mayor's aware of Taylor's tendency to sensationalize the facts, especially since he suffered it firsthand during his last election run. However, if you're having a relationship with Miss Raynes and it gets out, Taylor could use that fact to destroy our credibility. You're on a missing person case, not date night. You're to remain impartial and to help the victim's family. I expect you to remember and live by your Oath of Honor at all times."

"Sir, I've never forgotten my oath."

"Have you slept with the woman?"

Noah pressed his lips together to silence his anger.

"You know how the public will interpret such actions? They'll believe you took advantage of an emotionally fragile woman in her time of stress and pain."

Noah thought about denying it, but his picture with Teagan made the denial an obvious lie. The snapshot showed them as more than friends. "Sir, my personal life is not open to discussion."

The chief narrowed his eyes. "When you go to work each day in Hawick Falls, you not only represent the force, but you hold the trust and confidence of the people in our city. When you betray that faith by letting your emotions interfere with your job, then it is my business. I repeat, have you slept with Teagan Raynes?"

"Sir, my feelings have never interfered—"

The knock on the door interrupted them.

The chief snapped, "Come in."

Noah went to the window to give himself a timeout, but he felt his pulse leaping in his neck. Damn, Taylor. The man loved to stir up trouble. Where was the break in the investigation, that turning moment? Every investigation had one or else it became a cold case. The girls' predator was clever and egotistical. He lured the police to Pretty Park to find Clark's car. The action reeked of "I got you."

But he was going to make a mistake if he hadn't already. Noah just had to discover it. Yes, he had to find Lisa's abductor before the lab confirmed her DNA from the next homicide victim.

Paul entered and threw a glance at the chief then at Noah and back to the chief. His brows rose together questioning what he had walked into.

"Well?" the chief demanded.

"Ah, sorry, but 9-1-1 received a report of a white-haired man shoplifting at Muffy's and causing a disturbance. The patrol is on its way and will pick him up, but the officer who relieves me at Miss Raynes filled me in that a suspect of the same description tried—"

"Bring him in. Take care of it."

"Me?" Paul sent Noah a searching look.

"Anything else?" the chief barked.

"No sir. I'll go." Paul's lips thinned, and he closed the door with a click.

"Cassidy, you're now in charge of the Meter Feeders."

"What? I thought we made a deal with them."

"You were wrong. The arrogant sons of—"

"Sir, we reached an agreement with the Meter Feeders that if they cooperated, no charges would be brought."

"They haven't. They returned to feeding the meters and giving out their propaganda this morning. Those kids have robbed us blind." The chief waved his cigar through the air. "Consult with the DA on bringing indictments against the gang members. I'm handing the case over to you. I'll increase my presence on the Grant investigation while you work with Paul. Wrap up the Meter Feeders. Quick."

"I'm working with the kid?" Noah had to lift his jaw from the floor. "What about Lisa Grant?"

"You're still on her case, but first, get these teenagers off the streets and our traffic funds in the black. I hope to God nothing else comes out about you and Teagan Raynes or we can expect worse than a sarcastic comment on offering comfort."

No sense arguing with the chief on his assignment. The man could win an award for most hardheaded. Noah left the chief's office with his mind reeling with protests. "The kid! Mercy," he muttered as he stomped through the squad room where he felt the stares of the men on him.

Yeah, take a good look.

He was having a bummer of a day. He needed to bust the Teenage Mutant Meter Feeders and get back where he belonged. He'd bring those punks into the station again, and while he held them, he'd grill each member about the night Lisa Grant disappeared.

Noah paused to text Hines his new assignment. Finished, he grabbed the handle of the rear exit and yanked it open.

He'd gone six feet toward his car when his cell vibrated in his pocket. Must be Hines.

"Cassidy!"

Noah turned to find Paul behind him.

"Seems the men already had the Muffy shoplifter in a cruiser when I talked to the chief. They're bringing him in to holding now."

What did that have to do with him? "And?"

198

Paul shrugged. "I thought you might want to question him since I'm on duty at Miss Raynes' in a few minutes. I mean, he's the one who attempted to break into her house, right?"

His morning wasn't so bad. "I can do that for you." Noah let the door slam and turned around to interview his suspect. Maybe his turning point had arrived.

CHAPTER 33

Matt showed up at Teagan's house late in the afternoon. His familiar face was welcome. She'd spent the hours screening calls from the neighbors and press about her relationship with the detective.

Matt gave her a hug after he told her he'd watched the noon newscast confirming Kara's death.

They sat in the kitchen, and Teagan heated the water in the microwave for tea and then passed a mug to Matt.

"Thank you," he said as she slipped into a chair beside him with her own cup.

She sensed her picture with Noah was on his mind, and his polite façade hid his disappointment in her.

Aunt Sophia's phone rang from the other room.

"I better get that." She raced into the living room and swept up the cell from the sofa cushion. It must be Noah.

"Teagan? This is Chelsea Hines."

Was she upset about the note she'd left? "Chelsea, I apologize for leaving without thanking you in person."

"No problem. I called because I'm concerned about Noah. Denny told me they argued. I mean my husband's not a worrier. If he's concerned about his partner, then something big happened."

"I spoke to Noah this morning, and he was fine."

"Whatever's going on might be connected to the pictures in the paper. Did you see them?"

"Yes." Her stomach jumped with nerves. "And I thought no one read newspapers nowadays."

"Mr. Taylor posted the article on his blog for those who don't do print. Denny hasn't been able to talk to Noah. Do you have any idea where he is?"

"I don't, Chelsea. I assumed he was at work."

"If you see him, ask him to call Denny or me."

"I will. Thanks for looking out for him." She hung up before Chelsea could raise more questions.

Her cell buzzed and Noah's name appeared on the screen.

"Are you okay?" she asked, omitting the hello.

"Yes. I only have a few minutes. The chief assigned me to work on the Meter Feeder case."

"I heard something was up. Chelsea Hines called. Her husband is trying to reach you. Are you still on Lisa's investigation?"

"I plan to take care of the teenagers, right away, and I'll be free to concentrate solely on finding Lisa. I wanted you to know. Keep the faith."

"The pictures caused trouble, didn't they?" Guilt began to whisper in her ear. *You slept with him when you should have been working on saving Lisa.*

He sighed. "The chief wasn't happy to see his lead detective splashed on the front page instead of news of an arrest."

She had to fix her mistake. "I'll speak to him."

"You talk to my boss?" He let out an utterance she'd swear was a chuckle. "I'm a big boy, Teagan. Sit tight and concentrate positive thoughts on bringing Lisa home."

From the mantle, Aunt Sophia seemed to be frowning at her again. Yes, she'd be lecturing Teagan on public displays of affection and asking why a detective involved in finding Lisa was wasting investigation time with Teagan when every minute counted. A pit of guilt opened in her stomach.

Maybe Matt was right. A few days apart would be good for them until she could sort out how to repair her slipups. "Noah, I was thinking. We should take a break, starting now. A short one until life is normal again."

"Break?"

"Teagan," Matt said as he walked into the room. "Your tea is getting cold. Is everything okay?"

"The priest is there?" Noah asked.

His accusing tone increased the awkwardness of the moment. She nodded to Matt but waited until he'd returned to the kitchen to answer Noah. "He is, but—"

"I got to go. Stay safe."

"Wait, Noah." He'd hung up. Her hands shook with an overflow of hurt and irritation. He was blaming Matt for her decision. He acted like she didn't have a thought in her head. Yes, Matt had expressed his opinion, but she reached her own conclusion. She resisted the temptation to stamp her foot, and walked back into the other room.

She wiped a hand over her hair and walked back into the other room.

"Any news?"

"Nothing." She microwaved her mug of tea again to avoid Matt's gaze.

"We searched for Travis on the hiking trails today," Matt said. "We didn't find him, of course. Seth was disappointed, but he's vowed to continue looking for the boy. I was impressed with his concern. The volunteers will walk the tougher paths on the west side tomorrow. The planning meeting is in an hour. If you made an appearance before they left, it would boost the searchers' morale, especially with the bad news on Kara Linn."

"Has Seth formally reported Travis missing?"

Matt folded his hands on the placemat. "If he hasn't, I will encourage him to do it today."

"Thanks, Matt. Have you spoken to Kara's mother?"

"She's not speaking to anyone. I'll try again in a day. Come to the planning meeting. You'd get the bonus of not sitting idle in your house."

"You just want to make sure I'm not alone. Besides, I'm not Seth's favorite."

"He'll behave, and you understand me too well. Coming?"

"I'm not up to it, Matt."

"I saw the picture of you and Detective Cassidy in the paper."

She flinched even though she expected the news. Her throat tightened with guilt. "It's not…quite what it seemed." The heat crept up from her neck and across her cheeks.

"Teagan, you're getting involved with a man when your

emotions are all over the place. Slow down. Be certain."

"Noah didn't hit him. Vic Taylor wrote the piece to sound like he did, but Noah never raised a hand to him. I was there."

"How do you explain the picture with the detective's arms around you printed on the front page?"

"He was consoling me about Lucy and Lisa." Teagan hoped her cheeks didn't flush scarlet.

Matt sat with his lips pressed together, censoring himself.

Why did she have such a bad case of the guilts? Because the picture didn't show a person being reassured, but more, and now Noah was in trouble. "I won't be seeing much of the detective in the future."

He didn't comment on that. Instead, he put his hand over hers lying on the table. "Just remember, I'm always near when you're ready to talk."

"I know, Matt." If only she felt a tiny measure of relief. Instead, once her mind got over the shock of ending her relationship with Noah, if that's what they had, she'd have a long cry. She should have taken a deep breath when he asked about Matt instead of blurting out the first thought in her head.

Matt brought his mug to the sink. "Will you be okay? Stacey can stay with you."

"I'll be fine. There's an officer outside my house."

"Is it the same patrolman who was on duty when the homeless man broke in?"

"He's been replaced." She'd no idea if he had, but it sounded like a reasonable reply.

"I can cancel if you want company."

"No, I'm exhausted. I'm going to lie down upstairs."

He searched her face. "I'll come back. I should have news on the Travis search later."

"Don't bother. I'll be sleeping. I'm turning in early." She needed to be alone to get rid of the gnawing sense she'd made a huge mistake with Noah, one he wouldn't forgive.

I'm not the forgive and forget type.

Matt laid a hand on her shoulder. He looked doubtful. "Please answer your phone, or I'll worry about you."

She started to rise, but he gestured for her to stay seated.

"I'll see myself out. You rest."

The sound of his footsteps faded away, and she let the tears run down her face. No, she'd had enough of crying and whining. She swiped her eyes and nose with a tissue, wandered into the living room, and sank onto the sofa.

"Please, St. Jude, help me find Lisa and watch over Noah." If she had her St. Jude's medal, she'd feel better.

Teagan picked up Aunt Sophia's phone and glanced at the number of messages for her aunt. The woman had been a leader, a doer. Why was she sitting around looking at ancient texts? She needed to be involved. Maybe she'd find a clue and help Noah. She'd shower, change, and attend the search meeting.

CHAPTER 34

Paul followed Teagan to the door of the church office where she told him she'd be at least an hour at the meeting. He reassured her he'd be gone only a few minutes to pick up coffee at the drive through next door. After, he'd wait for her in the parking lot.

"Thanks, I'll find you." Teagan walked up to the desk where Stacey slid her a glance and continued talking on the phone. Teagan watched the minutes slip by on the digital desk while the secretary ignored her. It was hard to justify Stacey's action since she was discussing the sale at Hawick Falls Fashions.

She might as well interrupt. "Stacey, where's the search meeting? I didn't see any cars outside for it."

"Hold on," Stacey said into the phone. She pushed the mute button. "Matt had an emergency. The meeting's rescheduled for tomorrow at eight p.m. I contacted everyone who volunteered about the schedule change. Your name wasn't on my list. Next time, make sure you're on the sign-up if you want to be updated."

Teagan's patience dropped a level at the reprimanding tone. "Is the church open?"

"Until Matt returns and locks it."

Teagan whirled around and left, her patience frayed over wasted time. Outside, the damp air and fog refused to budge. The church bells pealed out the hour. Teagan stopped in the middle of the parking lot. While she was here, she'd light a candle and seek a moment of peace. Halfway across the lot, the idea of looking for her medal floated into her mind. She'd need her flashlight in the glove compartment for the closet since the bulb probably hadn't been replaced. Reversing direction, she caught sight of Vic Taylor's compact car sailing past. Where was he going?

What gave him the right to cause grief in Noah's life? Her anger flooded back. She jumped into the driver's seat and met the patrol car pulling into the entrance. Teagan didn't have a minute to spare if she was to catch Taylor. She signaled Officer Paul to follow and set off.

She tailed Vic through the village before the truth struck her. He was driving toward Pretty Park, but wasn't the park still closed? His sister lived near there. Maybe he was going to her house.

Taylor's car came into the view near the park entrance. The fire had destroyed at least half of the trees in the wooded section. The odor of charred wood permeated the air vents. Teagan slowed. Taylor was driving between the sawhorses used to block the road with barely an inch to spare.

By the time Teagan banged a U-ey, and waved at Paul to do the same, Taylor had disappeared inside and around a curve in the park. She prayed she could locate him before he detected she was shadowing him.

She entered the park, rounded the bend, and braked. Paul flashed his blue light. He must have a few questions about their chase, but where had Taylor gone? She'd drive a few more feet. The paved road had turned to dirt before she pulled over and cut the engine. Paul parked behind her, hopped out, and strode to her.

She opened the window and leaned out. "I was trying to figure out what Taylor was up to and where he went."

"Vic Taylor?" Paul said.

"Yes, but he's disappeared." She blew out a breath of disappointment.

"Why would he come here?" Paul scanned the deserted area.

"Maybe he wanted to write a piece that blamed the firefighters for the woods burning." She shook her head and stared across the old athletic field to the boarded up snack shack that budget cuts had forced the rec department to close.

The tail end of a vehicle was visible behind the end of the building. "Is that Vic's car?" She pointed to it.

Paul moved closer and strained to see.

"He told me he hung out at the park investigating his niece's disappearance. I bet he's inside the old snack bar spying on us with binoculars." A new thought hit her. "Paul, he might have held Kara and now Lisa in there."

Paul's eyes widened. "You should go home. I'll call in a trespasser at the park and join you later."

Nerves fluttered in Teagan's stomach. "But the searchers went through the park."

"Doesn't mean someone can't squat here after we went through the area." Paul's lips tightened. "We should head to the entrance. I'll call in." He walked back to his cruiser.

Her hand hovered over the ignition. Was Taylor inside the abandoned refreshment stand with Lisa? If only Teagan could look.

Movement at the edge of the woods snared her attention. A form emerged. The man's side-to-side sway gave away his identity. Travis.

Goose bumps popped up on her arms. Paul was already in his car and probably waiting for her to turn hers around.

The teen paused, and his gaze focused on her. At any moment he'd run and her one chance to question him about Lisa would be gone. She jumped out, leaving her door open, and the car beeped its warning that she'd left her key inside.

"Travis, wait." She ran toward him. "Where's Lisa?"

He turned to her. "Teagan?"

She stopped a few feet from him.

Travis' stare held a glazed, glassy look that made her want to run away. "What are you doing here?"

A musty, foul smell rolled off him. His jeans and T-shirt were mud-splattered and slept in. His uncombed hair stuck up on his head in odd places, and in his hand he clutched a knife.

Whoa! She retreated two steps. "I'm looking for Lisa. Where is she?"

"I haven't seen Lisa since we fought." He inched closer.

Could she escape if he chased her? "What are you doing at the park?"

"My uncle told me I had to get out of his house. I was causing too much trouble with the cops. I tried to sleep down by the lake on the beach. It was too cold. I moved to the snack hut after my uncle told me they'd searched the park."

"I saw you at *my* house after Lisa disappeared. Did you come to steal another of my aunt's dishware?"

"I didn't steal it. Lisa gave it to me. She said Mrs. Raynes was dead so it was up for grabs. I promised to split the money with her."

"Why did you come at night after she disappeared?"

"We used to meet last at your house." His mouth pinched together. "I kept thinking about her. I had a weird thought she might be playing a joke on us and be hiding at home. You know, she's like that."

"You thought she wasn't missing?"

"I thought she might surprise me and come out. We used to stay in the cellar and pretend it was our place. I know it was dumb. I loved her. I miss her." He lowered his weapon and collapsed on the ground. "Why did she leave me? Everyone thinks I hurt her. I never would. I wanted to marry her." Drawing his legs up to his chest, he rested his head on his knees and cried.

Fear and sadness jumbled in Teagan's mind. Travis' sobs and his crumpled form tugged at her heart, but the knife in his hand warned her to stay away.

"Travis Bodell, I'm making a citizen's arrest."

She spun around to Vic Taylor, but standing behind him was Paul with his gun leveled on Taylor.

"Taylor, drop your weapon and kick it to me," Paul said.

Taylor turned around. "Are you arresting me? I didn't hurt anyone. Take the kid."

"Drop it, Taylor."

Vic released his gun to the ground with a thud and booted it toward Paul. "I've been searching for this boy. He's the one who killed my Kara and probably Lisa Grant."

"Miss Raynes," Paul said, "come stand behind me."

Teagan joined him while keeping her eye on Taylor and Travis. Had they finally found the key to Lisa? Her heart pounded in her head.

Paul scooped up Taylor's weapon and kept watch on everyone. "The patrol is already on the way. When they arrive, we're all going to the station to talk. Travis Bodell, drop your weapon."

Travis raised his dirty face streaked with tears. "It's just a knife." He tossed it on the ground near the officer.

"He probably stabbed my Kara with that knife," Vic yelled.

"I don't know any Kara," Travis said. He burst into louder bawling. His cries filled the air until the wail of a siren drowned them out. Relief rolled through Teagan. She whispered a prayer that Travis would change his denials and lead them to Lisa.

****

Noah's energy was running at peak level despite the fact the interrogation room would need a good fumigation after he finished.

Teagan's announcement about a break hovered on the edge of his mind, daring him to think about her and forget his job. No way could he let her in and feel that stab in his chest.

He'd already wasted most of his afternoon on the Albino Man, whose legal name they'd discovered was Mr. Alfred Moore through his Vet records.

The guy laughed and grunted answers to questions. The clock in Noah's head ticked away, reminding him Lisa Grant needed to be found while this guy played him for a fool. Noah shoved a picture of Kara Linn at him and asked if he'd seen the girl. The homeless man shrugged and shook his head. Noah followed up with a photo of Lisa. "Did you see this girl at the park?"

The homeless man nodded and sat grinning at him.

"Did the girl get in a car?"

Moore gave him thumbs-up.

Was he just gesturing or was that a yes? "How about you describe the vehicle? Truck? Car? Bike?"

Moore rocked back and forth in his seat.

Hell. Noah ripped a piece of paper from his pad and handed it and a pencil to Moore. "Draw the girl leaving the park."

After several silent minutes, Moore produced a stick figure and a rectangle with four circles.

Noah gritted his teeth. What had he expected? Did Moore suffer from more than a stroke and PTSD, or did he just enjoy torturing a detective of the Hawick Falls Police Department?

Noah needed a new tact. "Hungry, Mr. Moore?"

The older man raised his eyes to Noah. His lips parted.

Now he'd gotten through to him. "You know what I like? That fast food place near the plaza. Their hamburgers are three inches thick, juicy, and on homemade rolls. Mmm. Ever taste one of those?"

Moore shook his head.

Now they were communicating. "We can finish up with you drawing or printing the name of the person who picked up Lisa Grant. Then I'll buy us some burgers."

Moore licked his lips.

What was going on in his brain?

Moore reached for the pencil and went to work scratching out something on his sketch.

What was he doing? Noah placed his palms on the table and leaned toward him. "What happened to Lisa Grant? Did she get into a car?" Moore seemed to be retracing his lines.

Noah pointed to the drawing on the paper. "Is this the vehicle?"

Moore added lines to the rectangle.

Mercy. This was useless. Noah's thoughts drifted to Teagan. Time apart. Why didn't she just say get lost? The priest was at her home while she ended it with him. Had she confessed her sin of sleeping with him and her penance was telling him to stay away? Pain stabbed him. He wasn't ready to date again. He didn't need the grief.

Across from him, Moore held up his picture. A series of Xs covered the shape.

Great, X marks the spot. Noah shoved away from the table. He needed to do something productive, and questioning Moore wasn't it. He'd cruise over to Muffy's and to the homeless shelter to ask a few questions about Moore. Maybe they'd been chasing the wrong suspects, and this man was involved in Lisa's disappearance.

"I'll order your burger before I leave." Noah went to open the door and hesitated. "How about a side of fries?"

Moore's eyes grew large.

"Try and tell me one more thing. Did—"

A knock interrupted his last question. Noah opened the door to an officer in the hallway.

The uniform gestured for Noah to step into the hallway. "I've something you should know. When the suspect emptied his pockets in booking, he had a wallet and key inside. I thought they were his and checked a few seconds ago. He had the missing girl, Lisa Grant's, billfold with her license and a couple of dollars. The key was inside with the bills. It could be hers too since he doesn't rent or own a home or car as far as we know. There's a pink heart on the top of the key, which indicates probably belonged to a female."

"Are you kidding me?" The Lisa Grant case grew stranger by the second or by the suspect. It explained why he chose the Raynes' house. "What else did he have?"

"Nothing except the stolen food from Muffy's."

"Send a picture of the wallet, license, and key to my phone."

The officer left. Noah waited until he heard the ding on his phone and marched back into the interview room.

"Okay, Mr. Moore. He pulled up the first photo on his cell and held it up to him. "Where'd you get the wallet?"

Moore tapped his mouth with his fingers.

"Did you find it?"

Moore gave Noah his vacant look.

He swiped to the next image. "How about the key? Did you use it to try and enter the Raynes' residence?"

Moore stared back without recognition. Noah asked a few more questions, but Mr. Moore was done.

Noah dropped his arm in frustration. "I'll order the food." He had to talk to Teagan about the wallet. Would she act different around him now? What had happened to change her feelings for him from this morning? It had to be Father Matt.

Mentally, he shook his head. What had he expected? One night together didn't mean they were going steady. Geesh, he'd lost it and over a woman who believed in saints and miracles. *Get your head into the case.*

Moore was smiling as Noah left the room. Noah told the officer outside the room to order some food for Moore and to charge it to Noah before Moore returned to the holding cell.

Noah walked into the squad room where half the desks stood empty.

"Hey, Cassidy." A young woman in uniform waved him over to her desk where she was closing down her computer. "I heard Paul found Travis Bodell."

"Paul? I thought he was at Miss Raynes' home?"

"Guess you'll have to investigate, Cassidy. I've got to go. A bear is emptying the bird feeders on Elm Street. Animal Control called for assistance with the crowd."

"Thanks." He whirled around and missed colliding with Teagan.

Her mouth opened with a small gasp of surprise as she recognized him.

They stood staring at each other. Stray strands of hair clung to her flushed cheeks. Her gaze of shock smoothed into one of confusion. She was embarrassed to see him again.

"Noah, I…"

"Are you with the priest?" He struggled to speak in a low voice.

"Matt? He's not here. Why?"

"You seem attached to him."

"I don't understand." She shifted and her shoulders slumped forward. "Noah, I…" Her voice trailed away. She lowered her eyes and twisted her ring.

He wanted to touch her, to reassure her, and watch a smile of relief and happiness spread across her face before he kissed her one last time.

But he wasn't asking for another knife in his chest. "I'd like a moment to show you a couple of pictures." He motioned for her to move to an empty desk and took out his phone. In two seconds, he brought up a photo of the Mr. Moore.

"That's him. That's the man who tried to get into my cellar."

He swiped to the picture of the blue wallet with the initial L on it. "Look familiar?"

Teagan's shoulders rose as she nodded. "It's Lisa's. Where did you find it?"

"Your homeless man had it in his possession. Could he have taken it from your house?"

"Only if he came inside before I reported Lisa missing. The police searched the house, and it was gone."

"I just wanted to make sure. We don't know how he got it, or if he met Lisa. He's not talking. I've another picture." He brought up the key.

Teagan twisted the ring on her finger round and round. "The key belongs to Lisa. She drew the pink heart on it with permanent marker. She kept it in her wallet. She was going to add the house key to a keychain when she bought her first car."

"We know why Moore didn't break a lock to enter. He assumed the key would work." Noah pocketed his phone. "That's all I need for now."

"Noah, I'm sorry about earlier when—"

"It's not important." He walked past her. He had to forget about Teagan, workplace politics, and even his own past. Self-torture wasn't his style. He had to do one thing. Bring down the predator who had killed Kara Linn and kidnapped Lisa Grant, and do it fast. Instinct told him it was one and the same person. But who? And how would he find the predator?

CHAPTER 35

The next day, Teagan entered the brick courthouse across from Falls Pizza for Travis' arraignment. Gray clouds blanketed the sky, threatening another storm. First they had a heat wave, and now downpours. The good news was the police might have a lead to Lisa, thanks to the homeless man.

Travis entered the oak paneled courtroom with his middle-aged public defender with a goatee. The charges of criminal trespass and destruction of public property were read aloud. A prosecutor explained how a search had determined Travis was sleeping inside the public building with clear No Trespassing signs.

Travis pleaded not guilty, and the judge announced bail and the next court date. The arraignment was over in minutes.

Teagan's stomach fluttered with nerves as she rose to leave. No one had mentioned Lisa. What if Travis hid her somewhere and she depended on him for food and water? They had to locate her and fast.

Where are you, Lisa? Teagan clenched her teeth against the frustration. Across the room, Seth sent her a furious look and stormed through the door.

She hoped she wouldn't meet him on the street again. Once she exited into the hall, she hit a long stride toward the elevator. No signs of Noah at the hearing. He must be on his other case.

"Miss Raynes," Detective Hines called out to her.

She stopped and waited for him to catch up to her.

"Thanks for coming today. I wanted to assure you we're working on bringing more charges against Travis. Today's arraignment maintains him on our radar."

"Do we know where he's been besides the snack shack? Lisa might be in one of his hideouts. He told me he moved around a lot to avoid the police."

"Travis insists he hasn't seen Lisa since the day they argued over paying for her hamburger. He claims he first stayed near the lake, then in a neighbor's boat that he kept in his yard, and finally the snack bar."

"Maybe Lisa's in the boat." Her voice rose with desperation. She blew out a breath.

"We went back and searched these areas again."

"Sorry, I was hoping Lisa and Travis were together and he'd lead us to her." She cleared her throat, trying to ease the fear closing off her breathing.

"Don't worry, Miss Raynes. We'll continue looking for Lisa. Yesterday we concentrated on the athletic field in the park, but we turned up nothing," he admitted. "We're bringing in machinery to dig in a few suspicious places."

They must be searching for someone buried. More news she didn't want to hear.

"I do need to inform you that the DA considered trespassing charges against you and Mr. Taylor, but has declined to bring them since you weren't living on the grounds."

"Please, thank the DA for me." She hesitated for a moment, and toyed with the idea of bringing up Noah's name. No, bad idea. She thanked Hines and stepped into the elevator. In seconds, she was exiting the courthouse. Humidity surrounded her once she left the air-conditioned building. She hurried across the pavement until she reached her car and paused to dig her keys from her skirt pocket.

"You bitch."

She whirled around. Seth Bodell was less than three feet from her. She flinched and shot a glance over the parking lot. No one was close enough to help if he whipped out a gun.

"You're ruinin' my nephew's life."

She had to get out of here, but Seth pressed closer to her. The odor of alcohol on his breath hit her cheek. She flattened herself against her vehicle to avoid touching him. Her purse served as a flimsy buffer between them. Unable to evade, she went as still as a cornered animal.

"You're goin' to hurt the way Travis hurts. You always hated him. I bet you're the one who killed Lisa to blame him. You're sick."

He was calling her a killer? Anger sizzled in her brain. Teagan shoved her hand into her purse. Her fingers wrapped around the butt of her weapon. "I have a gun in my purse. Touch me, and I'll shoot. But before I do, I'll scream and everyone will know you were attacking me and the shot was justified."

His eyes flicked wider with shock and dropped to her purse.

"Hey, Bodell," a skinny man yelled from the rear courthouse steps. "Let's leave."

He was a member of the men's group at church. No doubt, Father Matt sent him to support Seth.

Seth eased away from her. He walked a short distance and tossed her a glance over his shoulder. His surly expression had vanished, replaced by confusion and uncertainty. He crossed the pavement to his companion, spoke to him, and then jumped into his truck.

Teagan slid into her vehicle. *Guess I handled him.* Tears of relief and fear streamed down her cheeks. Should she call the police and report him? What would she say? He'd threatened her, and she'd done the same to him. What a mess. What was happening to her? Her fingers fumbled with the engine key. *Home. I just want to go home.*

Seth pulled away in the opposite direction. For once, she wished the cruiser that used to shadow her was still her companion. Paul had disappeared with Travis' arrest and gone to work another assignment.

The patrol drove past her house on the half hour. She wasn't completely alone, she reminded herself as she steered toward High Street.

At home, the silence was deafening. She sat listening to the sound of her own breathing.

Negative thoughts filled her mind. Lucy remained nonresponsive. Kara dead. Lisa gone. They were no closer to finding her than when she first vanished. If only Lisa appeared like Travis

If only Noah would call her. She couldn't blot him out in the quiet of her living room. She remembered him sitting next to her on the sofa. His warmth and reassuring voice helped her through the worst moments.

She remembered their last morning together, his kisses, and his touch. She replayed every microsecond they'd shared and ended with his cold expression when they met at the station. He wanted nothing to do with her.

Tears pricked her eyes. She scooped up her aunt's phone and found Chelsea's number. Teagan texted her hello and hoped she was okay.

Maybe Chelsea would fill her in on how Noah was doing. If only Aunt Sophia was here. Her aunt always said and did the right things. Maybe Teagan could find an old email from her aunt that would lift her spirits.

Teagan scrolled through them. Meeting reminders, doctor appointments, and friends' notes described Aunt Sophia's life. As Teagan moved down the screen, she uncovered a series of emails to Matt titled: The Next Bishop. They must be about his nomination. Aunt Sophia was his biggest supporter.

She paused over one with BISHOP NEVER in the topic line. Poor Matt. He'd been sure they'd be celebrating his ordination. She bet Aunt Sophia sent Matt a pep talk. The words might help her now. Teagan clicked on the message and read one word: AFFAIR

Huh? Wasn't much of an uplifting email. Teagan began to work through the following communications and shock spread through her until she stopped and sat back to process the meaning. Her aunt was accusing Matt of having an affair.

It couldn't be true. She jumped up and paced the room. What should she do? Nothing? No, she had to speak to Matt and listen to his side of the story. The mantle clock chimed five p.m.

She grabbed her purse and trotted to the car. The rain had brought more fog, and her headlights provided limited visibility on her drive to the church.

Stationed at her desk in the office, Stacey shot her a glance and continued talking on her cell. "I ordered six boxes, not sixteen. Yes. Yes."

"I need to see Matt," Teagan blurted.

Stacey rolled her eyes, moved her mouth away from the receiver to mumble, "He's not here."

"When will he be back?"

Stacey talked for another minute then hung up. "Really, Teagan, I don't have two sets of lips. Father Matt is at the ecumenical meeting with the other churches. They're discussing a bigger shelter for the winter. He's tied up at least until supper, and my work day is over." She pushed the monitor screen's button and it fell dark. "You'll have to wait until tomorrow."

Unsettled, Teagan whirled around and headed for the exit.

"Is it about the Vic Taylor lawsuit? Is he suing you, too?" Stacey yelled.

Teagan didn't bother to answer. Outdoors, a fine mist settled over her. Now where should she go? The messages from the phone streamed through her mind. It was probably good Matt wasn't here. She needed better control over her emotions before she spoke to him.

Noah. Find him. Talk to him, the voice in her head kept insisting. She was tired of drowning it out. While she was at the church, she'd look for her medal, and think about what to say to Detective Cassidy.

The sky spit large raindrops. Grabbing her flashlight from the glove compartment, she ran across the parking lot and into the vestibule. The next set of doors was shut. She scanned the floor. Most likely, if she'd lost her medal in the entryway or by the pews, it would have been found and returned already. The door to the downstairs was closed.

She pulled it open, turned on the light and wound her way downward one-step at a time while she hunted for the silver medal. At the bottom, she flipped on the overhead lamp for the hall. She hadn't walked too far inside the banquet room the last time she was here. She finished that search in minutes. The closet was the last place she'd gone.

She opened the door wide and used her purse as a doorstop. Experience did make you wiser. She entered, stooped down in front of the metal shelves and shone her light underneath the wire storage rack.

Something shimmered in the beam. She'd found it. One good thing had happened today. She stretched her hand beneath the lowest shelf. No deal. She couldn't reach it. In seconds, she'd hauled out the frame and scooped up St. Jude.

"I'll need you when I meet with Noah," she said, closing her fingers around the image. She stuffed the medal in her pocket and was about to push the shelving back when an indentation in the floor snagged her attention.

She stomped on the rectangular area. Her sandals made a clip-clop sound on the floor.

Strange. It sounded...hollow. She shrugged. Maybe they'd patched the floorboards, and they hid the repair job with the shelves.

Aiming the flashlight over the area, she saw a metal ring recessed into the floor. She bent, pulled out the grip, and tugged.

A piece of the flooring rose with a creak. Her breath caught in her throat. A door! She jumped back and peered into the hole. A dark, empty space was below. She flashed her light over the blackness. A ladder was attached to the wall.

"Teagan Raynes."

Seth Bodell's huge body filled the closet doorway. The icy gleam in his eyes sent gooseflesh rippling up her back. *Run*, screamed her mind.

But he blocked the one way out. Drawing herself up, she decided to fake confidence to escape. "Seth, move aside. I'm leaving."

His fist shot out before she could duck. The blow landed on the side of her head. She staggered backward a step. The second punch stunned her senses and she toppled downward. Her arms and legs smacked against the edges of the opening and the sides of the ladder, but she continued to tumble into the black void.

She hit the ground with a thump. Vibes of pain ran up and down her body. She moaned and tried to clear her throbbing head. Blackness blanketed her surroundings. The rungs of the ladder shook with weight and the thump of shoes.

Seth was coming.

****

Noah walked past the holding pen on his way out of the station. Chelsea caught him as he exited.

"Denny was wrong," she said, walking beside him. "You do still live in Hawick Falls."

"Hines and I don't have many spare moments for talk. How are you, Chels?"

"Pregnant."

He stopped. "You and Hines?"

"Yup. Did you expect a different father?"

"Congratulations. Your baby is one lucky kid to have you for a parent."

"I plan on whipping Denny into shape. He's been really overprotective of me, and I want to apologize for my thickheaded husband for yelling at you about Teagan staying at our place."

"Guess he's human like the rest of us." He wished Hines' anger was the worst thing in his life. Noah started toward his car.

She kept pace beside him.

"Have you seen her?" he asked, unable to control his urge to know.

They paused next to his vehicle while Noah waited for his answer.

"Teagan texted me today."

"Oh, yeah, how is she?"

"She didn't say. Denny saw her in court. He told me she looked awful. You should see her. I'm sure you can come up with a reason."

"Teagan wanted us to take a break"

Chelsea shrugged. "Women change their minds every day."

Noah opened his door. "Take care of yourself and the little one."

"I speak for my husband too, and Denny wants you to come over to the house. Save a little energy for your friends." She leaned up on tiptoes and kissed his cheek. "June was my best friend. She'd never want you to be alone, Noah. She'd want you to be happy. And remember, Denny and I love you."

For once, Noah thought he'd blush, but Chelsea was already moving away. He climbed into his front seat. Chelsea's words repeated in his mind. She'd told him the truth. His sweet wife only wanted him to be happy.

But Teagan wasn't the answer. She'd chosen a different path that didn't include him. He had to forget her. He ran a hand over the back of his neck. If only forgetting was easier. He woke up in the morning and promised himself he wouldn't let her into his head. And then he realized, it was too late. He'd spent the last few minutes thinking about her.

He missed her hopeful theories about the case, as off as they seemed to him. He missed her enthusiasm and readiness, and the anticipation he felt when he was about to see or talk to her. He even missed the way she moved her hands around when she was excited. Worst, the morning they'd spent in her bed was burned into his memory and he'd been unable to shake the images of her in his arms.

Now in his car, his willpower weakened and he grabbed his phone and searched his messages. Nothing from her. His finger hovered above her name on his contact list. Then he clicked off and started his engine. He should ride down Main Street and check if the Meter Kids were hanging out yet.

His phone buzzed.

"Cassidy," his partner said. "Lucy Watson is awake and able to have visitors."

"I'm glad to talk to you too, Hines. Hope your kid takes after your better half."

Silence filled a beat before he asked, "Chelsea told you? We were waiting to announce it. She's had a few problems in the past. Look, if you're at the hospital in ten minutes and happen to visit Lucy—"

"Got it. And Hines. Thanks." Noah jammed the pedal to the floor as he raced to question a key person in his case.

At the hospital, Lucy's pasty white skin and rail thin frame reminded Noah the woman had barely escaped death.

Hines asked the big question. "Who hit you, Miss Watson?"

Her answer was an unclear murmur. Noah exchanged a look with Hines who shrugged.

"Who'd you visit in Hawick Falls?" Noah asked, hoping his trip to the hospital wasn't a waste like the Moore interview.

The fog lifted from Lucy's eyes. She waved him closer. He bent toward her. She whispered the name.

CHAPTER 36

Seth was coming. Her gun was gone. Move. Gotta move. Get away. But where was she? She squinted into the dark. She wobbled to her feet. Her left leg throbbed and gave out. She listed sideways and hit the cold wall. Nightmare!

Seth landed with a thud close to her.

Please, God, where's the door? Her weapon was stowed in her purse upstairs. Sweat dripped off her chin. She held her breath and prayed Seth wouldn't find her. How big was this room? *Don't breathe. He'll hear you.*

The swish of fabric against fabric alerted her Seth was on the hunt. She crept forward, stopped and listened. Where was he now? She inched along the wall. The ladder must be close. *Don't let me run into Seth.*

A light flashed on overhead, and lit the small hall opening into a square room.

Seth stood across the room by the wall switch. His eyes glowed eerily as he leered at her. She flinched and desperately looked for an escape. Granite slabs made up the foundation and walls. The only way out was the way down.

She darted into the larger space and stopped on the opposite side of a workshop table.

She shot wild glances around the room. *No way out*!

Seth's lips twisted into a sick grin. "Goin' to shoot me now?" He lunged.

She screamed and ran for the ladder, but he blocked her route. Panicked, she jerked her gaze around the chamber. No escape. Not even a heat register. Shelves lined with yard tools filled one wall. She was alone, with Seth. She clenched her teeth against the bitter truth. He meant to kill her.

"You ain't goin' nowhere." Seth crept toward her with a sick smile.

She closed her eyes for one last plea, her only hope was a miracle. *Please, St. Jude, get me out of here.*

Seth charged. Teagan whirled around, grabbed a rake from the corner and swung the handle at him. Whack. It cracked against his cheekbone. He drew up short. His face reddened and then he tore the weapon from her hands with a roar. The hair on the back of her neck stood up in horror. He was like a wild animal.

Desperate, she snared a pair of clippers from a wall shelf.

She snipped at the air in front of her. "Go away. Father Matt will come looking for me any second. You'll be arrested. He'll be my witness."

"You're full of it. I ain't fallin' for your lies, bitch. The cops want to put Travis away forever." He dove for her.

She snapped at him with the clippers. The metal jaws cut his hand, and he let out a cry.

Now. She ran for the ladder.

A blow knocked her off her feet. She dropped to the ground. The room grayed and spun.

He hooked his arm around her and lifted her off her feet like a doll.

Her senses pulled together. *Fight. Fight.* She clawed and kicked, but nothing slowed him as he carried her to the table. He shoved her against the top and pinned her arms behind her.

"Let me go. Let me go!"

He pushed her face onto the wooden surface and pressed his body against her legs and bottom. A wire attached to an overhead pole came around her neck and held her like a soon-to-be slaughtered animal. The yank on her waistband sent her pants button popping off.

"No!" Hot tears rolled across her cheeks. She stomped on his foot but it was like an ant attacking a rhino. It was over. She was going to die. *Never to find Lisa.*

His arm circled her waist and pulled her to him.

Never to see Noah. "No." Oh, my God. She struggled until the collar dug into her throat, cutting off her breath. *Can't breathe.* Struggling to inhale, panic rippled through her. *Don't let me die this way.* "St-op."

"You heard her. Stop."

Noah! Was she hallucinating? No, he was standing there. His jaw clenched. Anger blazed in his eyes. In his hand, he clutched a flashlight aimed at the floor. "Drop the ax and put your hands up, Seth."

She gasped short breaths, while Seth stepped toward Noah. Where was his gun? Now they'd both die. "Run, No-ah."

"Let me see you turn tail." Seth smirked.

"Seth, from what I see, you've been lying to me. I warned you I don't like people who lie, and I warned you to stay away from Teagan. You didn't."

"What are you gonna do? Blind me to death with your flashlight? Go ahead."

"You got it." Noah raised his flashlight. A beam arced across the room with a crack. Teagan squinted against the brightness. What in the world?

Seth collapsed to the ground with a thud. The illumination vanished, and Noah clicked off his light and strode across the space to her.

What... what happened? She blinked in shock at Noah.

"My stun gun. Always obey law enforcement, Bodell." He tossed a glance at the prostrate man. "Are you hurt, Teagan?" He sent a searching gaze over her.

"Okay," she croaked.

Noah grabbed the clippers from the floor and snapped the wire around her neck. She gripped the edge of the tabletop and breathed.

Noah wrapped his arm around her waist. "Will you okay for a minute?

She nodded and Noah crouched beside Seth.

"Is he...alive?"

"He should be." Noah had his handcuffs in his hand. "Seth Bodell, you're under arrest." He cuffed the man while reciting his rights and straightened. "We'll read them again in a few minutes when he's regained his senses, but I enjoyed the moment."

Noah's arms circled around her, crushing her to him. Tears filled her eyes and she clung to him, feeling his warmth, each of his breaths. They were both alive and together.

Too soon, he released her. "There's a chair beside the shelving. Sit while I call in."

She nodded and he supported her across the few feet to the bookcase and released her when she sank into the seat. Was he real? Was anything real?

Noah spoke into his cell phone. "Backup and ambulance requested at..."

His words faded as she hugged herself against the chills racing over her. She'd never feel safe until she escaped this hole. She wanted to go miles and miles from the church dungeon.

Noah was patting Seth down. "Hines and his men are close. They'll be here in minutes." He glanced at her. "You doing okay, Teagan?"

"I—"

Pounding drowned out her words. What was that? The sound came from somewhere near her. It grew louder and louder until she leaned closer to the noise. It came from behind the bookcase. Was she crazy? "Noah, someone is in the wall."

She didn't wait for an answer but thumped three times on the granite near the shelves. Knocks echoed hers.

"Noah! There's a person on the other side of the wall." Thudding against the spot, she held her breath until the echo of her taps repeated.

"Maybe it's Lisa. Lisa? Are you there?" Teagan shoved the tools from the shelves, letting them clatter to the floor. "Lisa!" She paused. Thumps answered.

"It must be her." Teagan rose up on tiptoes to the next shelf and threw off cords, dustpans, and batteries, anything in her way.

"Police." The shout came from above.

"Clear below, Hines," Noah shouted.

Officers led by Hines streamed down the ladder. They surrounded Seth, who began to make guttural noises. Noah filled in his partner while Teagan yanked on the metal frame to give herself better access.

Suddenly, Noah was beside her. "I'll do it."

"Hurry," she begged. "St. Jude, help us find Lisa."

With one swift jerk, Noah dragged the unit next to the table to reveal a small door in the wall.

Noah pulled on the handle. Nothing budged. He grabbed a shovel from the floor and hacked at the wall. Two other officers joined him with shovels and rakes.

"Hurry," Teagan urged and strained to see past the men in front of her. The sounds of their metal tools hitting and breaking the wall filled the silence in the chamber.

Let it be Lisa, Teagan prayed.

"It's open," Noah shouted.

She pushed forward and peeked through the officers. Noah was shining a flashlight into the hole in the wall.

"Do you see Lisa?" Teagan shook with nerves.

"Hold on. I'm going in." Noah disappeared into the dark space.

"What's happening? Noah?" Teagan clenched her hands until they hurt.

"I got her," he shouted. "Bring me the tarp."

"Will do." An officer grabbed the blue covering hanging off a corner of the table and passed it through to Noah.

Tarp? Was she injured? Nausea worked its way up Teagan's throat.

Hines appeared at her side. "An ambulance is almost here. You should be seen by a doctor. I'll take you up after Seth."

"I'm not leaving without Lisa."

More uniformed officers arrived. They surrounded Seth and pulled him to his feet. A crowd of uniforms formed a wall around him, blocking her view. They escorted him to the ladder.

What was taking Noah so long? "What's happening?"

He stuck his head out. "She's breathing, but in bad shape." He inched aside, and she leaned into the gap. Noah's flashlight lit the hole. A form under the tarp lay on what looked like a ledge.

The beat of Teagan's heart drowned out the shouts of Hines, directing the men who were taking Seth away.

"Lisa. It's me. Teagan. We're bringing you home."

The girl didn't answer.

"Lisa, Lisa."

The girl stirred with a groan.

"She'll need medical care," Noah said. "You'll go to the

hospital and get checked, too."

"No, I want to sit with her. I'm fine." She climbed inside after Noah exited and crouched beside Lisa. Her face was ashen, and she mumbled, "Home."

Lisa was alive! A miracle had happened. Tears rolled down Teagan's cheeks and chin. She folded her knees beneath her and held Lisa's hand. She swallowed and whispered, "I'm so happy to see you. We've been looking forever."

An eternity later, the officers who'd removed Seth returned. Teagan crawled out and Noah joined her while they waited for them to pass Lisa out of her hellhole on a backboard. At last, she appeared. A blanket replaced the canvas over her limp form. Her filthy hair clung to her wan, dirt-streaked face. She lay motionless like she was sleeping. Only the movement of her chest reassured Teagan that Lisa was alive.

The EMTs pushed past Teagan and worked together to lift Lisa up to the next level.

"We'll wait and they'll return to carry you up," Noah told her.

"No way. I'm going up on my own."

Noah frowned but he let Teagan head up the ladder while he shadowed her behind as they climbed. When she finally stood in the silence of the upstairs storage room, excitement raced through her and drowned out the throbs of pain in her legs, neck, and head. Teagan and Noah wound up the stairs to the empty church entryway.

"Noah, where did they take her?"

"This way." He wrapped an arm around her shoulders and walked with her to the front steps. The ambulance sat in the lot. Its light flashed in the night. A group of spectators gaped at them from the sidewalk where officers ordered them to stay.

Ahead, the EMTs carried Lisa to the emergency vehicle. Teagan broke away from Noah and ran to her side.

"Teagan." Lisa opened her eyes dark with pain and looked up at Teagan.

The medics carrying the stretcher paused while the emergency vehicle pulled closer to them.

Teagan bent down toward the teenager. "Seth is going to jail for a long time. He can't hurt you anymore."

Lisa's lips moved. Teagan leaned down to hear her.

"Matt…monster."

"What?"

"Matt…police. Please. Too." Her eyelids fluttered closed.

"Lisa?"

An EMT placed a hand on Teagan's arm. "Please, move aside while we load the ambulance. You can get in after she's secured."

She nodded and he turned away.

What did Lisa mean? Matt police too. Monster? Had Seth hurt Matt? A fear whirled in her head. Across the lot, Noah and his team were surrounding the rectory. Matt had been at a meeting, hadn't he? Maybe not.

She raced to the rectory. An EMT shouted to her the ambulance was leaving, but she didn't stop. "Noah. Noah."

He turned to her and lowered his drawn weapon. "Teagan, what are you doing? Go to the hospital with Lisa."

"Not yet, Lisa said two words to me. Matt and monster." Teagan paused to catch her breath. "I'm guessing if Matt returned, Seth might have hurt him. I don't know."

"She could be delirious, Teagan."

"Maybe." The ambulance pulled out to the street. The strobe lights rolled over them in the darkness, and she became aware of the men waiting for Noah. "What are you doing?"

"We're searching the grounds, Teagan. It's a crime scene." He laid a hand on her shoulder. "Go back and wait by the steps." He ordered two of his men to escort her.

"But I know the floor plan," she yelled to him, but he was already leading his men forward.

The officers flanked her sides as they led her to the front of the church, and the rectory was out of sight. Clutching her medal, she paced the walkway until Noah returned.

"No signs of the priest," he said before she asked. "I'll take you to the hospital. You're in no condition to drive." He took her arm and guided her toward the lot.

She glanced back for one last glimpse. The rectory was dark. Should she feel relieved or afraid?

Matt monster. The words shouted in her mind. She had to be wrong.

CHAPTER 37

As Noah drove the legal thirty miles per hour to Teagan's house, his mind cruised full speed ahead. A day had passed since the arrest. He'd grabbed a few hours of sleep after booking Seth Bodell who'd refused to answer questions. They'd have to connect him to Kara Linn, but he held onto the hope Seth would spill his guts when his future life choices were explained to him.

His thoughts turned to Teagan. He and Hines had taken her statement after the doctor cleared her and then left her with Lisa. Both of them were safe, but he'd wanted to stay with her. Put his arms around her and whisper words just for them.

He hit the accelerator and headed through the roundabout. Most of the tourists were headed to the lake on this sunny weekend, and traffic was sparse.

Residents were off with friends and loved ones. Loved ones. Any doubt that he had strong feelings for Teagan vanished when he'd entered Seth's lair to find her collared like an animal about to be slaughtered by Bodell. Noah hadn't felt the rage that flooded him for a long time, but he'd kept control and taken Bodell down.

Noah spent the past hours thinking about what his life would be like if he'd arrived too late for Teagan. He knew with clarity he didn't want to go back to his empty days, which meant never seeing her again. His anticipation lifted when he pulled into her drive; although, he dreaded what he had to tell her. She'd had enough suffering. Too bad he was bringing her more. He hoped she didn't blame the messenger.

****

At the ring of the bell, Teagan paused in her dusting and glanced out the front window. Noah had arrived. A wave of excitement flowed through her until she realized he was here to report on the case, not to visit her. Still she couldn't stop the happiness flowing from the top of her head to her toes.

She opened up. "Good afternoon, Detective Cassidy. You found a way to escape your fans?" Since arresting Seth over twenty-four hours ago, Noah had become an instant hero in Hawick Falls.

"The chief is handling the media. I couldn't speak to you earlier because I was doing reports, and you were at the hospital with Lisa. Can I come in?"

"Yes, of course." She stepped aside.

He walked past her with his usual scent of fresh soap and determined gait. He stopped in the middle of the living room and scanned the furnishings with his intense stare.

"Is something wrong?"

"The place is different. It's —"

"Neat and clean? I'm picking up this morning before I go back to the hospital. I rearranged the furniture and was vacuuming when you arrived."

Jogger appeared on the threshold, sat,

"Morning, Jogger." Noah fished in his pocket. He tossed a small object to the cat who batted a felt toy into the other room and scampered after it.

"You bought her a fake mouse?"

"Is that what it was?" He shrugged.

"Thanks, Noah." She'd never expected him to give her pet a second thought.

"The mouse was on sale at Muffy's. You're busy. Jogger's doing well, and you look happy." His gaze roamed over her.

Her hand went to her hair. She should have looked in the mirror before she let him inside.

"Your eyes are…brighter." He broke into a grin. "I'm glad."

"My eyes? Thank you." It was a strange compliment, but her

pulse raced faster. Now she had no excuse but to confess her thoughts to him. "Come sit, please." She limped across the room to the sofa.

"You're hurt. I'll take you back to the doctor."

"Don't be silly. I'm just bruised." When her adrenaline had been pumping through her, she'd felt nothing. No such luck today. Her body ached everywhere, but her happiness overrode the pains. "Lisa's alive. Seth's in jail and Jogger has a new toy. I'm super. Why don't you have a seat?"

He sat in the chair.

"First, what's happening with Seth? He's not getting out, is he?"

"Travis refused bail. He and his uncle are enjoying the family rate behind bars. Except for protesting his innocence, Seth has turned into a mute, but we have a stronger case against him every hour. He worked on repairs to the church basement before construction of the Activity Center. We theorize he became familiar with the old cellar and built his separate chamber at that time. The building is open during the day, giving him access. We searched his house for a key to St. Jude's but nothing, yet."

"So he's planned the chamber for a long time."

"Don't worry. Once the doctor gives the green light to question Lisa, we'll nail the guy."

"Thanks. Noah, I found threatening emails on my aunt's phone." She rose, ignoring her pain and grabbed the cell from the mantle.

"Someone threatened your aunt?"

Teagan wet her dry lips. "No, Aunt Sophia warned Matt she'd reveal his affair with Lucy unless he withdrew from the list of candidates for bishop." She held out the phone to him, waiting for his surprise.

"I know about Lucy's affair with the priest," he said, accepting the cell. I'll need to keep your aunt's phone." He slipped the cell into a plastic bag from his pocket. "I'll send yours back today."

"Matt and my best friend." She sank on to a sofa cushion. When would the world return to normal?

"Lucy regained consciousness. She named the priest as the man she returned to meet."

"Thank God she's conscious." Teagan released a sigh of relief.

"Why was she here?"

"Lucy came back because she wasn't dealing with the guilt and wanted to confess her sin, but not in confession. She'd already done that and was still suffering. She met with the priest and they went round and round. I'm guessing when he couldn't talk her out of acknowledging their involvement, he hoped to silence her."

Teagan tapped her fingertips on her knee. "None of this sounds like Matt."

"I'm sorry. Lucy identified him as the driver who hit her."

"I can't believe Matt would hurt anyone."

"We believe he and Seth worked together. Matt was the brains, and Seth the brawn. How long they've been a team, we don't know yet. We studied timelines, opportunities. First we questioned how Seth would know Lisa went to the park that night. Travis could have told him, but since he wasn't going to meet her, probably not. Lisa might have mentioned it to Matt when they spoke after lunch. Either one of them could have picked her up. The key will be Lisa."

Lisa held the missing pieces.

He rose and moved to the couch. His knee pressed against her, reminding her of how much she wished they were together.

"We collected a lot of items for the lab from his underground lair. Forensics will help us with convictions. We found one of Father Matt's half-smoked cigarettes in the chamber. It's at the lab, but it's his brand. Seth doesn't smoke."

Her head ached with doubts. "Matt and Seth seem a strange duo to me."

"We learned Matt was paying Seth's mortgage under the guise of the church's help. I'm sure that's how the relationship began. Now no one has seen Matt. He's been missing since he left his meeting at noon, the day we found Lisa."

Teagan let the reality sink deeper into her mind. "Matt pointed out to me that my aunt wasn't perfect. I bet he was referring to her threat to reveal the affair." He'd been her trusted friend and family.

"Why would Sophia hurt Matt by revealing the truth about his illicit relationship?" Noah asked. "She and your priest were close."

"He betrayed his vows. It was that simple." At least she understood her aunt's actions. "I'm still processing Matt hurting Lucy and possibly Lisa and Kara. He did know where to get Jake's car and his keys."

"We're looking into other missing girl cases to see if there are connections."

"Others?" Her stomach did a flip, and her jaw dropped in shock. She rose, stopped a few feet from him, and threw out her hands. "The nightmare never ends."

Noah crossed the floor to her. He took her hands and held them still. "I'm sorry, Teagan, but there's more. We discovered a notebook hidden in the floorboards of Matt's bedroom. The book contained years of news clippings of girls who had disappeared within a hundred mile radius of Father Matt's churches. Almost all of them were homeless, making them difficult for the police to track. I'm afraid these saved articles are Matt's trophies of his victims. We're re-investigating all of them."

Matt. Monster. Lisa's words burst into Teagan's head. The man she'd known was good and kind. Who was Matt the Monster? "You think he sent me the death threat. Why?"

"He used the threat to tighten his power and control over you. You'd be surprised at how these types of organized predators interject themselves into an investigation. They do it for different reasons. Father Matt used you to find out where the investigation was headed and keep himself in the center of the activity.

She frowned. "I wanted him with me."

"The priest took advantage of your relationship. He knew there'd be no ransom call and believed the investigation would slow down or change. He wanted to kick the excitement back up a notch. Teagan, for your own safety, do not allow him in your home or aid him in any way. Call 9-1-1 immediately if you hear or see him."

"I'll try."

He lifted her chin and forced her to look at him. "Denial will not protect you. Promise me you won't let him inside, and you'll phone me the second he contacts you."

Lisa had returned, but she had lost Matt.

"Teagan." Heat darkened his eyes, and her heart slammed against her ribs.

Did she have another chance with Noah? She'd prayed for one, and instinct warned her that in their mixed up lives of death, threats, and stalker, this was it. She ignored the panic filling her mind with doubts and locked onto his gaze. "I promise."

He released her and she blurted, "I-I told you we should take a break."

He stared at her with such concentration. Her thoughts threatened to desert. She should stop now before she looked like a fool.

"I've respected your decision."

"Noah, I was wrong."

He raised one brow.

Okay, say it. She inhaled and forced the words out her tight throat. "I want you and me to be together. I'll understand if you don't or have doubts. I know I have a lot of flaws. I can be impulsive. I have the whole guilt trip thing down to perfection, and I worry too much about what people think of me. I even agonize over what my aunt thinks about me and she's gone."

"Thinking about your aunt isn't strange."

"I guess it's normal for someone who has lost family. But I'm going to make my own decisions and not stress over the opinion of others. I should have kept my faith in you, and I understand if you have doubts about us. I—"

He tugged her close, crushed his mouth against hers, and then let go of her. Shocked, she put her fingers to her tingling lips.

"I've no doubts." A smile spread across his face. "It feels right."

Felt right. Sometimes it was that simple.

"Listen, Teagan. How we live our lives is our decision, no one else's. Agreed?"

"Hmmm, I might need more convincing."

He leaned down and captured her lips in one of his mindless, drugging kisses that left her shaking, breathless, and wanting more. He grinned. "Did I convince you totally?"

"I don't know, Detective. I think I need more persuading."

His phone buzzed. "Hold onto the idea." He stepped into the hall.

She stood, afraid to move, or talk and ruin the moment. It was too much like a dream. They were going to be together. If only his phone hadn't rung.

He returned in seconds. "I'm sorry, Teagan. I have to leave. The parents of the Meter Feeders want a meeting at the Station.

They seem ready to talk and make sure their kids will have clean slates for their college applications. I'm just happy we'll be able to settle back to normal. I'll be back. I give my word." He pulled her into his arms and held her.

She leaned into him, buried her face in the hollow of his throat, and soaked in the hardness of Noah Cassidy. The boy, now the man, she'd loved. Raising her head, she said, "I wish you didn't have to go."

"Me too." He slung in his arm around her shoulders, and they walked to the door where she faced him.

"Noah, I've one more question. How did you find me with Seth?"

He sighed. "I interviewed your homeless man about the vehicle he saw Lisa get into the night she vanished. He drew a box for the car or truck and added a bunch of Xs. After Lucy confessed her affair, I thought maybe the Xs were crosses and headed to the church to question Father Matt. That's when I spotted your vehicle in the parking lot and went to look for you."

"Seth and I had an argument. I threatened to shoot him."

"What?"

"I guess he was following me."

"He never will again, but in the future, remember to let the police handle these type of incidents." Noah moved closer and brushed his fingers over her cheek, heightening the beat of her pulse. "I wish I'd found Lisa and saved you the terror of Seth."

"I got a miracle," she whispered. "Few people can say that." An idea flashed in her mind. "Just a minute." She ran to her purse, fished out her gift, and ran back to him. "Take this."

She pressed her St. Jude's medal into his hand. Would he accept it or laugh at her? "It's not a rabbit's foot, but the medal is better." She bit her lip and waited for his response.

He closed his fingers around her present. "I'll keep it over my heart." He tucked it into his shirt pocket and laid his palm over it for a second.

Teagan's throat clogged with emotion.

"Stay safe, Teagan."

She watched him jump into his vehicle and drive off to work. He'd come back to her, not because of the case, because he cared about her.

The mailman's truck pulled to a stop in front of her house. She waited for him to give her the letters and bills. She should call Noah and tell him they'd meet at the hospital.

The uniformed carrier handed her the envelopes. She closed the door.

A piece of mail caught her attention. The printed label was familiar. She tore open the flap. A holy card was inside. Oh, no, not again. Nausea cramped in her stomach. Under the picture of Mary Magdalene, she read, "To err is human, forgive divine."

She flipped the card over. *Vale, Matt.*

CHAPTER 38

Lisa woke. Where was she? She sat up. A plastic tube ran from a vein in her hand to a hanging bag by the bed. Oh, she was in the hospital. She was free!

Happiness flowed through her. Inhaling the fresh scent of laundry detergent, she snuggled into the clean sheets and blanket. Bright electric lights burned in the ceiling. The blackness was gone. Teagan had kept her promise and found her. Soon she'd bring her home. They'd be a family. Finally, Lisa's dreams would come true. Except for Travis.

If only Travis had been her hero. But that detective, he'd appeared in her tomb to take her home like a super hero from Comic Con. Fighting tears, she glanced out the window. Green grass grew beyond the parking lot, and trees with leaves lined the sidewalk. She sighed in awe and wiped her face with the edge of the sheet.

The sky. She wanted to see more of it. She slipped her feet over the side and fought the wooziness until her legs felt steady. She stood. Her IV didn't reach far. She managed another foot forward and tilted her chin upward.

Blue heavens with soft fluffy clouds stretched overhead. She smiled and her gaze fell to Earth. A figure dressed in black had stopped in the middle of the walkway and stared up at her.

She froze. The man raised his palm and made the sign of the cross in the air. Her mind zipped to the night at the park.

She'd hurled herself into the front seat of Father Matt's car. Her savior had worried she'd snuck out to meet Travis. He was here looking for her, making sure she was safe.

Only he wasn't here to help.

She hadn't wanted to go home right away, and he'd brought her to the rectory where he insisted she drink and eat. She had woken up in her tomb, the torture chamber with Seth and his tools, and Matt, not the girl, watching her suffer.

Lisa stumbled backward, knocking a cup off the rolling tray. The goblet crashed to the floor and bounced with several plops.

"What are you doing?" A nurse in her flowered uniform appeared in the doorway.

"I was looking out the window." Lisa climbed into the bed and tugged up the blanket to her chin. Would he come hunting for her in the hospital?

"Rest for now. You'll be up and walking around later."

"I saw a priest outside. He was making a big cross in the air."

"Oh, that's not a priest. It's a man whose daughter died here a few months ago. He prays for the sick and blesses the patients. They won't let him in. Don't worry, he's harmless. I feel kinda bad for him." She took Lisa's vitals and scribbled on her chart.

After she left, Lisa closed her eyes, but visions of the father dressed in black prevented her from sleeping. He'd looked like Matt.

Matt. She shook as she remembered her last normal afternoon. Matt tried to calm her down from her fight with Travis. She'd poured out her problems to him in the church parking lot.

In return, he'd preached to her about goodness and virtue. He'd told her Travis was not for her. Then he'd really ticked her off by listing her faults as reasons they weren't a good match, until she blurted it out. She'd read Aunt Sophia's texts about his affair, and she'd announce his faults, his big sin to everyone.

"Don't." His voice was flat and cold.

She'd laughed. "And I can meet with Travis anytime or anywhere. In fact, I'm meeting him late tonight at the park. And you can't stop me or tell anyone or I'll tell on you." She'd walked away, feeling his angry stare on her back. What would he do? He was a priest. Matt was harmless.

But she had been wrong. He was clever and evil.

****

Two blocks from Teagan's house, Noah's phone rang. He pulled to the side and answered. "Hey, Hines. I'm on my way to the meeting. What's up?"

"You need to hear this now. Matthew Hastings is dead."

"You found him?" Noah's hand tightened on his cell.

"Oh, we found Matthew Hastings all right. The problem is he died after graduation from Seminary School. He's been buried for over twenty years in a cemetery in the Bronx, which means Father Matt of All Saints Church—

"—doesn't exist." Couldn't be. "Hines, the man changed his name when he became a priest."

"Wrong, that was his legal name. The birth certificate he used matches the man's in the grave."

Noah let out a whistle.

"His DNA from the cigarette doesn't show up on CODIS either."

"You're full of good news, Hines. I can't wait to join you." Noah clicked the off button and sat with his thoughts spinning until he landed on the big questions.

"Who are you, Matt Hastings? Where are you?"

About the Author

Gone Before Goodbye is Nora's first book in the series— Love and Mystery in the 6-oh-3. She's hard at work on book two. She lives in New England where the changing seasons inspire her story ideas and her family keeps her grounded.

If you enjoyed **Gone Before Goodbye**, please leave a review at Goodreads.com or your favorite online retailer.

She would love to hear from you.
NoraLeDuc@yahoo.com
And be sure to check Nora's website:
NoraLeDuc.com